HAUNTED: POSSESSION

LEE MOUNTFORD

FREE BOOK

Sign up to my mailing list for free horror books...

Want more scary stories? Sign up to my mailing list and receive your free copy of *The Nightmare Collection - Vol 1* as well as *Inside: Perron Manor* (a prequel novella to *Haunted: Perron Manor*) directly to your email address.

The novel-length short story collection and prequel novella are sure to have you sleeping with the lights on.

Sign up now.

www.leemountford.com

1

THE ROOM WAS DARK. Pitch black. Cold.

Sarah Pearson was sitting cross-legged on a stone floor and her bum was starting to go numb, despite the layers of clothing she wore: a fleece-jacket, thin jumper, and under-shirt, accompanied by jeans and running shoes. The air around her bit at the exposed skin of her face and hands. However, she had to push those things to the back of her mind and concentrate—to try and tap into whatever gifts Father Janosch believed she now had.

Ones she had gained after Perron Manor.

She was on the top floor of Chillingham Castle, an old, medieval castle in the north of England.

Northumberland, to be exact, the same county as the home she had inherited the previous year—the one that had changed her life forever.

Ruined it.

The bedroom was dark, lit only by a sliver of moonlight that seeped in between the thick curtains which covered high windows. The only sound was her breathing, which was a little more rapid than she would have liked. She had been alone in the bedroom for almost fifteen minutes now, just waiting for something to happen.

Sarah tried to keep herself calm by concentrating inward; she focused on her body, trying to pick up on any change in feeling or sensation. It was her third investigation since she and the team had finally closed the door on Perron Manor, but nothing had come close to that experience.

There had been experiences to note, however, including a small, cold flare in the pit of her stomach that always preceded contact with a spirit. So far since they'd arrived at Chillingham Castle earlier that day, she'd felt nothing, and the only cold was the kind that seeped into her bones from the surroundings.

The bedroom was quaint, with bare stone walls painted white and exposed timber roof beams above. A large floral rug was laid over part of the stone floor, just below a double bed that was adorned with plain white sheets and pillows. There was even a writing desk pushed up in front of one of the smaller windows. Pictures hung on the walls—mostly paintings and old photographs of local landmarks. The room had its own fireplace as well, but it remained unlit like every other fireplace in the castle that night, save for the one in the living room that was being used as a base of operations.

A burst of static from the radio in her left hand caused Sarah to jump. Then, the voice of David Ritter came through.

'Anything?'

'Nothing,' she replied. The others were watching her via a camera mounted in the room. However, cameras couldn't pick up on what Sarah was feeling, nor what she could sense. *That* was the point of the vigil: to test those abilities further.

At least, that was her theory on what the Church was doing with them. It had been clear that none of the locations they'd investigated had been a doorway to Hell. None were what Perron Manor was. Ever since she'd exorcised her now-abandoned home, Sarah hadn't again felt that searing sensation, like fire on her skin.

'Okay,' David said, 'we'll give it another ten minutes, then try a different room.'

'Fine,' Sarah replied. She wanted to say more, since the brief contact with David had helped break the silence that was beginning to feel overwhelming.

The waiting was what she hated.

In the previous locations the group had visited, they'd actually found some success. It turned out that spirits seemed to gravitate to Sarah, like she was a beacon in the mists of the afterlife. None of the interactions had been dangerous, thankfully, but that didn't make them any less unsettling. Even after the horror and danger of Perron Manor, Sarah still wasn't used to her new life now... her new calling, if that's what it was.

The other reason she wanted to keep talking to David was to try and thaw the ice that had built up between the two of them—hell, between Sarah and the *whole* team, save Father Janosch... and possibly Ralph. She couldn't blame them for it, of course, but she had noticed a definite divide in the last three months, ever since she stabbed and killed Jenn.

Sarah was also the reason Jamie had been killed as well, though not as directly.

She hadn't been herself then, and hadn't been in control of her own actions. She had been possessed, with one foot in Hell, coming within a hair's-breadth from becoming the key to destroying the world.

Clavis.

What Sarah thought she knew about herself and her past had proved to be a lie. Her father wasn't actually her biological father. She was the daughter of a man named Marcus Blackwater, the person responsible for a massacre at Perron Manor in 1982. As such, it was her bloodline that made Sarah special, though she didn't feel that way. She felt cursed. To her, that bloodline was a tainted one. It was a concept she still struggled with.

It was precisely because of her tainted blood that things had spiralled out of control at Perron Manor. Sarah had become possessed and acted under the influence of evil. Thankfully, the ritual of *Claude Ianua* had been completed in the nick of time, therefore closing the Devil's Doorway, allowing the real Sarah to be pulled back. However, she came back with a certain gift for sensing things beyond her own world—a gift she was still trying to figure out and master.

Another fifteen minutes passed with nothing but silence. Eventually, Sarah herself called time on the vigil. She lifted the radio to her mouth.

'I think we're finished here,' she said. 'I need a toilet break, anyway.'

'Understood,' David replied. He offered nothing else.

Sarah got to her feet and stretched out her back, letting the blood flow again after being sat cross-legged and stationary for so long. She turned and walked to the door. Just as she reached for the handle, however, she got something… a feeling in her gut.

It was small, little more than a flutter, but noticeable nonetheless: an ebbing feeling of cold that radiated outward. She had experienced that a few times before at the two prior locations, as well as in everyday life when she would spot ghostly figures watching from the shadows, or dark clouds hanging close to certain people. She didn't fully understand it all yet, but was trying hard to.

'Hello?' she said out loud to the dark room. The radio crackled to life again.

'Sarah? Can you see something?' David asked. The camera was accompanied by a mic, so the others could hear what she was saying. She ignored the question and instead concentrated on the icy feeling in her stomach.

There was a creak from just outside the door, like the sound of a foot pressing on a loose floorboard. Sarah's heart-rate increased and the cold within her grew.

Something is out there.

As if to confirm her suspicion, she heard a low, throaty moan.

2

'SARAH?' David said into his radio again.

The laptop before him showed a live feed from the bedroom on the top floor. Sarah was on screen and had her head pressed to the door, clearly listening to something on the other side.

However, she wasn't responding to him.

'Can she hear me?' he asked, turning to George Dalton, who was seated beside him.

'I think so,' George replied. 'Something must have her attention.'

'Can you hear anything in the room, or see anything?'

A few clicks on the keypad later, the image on screen switched to the corridor outside of the room. Both David and George peered at the screen, as did Ann Tate, Ralph Cobin, and Father Luca Janosch, who all stood behind David.

'I'm not getting anything,' George replied. George had in earbuds to help him pick up on sounds the laptop speakers might not convey too well.

The group was situated on the ground floor of the castle,

in one of the living rooms. The walls were made from bare-faced stonework and a fire had been lit in the large fireplace, pushing out a generous amount of heat. The wall decorations seemed cluttered and mismatched, with different-sized pictures and paintings covering most of the stonework. However, to David, the unordered arrangement had its own charm.

In many respects, Chillingham Castle reminded David of Perron Manor, with its old-world feel, stone walls, high windows, and fireplaces in every room. It was a similar age, too, though Chillingham Castle was much bigger—likely more than twice the size of the Manor.

Chillingham Castle was also well known in the paranormal community as one of the most active locations in the country, with a number of spirits alleged to roam its halls, including a child-like wraith and the ghost of Lady Berkeley.

It was the third location the team had been instructed to investigate in as many months. All were known as being haunted, and the team's job was to determine if any had the potential to be a Devil's Doorway. In reality, all that meant was going inside to see if Sarah was able to pick up on anything. David felt his involvement, as well as that of his team, was superfluous. However, it had been interesting to witness Sarah coming to grips with what she could do, slow though it was. Still, in his time since Perron Manor, David had experiences in each location they had been sent to, and he knew that was because of Sarah drawing out whatever resided within.

He had a feeling that the same thing would happen tonight at Chillingham Castle; he'd get something worthwhile from the whole experience—even though he felt pushed to the side—and then they would all go about their own business until called on again. During that time, he would have no contact with Sarah at all.

None of them would.

But that wasn't exactly her fault.

She'd apologised to them all, tearfully, on that fateful night as the police dragged her away. She'd apologised again when they met up again for their first investigation under the employment of the Church—Sarah having 'miraculously' escaped a conviction or jail time. The knife she'd used to stab Jenn had apparently gone missing, and some of the evidence collected had conveniently become contaminated as well.

David had appreciated the apologies, and his logical brain knew they were genuine. It wasn't *really* Sarah that had killed Jenn. Nor was it really her fault that Jamie had died in such a gruesome manner.

However, David just couldn't shake the image of Jenn's eyes widening in surprise as she slowly realised what had happened, and of her then dropping to the floor of the dark basement, bleeding out as chaos ignited around her.

The image that stuck with him most, of course, was the look of absolute glee from Sarah as she carried out the will of those demonic forces. Despite what logic told him, it was still difficult to remove that girl from the one who had been so tearfully apologetic later.

'She's opening the door,' said Father Luca Janosch. He leaned over them to get a better look at the screen.

They watched the image from the hallway as the door continued to slowly open. Sarah was peeking out, looking both left and right. Her voice then sounded out through the speakers.

'*Hello?*'

David intently scanned the feed, searching for any kind

of movement or flicker that could indicate *something* was there with Sarah in the hallway.

Sarah carefully stepped out of the room, one hand pressed gently to her gut. David saw her attention then drawn to the far end of the corridor. Her body seemed to stiffen.

'*Who... who are you?*'

3

SARAH'S BREATH was caught in her throat. The light in the corridor was poor, but she was still able to make out the figure at the end of the hallway, though it was dressed mostly in shadow.

It was a child—a boy, decomposed and almost skeletal. She could make out one good eye that glinted like a coin in the darkness. Sarah could also see the bone of the boy's jaw and the grin of his skull, layered only partially with dry flesh.

The boy was motionless and dressed in simple, dusty clothes: grey shorts and a dirty white shirt that was ripped and torn. The cold sensation was now extremely strong and absolutely unmistakable.

Looking at the child that stood in the shadows up ahead, Sarah doubted she would ever get used to seeing the dead.

'Can you hear me?' she asked.

The boy continued to stare but didn't answer. After Sarah took a few slow steps forward, though, she heard him emit a moan. It sounded pained.

'Are you okay?'

It was such a stupid question, and Sarah winced as soon as she'd asked it. *Of course he isn't okay. He's dead.*

'You... can... see me?' a disembodied voice said. It had a strained, echoey quality to it and came from the direction of the child, though his jaw hadn't moved.

Sarah nodded and kept walking slowly forward.

'I can,' she replied. 'And you can see me as well, can't you?'

The boy shook his head.

'I... can... hear you.'

Sarah stopped for a moment, confused, and once again stepped closer to the boy. Though she had seen spirits in the previous locations since Perron Manor, she'd never actually spoken to any. 'What *do* you see?' she asked.

The boy paused before replying. '*Darkness, coming towards me. Is... is that you? Are you in the dark?*'

Darkness? Was that what she looked like to him?

'I don't think so,' she said. 'But I won't hurt you.'

He didn't respond. Without knowing exactly what to do, she decided to continue closer, hoping David and the others didn't try to speak to her again and potentially scare the boy away. Thankfully, the radio stayed silent.

'Do you know where you are?' Sarah asked. *Does he even know* who *he is?*

The boy slowly shook his head. As he did, more of his face was revealed from the shadows for a brief moment. He had no nose, only a hole in the grey skin, and his right eye was also just an empty socket.

The sight of him unnerved Sarah, but also made her feel pity for the poor lad. *What a horrible existence for him.*

'You're in a place called Chillingham Castle,' she said. 'Have you heard of it? Did you used to live here?'

There was another moment's pause before he said, '*I... don't remember.*'

'What *do* you remember?'

'*Nothing. I don't remember... anything.*'

'Surely you remember something?' Sarah pressed, keeping her voice as kind and gentle as she could. 'What about just now... what were you doing before you were here, in this corridor?'

'*I... don't know.*' He sounded sad. Scared, even. '*Please don't hurt me.*'

Sarah stopped, surprised. 'I won't,' she said. 'I'd never hurt you.'

'*Leave me alone. Please. Go away!*' Now the boy was beginning to sound frantic.

'Why? There's no reason to be scared of me.' Sarah was confused. What had caused the sudden change in his attitude towards her?

'*I... can see you in the dark now,*' the boy said. His voice had become little more than a frightened whisper. '*Something is in there with you.*'

Sarah was blindsided. She looked, but couldn't see anything around her. The boy was the only other presence in the corridor, other than herself. 'There's no one else here,' she said.

But when she turned back, the boy was gone. The cold sensation that had flowed through her dissipated in an instant as well, leaving her feeling alone and empty.

4

MORNING LIGHT HAD BROKEN through the dark, burning the skies a beautiful orange.

Father Luca Janosch stood with Sarah as the other members of the team loaded up the vehicles with their equipment. Luca could tell David and the others were a little disappointed they hadn't picked up any hard evidence, having only caught Sarah on camera speaking to what seemed to be an empty space. But Sarah's recounting of what she'd seen had been markedly different.

Her experience seemed to have troubled her as well.

However, it was further proof of her abilities, and the Council of the Church would likely be pleased.

Luca and Sarah gazed up at Chillingham Castle. It certainly lived up to the name, being a genuine castle with battlements across the top and thick corner towers that protruded a full storey above the centre section. It was an impressive sight when framed against the amber sky behind it.

He worried for Sarah. It was maybe a stretch to say Perron Manor had completely broken her, but it had certainly pushed her close to the edge. The guilt she carried shone through in her appearance, with her normally sparkling blue eyes just looking tired more often than not.

'How are you feeling?' he asked as he pulled the parka jacket he wore a little tighter around himself. As he did, he felt the cold metal of the small crucifix he wore beneath his shirt press into his skin. The incoming morning was slowly pushing away the chill of the night, but it was a slow process, and the air around them still had a bite to it.

Sarah seemed to consider the question for a moment. 'Fine,' she responded flatly.

Luca chuckled. '*Fine*. Does anyone ever really mean that when they say it? To me, it always seems to say, '*I'm not fine, but don't ask me about it.*'

A small smirk crept over Sarah's lips. 'So then don't ask me about it.'

He saw her cast a glance toward David and the others, which was followed by a forlorn expression.

'They'll come around, you know,' he said.

'Will they? And can I really expect them to, considering what I did?'

'We've been over this, Sarah. *You* didn't do anything. You were—'

'Possessed, I know. But I was still the one who brought everyone to the house in the first place. I lied about how serious things really were. And, possessed or not, I was still the one that stabbed Jenn...' she trailed off for a moment. 'I still see her face. How shocked she seemed before she died.'

'I'm sorry you have to go through this, Sarah,' he said. 'I really am. But if you feel you need redemption, though I'm not so sure you do, then you have a chance at it. The work we are now doing is extremely important.'

Sarah scoffed and shook her head. 'Hardly. We're just

running around finding a few ghosts. We haven't exactly found anything approaching what Perron Manor was, have we? I mean, what have we really gotten from Chillingham Castle? A conversation with the ghost of a child is hardly a breakthrough. We already know that spirits exist. Seems more like the Church is messing us around... or seeing what I'm capable of.'

As much as Luca wanted to refute what Sarah was saying, maybe even reassure her, he simply couldn't. He had been thinking the same thing as well. Their investigations, while interesting, were certainly not at the level he had been expecting. He, too, had the impression the Church was testing Sarah, to see what she was really capable of, and how much use to them she could be. Sarah was always the main point of discussion in any of the debriefing meetings.

'Well, at least you are a free woman,' he offered after searching for something—*anything*—to respond with.

'Funny about that evidence going missing, no?' she replied sarcastically. 'And a hotshot barrister, who I had never met before, taking my case. The Church bailed me out, Father, we both know it. Now, let me ask you this'—she turned to face him—'was it the right thing for them to do?'

Luca frowned. 'What do you mean? You *were* innocent.'

'Debatable. But clearly the Church has subverted the course of justice here. They made the whole thing go away, yet people died, Father. Hell, somehow, none of the others,' she pointed to the rest of the group, 'were even called to the stand to testify. How is that possible?'

Luca remained silent. That was something he had been struggling with as well.

'So,' Sarah went on. 'Is that really ethical? Whether you believe I was innocent or not, enough people were 'influenced' so the problem just disappeared. That's a dangerous precedent, surely.'

The sound of Luca's mobile phone ringing saved him having to answer, and he was immediately filled with gratitude. He pulled the phone from his pocket and saw the call was from Bishop Turnbull, the Lord Bishop of Newcastle.

'If you'll excuse me, I have to take this,' he said with a polite smile.

'They checking up on us already?' she asked with a humourless grin.

'I guess so.'

Luca then walked away as he answered his phone. 'Bishop Turnbull, your timing is good,' he said. 'We've just finished our investigation. But why are you calling so early in the morning? Could it not wait until—'

'Luca, we need you to come in immediately,' Bishop Turnbull said. His tone made the statement sound like an order.

'For a debrief?' Luca asked. 'Can it wait? We've worked through the night. To be honest, I could do with getting a little sleep first. I thought we had a meeting scheduled for—'

'Luca,' Bishop Turnbull again cut in, 'this isn't for a debrief. We have a situation and we need to see you straight away. The Council is already assembled, so how quickly can you get here?'

Luca felt his stomach drop. *What now?* He considered the travel time in his head. Fortunately, the roads would be quiet at this time of the morning.

'A little over an hour, I think,' he replied. 'What is it? What's the emergency?'

'Just get here quickly,' Bishop Turnbull said. 'The

Council will bring you up to speed once you're here.' The line went dead.

Luca's head was spinning. He had no idea what the meeting could be about. However, Bishop Turnbull not divulging any information was odd. Either it was classified to the extreme and couldn't be shared over the phone, or he had no idea of what was going on himself and was simply following orders by pulling Luca in. Either way, Luca had a feeling he wasn't going to like what the Council had to say.

5

Sarah watched Father Janosch as he spoke on the phone.

Though he was too far away for her to eavesdrop, she could tell by his expression that something was up. It piqued her curiosity. However, her attention was drawn away when the rest of the group—David, Ralph, Ann, and George—made their way over, since they'd finished packing up the van. She braced herself for what was coming: an awkward goodbye.

It had happened at each of the last investigations as well. The others didn't want to head off without saying goodbye, so they made polite and excruciating small talk for a couple of minutes before taking their leave.

Just go, she thought to herself. But they didn't, and Sarah felt herself give a forced smile as David reached her first, the others falling in behind him.

He returned her equally awkward grin. 'All packed up,' he said.

'Glad to hear,' she replied. 'I could have helped.'

He shook his head. 'It's fine, honestly. We're all pretty

adept and efficient at it, like a well-oiled machine, you know?' A fake, weak laugh followed.

Sarah nodded. 'I see. I'd only get in the way, I guess.'

Sarah surprised herself with the hint of venom that was evident in her voice.

David's eyes widened a little. 'No... that's not what I mean. It's just...'

'Don't worry, David,' Sarah said, raising her hand. 'I wasn't offended or anything, it just came out wrong. What did you think of the investigation?'

David shrugged. 'It was okay. We didn't really pick anything up this time, save for your conversation with the boy.'

Sarah had filled them all in on what she had seen shortly after her experience. Everyone believed her, of course, as none of them had any reason to doubt it. 'Nothing on audio?' she asked. 'Not even his voice?'

George shook his head. 'No, not that I've found so far. I'll study the recordings in more detail later, though, to see if I've missed anything.'

'Okay,' Sarah said. She then fell silent, not knowing what else to say. It was Ralph who spoke up next.

'How was the investigation for you?' he asked her. 'Did you pick up on any new sensations, or just the cold again?'

'Just the cold. Same kind as the last few times, but a little stronger,' she replied. 'Plus, the ghost actually talked to me this time. Though...'

'What is it?' Ralph asked after Sarah trailed off.

'The boy said he couldn't see anything besides a darkness getting closer to him as I walked. He also couldn't remember anything about himself, or anything before he appeared to me. It was sad.'

'Perhaps it's a repeating apparition?' David offered. 'Reliving the same thing every time he manifests.'

'Maybe,' Sarah replied, 'but he spoke, and even though he couldn't see me, he was definitely aware of me. Interacted with me, even.' She shrugged. 'Who knows. I wish there was something we could do for him. Seems like we just turn up at places, see something, then leave without ever actually *doing* anything.'

'What do you expect?' Ann asked, folding her arms across her chest. 'We tried to do something three months ago, remember? Jenn and Jamie ended up dying.'

David raised his hand to her. 'Ann, not now.'

'Be quiet, David. Someone needs to say it.'

'It's fine,' Sarah said. 'Ann has a right to voice her opinion. Besides, she's right. I know that. I'm sorry about it, about everything that happened back then.'

'Sorry doesn't bring them back!' Ann snapped.

Sarah looked down to the ground and slowly shook her head. 'No... it doesn't.'

With Sarah offering no fight or resistance, Ann paused. Sarah knew the woman wanted her to snap back so that Ann could let loose with her frustrations even more. But Sarah wouldn't do that. She didn't feel she had any right to defend herself against Ann's anger—the rage was justified.

'Besides,' Ann went on, 'we shouldn't even be doing *any* of this. It's pointless dragging us all out on these bloody ghost hunts. She's the only thing anyone cares about.' Ann thrust a finger towards Sarah. 'The rest of us just tag along, whether we want to be here or not.'

'That isn't fair,' Ralph cut in. 'No one is forcing you to be here at all, Ann.'

'Oh please,' she shot back. 'We're being offered a hell of a lot of money to keep silent and just keep showing up.

More than we can refuse. They're buying our compliance and our silence.'

'But you *can* refuse it, Ann,' Ralph replied. 'If you feel so strongly about it, just say no.'

'Grow up, Ralph. If they are willing to buy us out with that kind of money, I'm sure there are other lengths the Church would go to in order to keep us quiet.'

'Ann,' David cut in, 'that is ridiculous. It's the *Church* we're talking about, not the mob.'

'I'm not so sure about that. If they're so on the level, then how come we haven't met any of the people giving the orders? Everything comes via Father Janosch. So if it is all above board, then why the secrecy?'

'Your mind is running away with itself, Ann,' David said. 'This isn't some big conspiracy.'

'But it's hardly normal,' George countered. 'Let's face it, David, Ann has a bit of a point.'

The tense discussion—which was actually more interaction with the group than Sarah had had in a long time—was brought to a close when Father Janosch approached. He wore a frown that creased his forehead.

'Everything okay?' Sarah asked.

'I think so,' he replied. 'But I need to go. I've been summoned in for something important.'

'What?' David asked.

Father Janosch shook his head. 'I'm not certain. But I'd ask you all to be ready. I have a feeling we may be called into action again quite soon.'

6

LUCA FOUND himself walking down one of the lush corridors of Newcastle Cathedral. While he'd been to the impressive building in the past, it had never been as frequent as over the last few months—and never quite so early in the morning.

His footsteps clicked and clacked on the tiled floor as he walked, passing high, thin windows and a multitude of free-standing statues of various people of note in various poses. The walls were an off-white, lending the long corridor with its high ceilings a light and airy feel. The musty smell around him was faintly punctured by incense, but he could not see the source of the sweet and woody odour.

Luca soon reached his destination—the meeting room which was always used when speaking with the mysterious Council of Seven. He still didn't know the names of any of the priests who sat on the Council, and the secrecy was both odd and infuriating.

Such subterfuge was needless, in his opinion.

The only person he really knew in the meetings was

Bishop Turnbull. However, it was clear the Bishop wasn't on the Council, though Luca felt the man had designs to be.

The double door before Luca was high and wide. It had an arched head and the coving around it was ornate with intricate swirling patterns. He knocked twice on the thick wood of the door.

'Come!' he heard a voice call out from the other side, one he recognised as belonging to Bishop Turnbull.

Luca pushed the brass handle and the door easily and silently glided open.

The room inside had a polished hardwood floor and oak panelling to the walls. It was a fairly large space, with a long mahogany table inside.

Bishop Turnbull stood to one side, and seven elderly men sat at the opposite side of the table, all facing Luca. There was a solitary chair opposite them, which was intended for him.

The man who sat central at the table, with three others either side of him, looked to be the oldest of the group, and Luca guessed he could easily be in his eighties. He was thin and fragile-looking, with sagging jowls. He wore glasses, and what little hair he had on his liver-spotted head was grey and wispy.

Directly to his right was a priest who appeared a little younger, though was still in advanced years, perhaps in his sixties. He had broad shoulders, a square jaw, grey eyes, and a full head of white hair that sat in a side parting. This was the Eastern-European-accented gentleman who tended to do most of the talking in the meetings.

Next to him were two other men who looked of similar age and not too different in appearance, being mostly bald save for a ring of grey hair around the back and side of their heads. The one at the far end wore thin-rimmed glasses, which was one of the few differences between the two.

The three men on the left-hand side of the table were more of a mixed bag, with the first stout and squat looking, but with glasses, serious eyes, and a thick white beard. The next priest looked to be taller, but always wore a tired expression—when he wasn't scowling. He had a rather flat nose and letterbox mouth, with a hint of stubble around his chin. The priest at the far left was the only one who wasn't Caucasian: a black man with grey hair and bushy grey eyebrows. Out of everyone, he had the kindest face, but usually said very little. From the few words he had said previously, Luca had noted him to likely be from South America. All wore clerical collars with simple black shirts and suit-jackets.

Luca closed the door behind him as he entered then walked farther into the room. Each man at the table had a thin, burgundy-coloured folder in front of them. There was an extra file present as well, and also a black electronic tablet in front of the Eastern European priest with the broad shoulders. It was he who spoke first.

'Please, sit,' he said. Luca did as instructed and the man went on, 'How did the investigation go at Chillingham Castle?'

'About as well as can be expected,' Luca replied. 'Sarah was able to communicate with the spirit of a boy, but we didn't get any evidence other than that. The cameras and microphones didn't pick anything up. But it was clear from the get-go that the location wasn't a Devil's Doorway.'

The priest nodded. 'In all honesty, we assumed it wasn't. We needed to be sure, though.'

Luca considered for a moment. 'Can I ask a question? Of

the three places we have been to since Perron Manor, have you truly believed *any* of them to be a doorway?'

The Eastern European man looked to the old priest who sat centrally, and was given a small nod before turning back to Luca. The priest shook his head. 'No, not really.'

A frown crossed Luca's brow. 'Then why send us? Or do we really not have any true leads to go on?'

'We have some leads, yes,' the priest replied. 'But we... are hesitant to send the team to a place that might truly be a doorway.'

'Why?' Luca asked. 'Wasn't that the exact reason you put us together in the first place?'

'It was,' the man on the far right said, his accent a Scottish one. 'But as yet, we still don't fully understand what Ms. Sarah Pearson is capable of, or just how vulnerable she might be.'

Luca sighed. 'So the last few months have been what, exactly? Training?'

'In a way, yes,' the Scottish priest replied. 'But there has been a development which must put that training on hold.'

Now they were getting to the heart of the meeting, Luca realised. He was both eager and hesitant to hear what was so important that it couldn't wait.

'Go on,' Luca said. He leaned forward and placed his elbows on the table, lacing his fingers together with his palms flat on the wooden surface.

This time it was the Eastern European man who spoke again. 'We have reports of a problem in my home country, the Czech Republic. There is a cathedral in the town of Kutná Hora, a well-known one: the Cathedral of Assumption of Our Lady and Saint John the Baptist.'

Luca nodded. The name was quite a mouthful, but he

had heard of the place before. 'Okay. And... what? You think this cathedral could be a doorway? Surely we'd have known about a house of God being such a thing?'

But the priest opposite shook his head. 'No, not a doorway... we don't think. There's no real history of hauntings that we are aware of, so no reason to believe it is anything like Perron Manor. There is a church close by the cathedral that has an... *interesting* feature, but that's about it.'

The 'interesting feature' comment drew Luca's attention, but there was a far more pressing question at hand. 'So what is the problem at the cathedral?'

There were noticeable and uncomfortable glances between the seven men. The one that spoke this time was the American.

'There is a priest there—Father Josef Hus. A good man, very devout. However, we have received reports that he has... how to say this? Become possessed.'

Luca sat back in his chair. *A priest? Possessed?*

Possession itself was rare enough, but people who had taken up the calling were strong in faith, so they weren't usually susceptible to that touch of evil. Not genuine possession, anyway, though Luca was aware of some false claims from certain clergymen in the past who had merely been seeking attention.

Was that the case here?

'That is... interesting,' Luca said. 'Why is he believed to be under demonic possession?'

'His actions and behaviour,' the Eastern European priest went on. 'They have been troubling. Believe me, we have considered the reports closely, and we think they warrant investigation.'

'I can understand that,' Luca said. 'Of course it needs to

be looked into, but am I to understand you want *us* to travel to Kutná Hora?' To Luca, he and his team weren't the obvious choice to investigate this problem. Unless there was something else going on.

'That is correct.'

'Okay, but why us? Surely there are people in the Church who would be better suited?'

'Perhaps there are,' the priest replied. 'But there is a reason we want you to go over there.'

'And that is?'

There were more uncomfortable glances between the Council. 'Something Father Hus said when possessed,' the priest went on. 'He demanded to speak to Sarah Pearson... Sarah Pearson of Perron Manor.'

Luca frowned in confusion. 'He... what? How can that be? I thought what happened there was made confidential, including Sarah's identity.'

'That was our understanding as well,' the Eastern European man said. 'Though we could only suppress so much. I'm sure Ms. Pearson's name did get out there, to some extent.'

'Out there enough to travel to the Czech Republic?'

The priest opposite shrugged his shoulders. 'Possible, though unlikely.'

'So we need to determine if the possession is genuine?'

The man nodded. 'Yes. Because if it is, then the demonic forces have called out Ms. Pearson specifically, and we need to know why.'

'But surely it's far too dangerous to send her over there right into the dragon's lair. If we *are* dealing with possession, then we would be all but offering Sarah up.'

The old man at the centre of the table spoke next with a

frail voice. His accent was English, but generic, with no real regional dialect to it.

'Possibly. The Council isn't exactly unanimous on this... assignment. But the decision of our vote was to take action and see what we can draw out.'

The Eastern European priest took over. 'Inaction was what led to the situation at Perron Manor in the first place. We will not make that mistake again. We feel that with you by her side, and if we keep access to Father Hus limited, Sarah should soon be able to determine if what we are dealing with is real or a hoax. And if it *is* real, we can assess what to do next, and why these forces wish to speak to Ms. Pearson. If something is afoot, we need to know what. That means we need to be bold.'

Of the seven men seated across from Luca, two of them —the American and the Scot—looked down at their hands as their colleague spoke. If the vote wasn't unanimous, Luca could guess there were at least two dissenting voices.

'But we do recognise the danger,' the American said, looking up. 'Which is why we are only sending Ms. Pearson and yourself. The others stay behind. We don't feel there is any benefit of them tagging along this time.'

Luca considered this, then nodded. 'Okay,' he said. 'I think Ms. Tate will actually be happy with that, as long as she's still getting paid.'

'She will be.'

'Although,' Luca went on, 'I must insist David Ritter comes along, if he wishes to.'

'Why?' asked the bearded priest.

'Because he knows more about this stuff than any of us. It has been his life, studying the occult and paranormal. He was invaluable at Perron Manor and an asset to what we do.'

'More so than the rest of his team?'

Luca hesitated, but then nodded. 'I have great respect for Mr. Cobin, Ms. Tate, and Mr. Dalton. They have been through a lot and I consider them friends. But in all honesty, I think they feel forced into this whole endeavour—which isn't a million miles away from the truth. However, despite David Ritter still grieving over his lost friends, I do think he has found his calling in life. You would be wise to help cultivate it.'

His words seemed to be considered. The eldest man at the centre nodded. 'Very well, take him with you.'

'Thank you,' Luca said. 'Is there anything else to go on, any other information I need?'

'We can give you more particulars,' the Eastern European priest said. He took hold of the tablet that lay on the table and switched it on. 'First, though, we want you to meet someone.'

He then started up a video call, which was quickly answered. The face that appeared on screen was that of a woman who appeared to be in her thirties. She wore glasses, and her dark hair, which she wore in a simple bob, was showing hints of grey. Luca was able to see her clerical collar below her chin. A large, friendly smile crossed the woman's face and she gave a wave as the tablet was set down on the table, facing Luca.

'This,' the priest behind the tablet said, 'is Reverend Rachel Quinn.'

'Hello,' the Reverend said in a light and bubbly voice.

Luca smiled. 'Pleased to meet you, Reverend.'

'Please,' she replied, 'call me Rachel.'

'I'm Luca.'

'Yes,' she said, 'so I have been told. I think we may be working together quite a bit from now on.'

'Really?' he asked. 'Are you joining the team?'

'In a fashion,' the Scottish member of the Council interjected. 'Rachel is something of a historian, as well as a fine scholar and researcher.'

'Well,' Rachel said, 'I try my best.'

'She is in charge of studying the *Ianua Diaboli*.'

Ianua Diaboli was the book from Perron Manor and was based around the whole phenomena of doorways to Hell. It had helped them close the one at the house. Luca had wondered where the book had ended up after Sarah had agreed to hand it over to the Church, and it now seemed he had his answer.

'A little light reading for you, then,' Luca said with a smile.

She laughed and nodded. 'I'll say. To be honest, I still have to pinch myself that it's real.' Her smile then faltered a little. 'Same with the subject matter, too, I guess. Can't say it doesn't terrify me, knowing there are links to Hell in our world.'

'I know what you mean,' Luca agreed.

'And what you and your team went through at that house... it's just horrible. I'm sorry about what happened to Jenn Hogan and Jamie Curtis.'

'Kind of you to say. I suppose it just shows how important our mission is.'

'Rachel has been digging into the book,' the Eastern European priest said. 'Trying to determine its origin and author. It's a slow process, but she is our best hope, I believe. She is also looking into locations that could prove to be doorways, as well.'

'We have a list of some that look promising,' Rachel added. 'Though I believe you have another priority at the moment, in Kutná Hora?'

'It would seem so,' Luca said.

'Well, I'm told you will be given my direct line. So, if you come across anything you need help with while out there, please just let me know and I'll be happy to help.'

'I appreciate that.'

The American priest cut in, 'Lean on Reverend Quinn when you need to. We feel she could be an asset to you and your team out in the field.'

'Of course,' Luca agreed. 'I'll make sure to keep you updated as well, if we ever need to call on her.'

The American smiled. 'We appreciate that, but know the Reverend Quinn will do the same as well.'

Luca nodded. 'Understood.'

He had to wonder if this Reverend Quinn was as in the dark as he was about the Council and just *who* they were. She had an uncomfortable look on her face along with an apologetic smile.

'Those are the orders, I'm afraid. Direct from Bishop Turnbull,' she said.

Luca turned to look at the Bishop, who had so far said very little—almost a forgotten observer in the meeting. But it made sense. All the orders Luca had received had also 'officially' come through the Bishop. After all, how could the Council—whose rank and standing weren't clear—issue direct orders for him to follow? They couldn't, at least not without revealing exactly who they were. So everything officially came through Bishop Turnbull.

'I think that is all we need to discuss here,' the Eastern European priest said. He slid one of the burgundy files over to Luca. 'This has a little more for you to digest, such as information on the local area, as well as a list of other people who are residing at the cathedral. Sister Maria will likely be your primary contact when you arrive. She was the one who first escalated the problem after she became concerned with Father Hus' behaviour.'

Luca picked up the folder and flicked through it. Getting information and being sent off on a mission like this seemed strange to him. It was *not* why he had taken up the calling to devote his life to God. He sometimes felt more like some kind of bloody secret agent than a priest. But what could he do? After Perron Manor, Luca knew the stakes, and he couldn't turn his back on the truths he'd learned.

'You'll leave tomorrow,' the eldest priest said. 'You fly out from Manchester. We will need to arrange another ticket for Mr. Ritter, if he agrees to go, but that shouldn't be a problem.'

'But tread carefully, Father Janosch,' the American member of the Council warned. 'You are to find out as much as you can, but don't put Ms. Pearson in any danger. She's vulnerable... and we need her.'

'I'll do my best,' Luca replied. He wanted to tell them not to send her in the first place if they were so concerned, but felt he would get nowhere if a decision had already been made. Luca got to his feet.

'And keep us up to date on all developments,' Bishop Turnbull added. 'We'll need daily reports.'

'Fine,' Luca replied. He turned to the Council. 'I guess I will see you gentlemen soon. Stay well.'

They nodded in response and said no more. Bishop Turnbull walked Luca from the room and out into the corridor. As they walked, Luca could not contain his frustration.

'I'm sorry, but I have to ask once more... why on Earth am I not allowed to know the identity of these men?'

Bishop Turnbull shook his head in annoyance. 'Not this again,' he said.

'Yes, this again,' Luca pushed. 'I'm sorry, but this whole

setup is beyond ludicrous. I seriously cannot see any reason why I'm not able to know who I'm taking orders from.'

'You take orders from me,' Bishop Turnbull stated firmly.

Luca bit his tongue. His first urge was to remind the Bishop that he seemed to only be a mouthpiece and puppet. Instead, he went a different route. 'But *you* take your orders from *them*. So it's the same point. What are they, anyway? Archbishops?'

'Drop it!'

'Cardinals?'

'Luca, I said drop it.'

'Some other secret arm of the Church I'm not aware of? I mean really, are we the hand of God or MI6 agents?'

Bishop Turnbull quickly spun towards Luca. His face was like thunder, his cheeks flushed, and he had a vein bulging on the side of his head.

'Luca, will you just drop it!' he snapped through gritted teeth. 'Your instructions come from me and that should be good enough for you. If not, hand in your collar or go back to your congregation. But do so with the knowledge that we are not as safe in this world as we thought we were. Yes, this whole thing is unorthodox, but the situation we find ourselves in is hardly something we are prepared for. We got lucky at Perron Manor, but we can't afford to come that close again.' The Bishop took a deep breath in a clear attempt to calm himself. 'So, what will it be, Luca? Are you going to help fight this evil, or are you going to step aside?'

Luca held Bishop Turnbull's gaze for a moment, but then looked away. He already knew the answer. As much as it would have been easier—and safer—to turn away, it wasn't something he could do. Not now that he knew the truth. Even if he strongly disagreed with how things were being run above him, it was just something he needed to accept.

'Fine,' Luca eventually said. 'I best go prepare myself. Looks like I have a job to do. I can see myself out.'

With that, Luca walked away.

7

SARAH WALKED STEADILY BACK over to the small table where David and Father Janosch waited. She carried a wooden tray with three drinks—two coffees and a tea—as well as some cakes and scones.

It had been an early start, with her, Father Janosch, and David driving down to Manchester airport in the early hours of the morning. The flight wasn't until midday, but the drive had taken a little over two-and-a-half hours. Because of the recent investigation into Chillingham Castle, the trio certainly felt some exhaustion.

Sarah set the tray down on the circular table the trio had occupied. They were seated in a coffee shop located within the check-in area of the airport. The shop was part of a popular chain, whose coffee Sarah didn't mind, though she tended to prefer the independent outlets.

The shop thankfully wasn't too busy, which Sarah appreciated. She really wasn't in the mood for the hustle and bustle of crowds.

She dropped down into her chair and slid the tray into the centre of them all.

'Tea for you, Father,' she said, handing him the cup, as well as the accompanying teapot. The thick, black wool coat he'd been bundled up in on the trip down was hanging on the back of his chair, and he wore a light blue shirt with his clerical collar. It was probably only her mind playing tricks, but Sarah couldn't help but feel he looked noticeably older since the first time she'd laid eyes on the man only a few months ago. The lines on his face seemed deeper, and his already grey eyes had dulled somewhat. Perron Manor had taken its toll on him.

Sarah passed David a mug. 'Latte for you,' she said.

'And a hazelnut latte for you, I take it?' Father Janosch asked.

Sarah smiled and took a sip of her drink. It wasn't perfect, but good enough. 'Yup,' she replied after smacking her lips together. 'I got some food as well,' she added, and motioned to the cakes and scones. 'Everyone dig in.'

Outside of the open-front coffee shop, travellers and commuters ambled by, carrying or dragging suitcases along with them—business people, families, couples, some clearly going on holiday, others obviously travelling for work. Sarah was willing to bet none were on their way to meet with a possessed priest.

It highlighted just how messed up her life had become now, ever since she and her sister had inherited Perron Manor.

David picked up one of the cakes and bit into it. Crumbs fell down to the table, as well as into his lap. He brushed them off his jeans.

He had dressed rather smartly for the trip, with a white shirt beneath a suit jacket. However, he still wore jeans and trainers, making him look smart-casual rather than full-on business like. Because Sarah was used to seeing him in a graphic t-shirt, it was still a bit of a change. He'd also opted to wear some kind of product in his brushed-back hair, giving it a shine, and his dark-rimmed glasses appeared newer and sleeker than the ones he'd worn at Chillingham Castle.

Is he trying to look more professional?

David had been pleasant enough with her on the journey down, though he was still withdrawn compared to how he used to be.

Luca squeezed the file he had with him on the table as best he could, shuffling the tray aside.

'I've told you what I know, but all the information I've been given is in here,' he said and patted the file. 'Feel free to read it if you want.'

Sarah shook her head. 'I trust you've told us everything,' she said.

'I may read it later,' David added, 'but I'm good for now. Though I have to stress again, I'm still not happy that the other three are being left out of this.'

'I understand,' Luca responded. 'I'm not either, but the orders were clear. Because Sarah's name was specifically used, and Perron Manor mentioned as well, then we think the potential for danger has increased. The Church doesn't want to expose anyone to unnecessary risk.'

'Other than us,' Sarah was quick to add. 'We seem expendable.'

'Quite the contrary,' Father Janosch replied. 'Without you, Sarah, we wouldn't really have an investigation at all, would we?'

Sarah shuffled in her seat and looked down at her coffee. She wasn't sure if that was supposed to be some kind of compliment, but the last thing she wanted was for her 'ability' to be the reason they were all put in harm's way.

'I thought we were *all* part of this?' David went on. 'The Church wanted us to come on board, and some of us have given up our former lives to do so. The others shouldn't be cast away on a whim. We're either a team or we aren't.'

'I understand, but the decision came from above me,' Father Janosch calmly stated.

'Well, it isn't fair. We aren't bit-part players in this.'

Sarah got the impression David was maybe speaking more for himself here than the others. Perhaps he was worried about being pushed aside.

'Again, I see what you're saying. But to be fair, the others didn't seem too upset when I spoke to them.'

'Ralph was,' David retorted. 'He called me about it after you two talked.'

Father Janosch nodded. 'Ralph was probably the most disappointed, I agree. But he was still okay with it. George seemed ambivalent, and Ann was almost relieved. I don't think her heart is in this, to be honest.'

David shook his head. 'Well, some of us are invested.'

'I know that,' Father Janosch said. 'That's why *you're* here. I need your expertise and dedication.'

David didn't reply, but the tension in his face relaxed. If he had been worried about his own position regarding their work, then Father Janosch's words seemed to have placated him for now.

During the drive down to the airport, Luca had brought both Sarah and David fully up to speed with the situation, and had stressed the urgency of the new development in the Czech Republic. Sarah's mind still struggled to comprehend why going out there was a good idea. If it was a hoax, as Father Janosch said it *could* be, then their time would have been wasted. More worryingly, though, if it *was* real, they would be marching to the beat of the demonic drum, and doing exactly what had been demanded of them. That seemed... naïve to her.

But, as Father Janosch had said during the trip, they were going to proceed with caution—observe and monitor, then report back. Sarah would be kept out of harm's way.

Yet that in itself annoyed her. While she didn't like walking into an ambush, she hated the thought that she was a liability, or someone that needed to be protected, even more.

It made her feel weak and fragile. That wasn't how she saw herself. Well, not before Perron Manor had fucked her life up. Since then, however...

'Now,' Father Janosch went on, 'the cathedral in Kutná Hora has no history of hauntings or anything of that nature—'

'The Cathedral of Assumption,' David cut in.

'That's right... I don't think I ever mentioned its name, though. How did you know that?'

'I've heard of it.'

Sarah noticed Father Janosch's eyes widen a little.

'How so?' the priest asked.

David paused, then shrugged. 'Nothing important,' he replied. 'You're right, there aren't any stories or legends of hauntings as far as I'm aware.'

'Is there something *else* we should be aware of?' Father Janosch asked. 'Forgive me, but if it is a place you've heard of, I can only think it has something to do with the paranormal.'

David chuckled. 'No, not exactly. It was the resting place for a famous Bible for a little while. I think there are actually two cathedrals in Kutná Hora, actually.'

Father Janosch frowned. 'When you referred to the famous Bible... you mean the *Codex Gigas?*'

'Yes,' David replied.

'I thought that was in Sweden?'

'It is *now*,' David confirmed. 'But it has travelled around quite a bit.'

'And, of course, you're aware of *why* that particular Bible is so well known?' Father Janosch asked.

David nodded. 'Yes, but I don't see a connection here. It just seems like a coincidence.'

Father Janosch thought on that, though Sarah felt distinctly out of the loop.

'Sorry, but you two have lost me. What is the *Gigas Codex* thing?'

'*Codex Gigas*,' David corrected.

'Yeah, that, what is it?'

'A Bible,' Father Janosch offered.

Sarah sighed. 'Yeah, I got that, but why is it so special?'

'It doesn't matter,' David said with a dismissive wave of his hand. 'It wasn't at Kutná Hora for long, anyway.' He looked over to Father Janosch. 'So, the Church doesn't think there is any chance the cathedral is a Devil's Doorway, correct?'

'Correct,' the priest answered.

'So, if a priest *was* possessed there, we need to find out how that happened, and what Sarah has to do with all this.'

'Aren't possessions random?' Sarah asked, still feeling slightly annoyed that her question about the *Codex Gigas* had been brushed aside.

'Often, yes,' David agreed. 'However, it just seems... coincidental... that we are called to a place of God so soon after what happened at Perron Manor, *and* so soon after you agreed to help the Church.'

'You think the whole thing deliberate?' Father Janosch asked. 'Part of some plan?'

'Wait,' Sarah butted in. 'These things we are fighting, they can plan like that?'

'Does that surprise you?' David asked.

In truth, it did, though Sarah wasn't completely sure why. 'I just thought demons, you know, popped up to wreak havoc wherever they could. I didn't think they hatched thought-out schemes.'

'Maybe they can do both,' David suggested. 'I'm not saying this is definitely part of some master plan, but we have to consider it. In fact, I think it's likely, especially considering this demon—or whatever it is—used your name directly, Sarah. It's the most obvious answer.'

'Which is why we are going to be careful,' Father Janosch added before taking a sip of his tea. 'We're just going to gather information, determine if the possession is genuine, and report back.'

'But why can't someone else do that?' Sarah asked. 'If the priest used my name, then send someone else.'

Father Janosch took another sip. It was clear he wanted to buy a few moments while he considered his answer. 'In truth, I think the Church wants to find out what it can from whatever we are dealing with. So in their view, this is a calculated risk.'

'It could be a stupid risk,' David stated. 'If you don't mind me saying so.'

Father Janosch laughed. 'Not at all. Never worry about speaking your mind with me. I understand your concerns, and I raised my own at the briefing. However, I think they may be right. The forces of evil lie and manipulate, but there can be truth in their words. We might be able to learn something from them, whether they want us to or not. Think of this not as walking into a trap, but as an opportunity to gather intel.'

'Intel?' Sarah asked, unable to hide her smile. 'Talking like a commanding officer there, Father. You going to send us out on manoeuvres as well?'

The priest chuckled and shook his head. 'Military work is more your thing, Sarah. But you get what I'm saying.'

She shrugged. 'Maybe.' Sarah hadn't thought of it like that before. She'd been too focused on what was waiting.

Perhaps Father Janosch was right. This could be a way to get on the front foot.

Or it could be a wild goose chase.

They talked for a little longer while finishing off the refreshments. An announcement soon came over the speaker system, calling out their flight.

Time to go.

Sarah quickly drained the last of her hazelnut coffee, and got to her feet. There was a buzz of nervous energy between them—similar to what she'd experienced during the last few investigations, only stronger.

She had a feeling this trip would be different.

8

DAVID HAD NEVER REALLY BEEN one for travel. At least, not international travel. He had seen plenty of Britain before, but when it came to visiting places overseas, the list of destinations he had ticked off was a short one.

So when they reached Kutná Hora, he was surprised at what he saw. He'd expected the Czech Republic to be all gothic architecture, narrow alleyways, grey clouds, old churches, and stone and brick materials everywhere. Where he'd gotten that expectation, he wasn't sure; however, the town they arrived in couldn't have been more different. The architecture _did_ have an overriding theme: off-white rendered walls and orange pan-tile roofs, with the buildings predominantly single storey. With the creamy white render dominating the views, Kutná Hora felt more like a Mediterranean village than a gothic town.

David was bundled into the back of a taxi with Sarah, and Father Janosch sat up front. The leather seat beneath David was cracked and torn, with the yellow foam beneath showing through. The driver, a stout man with thinning black hair, kept his dark eyes firmly fixed on the road ahead while staying deathly silent. He seemed interested only in doing his job, having given Father Janosch one-word answers in response to the priest's friendly questions—spoken in fluent Czech.

Polite conversation was not on the agenda, it seemed.

Their journey took the group up to the north-eastern part of town, driving along plain tarmac roads and passing more low-rise, rendered buildings.

Then David saw it. The cathedral.

Instead of being situated out in some remote location that would have cut them off from civilisation, this building stood proud, slap-bang in the middle of town, opposite a high street lined with shops. There was nothing remote about it.

'That's the place,' Father Janosch confirmed. They all glanced out of the window to view the building as they slowly passed by it.

The front elevation of the structure was grand to look at, and very striking amongst the plain buildings around it. It was faced with stonework, and there was a great, arched window which rose high up above an entrance door. A statue sat at the top of the tall, central section, though David couldn't make out what it was supposed to be. There were other statues close to the entrance, too, decorating the porch structure.

The main part of the cathedral was much longer than it was wide, and as the taxi ambled along the street, David was able to see two rows of large windows, one along the ground floor and one along the floor above. The heads of those windows were arched as well, with vertical and horizontal bars set within the glass. David could see the two roofs of the building. There was a main roof, and also a lower, lean-to one that covered a stepped-out section of the ground floor. It was a surprise to see that the roof tiles were a similar orangey-red as the other roofs in town, and not really in keeping with the traditional church building materials he had expected. They certainly didn't match the stone of the walls, and David felt slate would have been much more appropriate.

However, when he looked farther down to the end of the building, he saw what looked to be a newer extension split perpendicular in two directions. This section, though connected, didn't mesh aesthetically with the original structure. The wings were clad with the same white render as was seen throughout the rest of the town. At least that made the roof materials make sense—likely replaced when the newer section was built, David assumed. Despite the mix of styles, it was still an impressive building, especially with the stone steeple at the back, rising higher than the tall front entrance.

The car kept on going.

'We're passing it,' David said, confused.

'Yes,' Father Janosch replied. 'I have accommodation arranged for us a little farther down here.'

'We aren't staying at the cathedral?' Sarah asked.

Father Janosch shook his head. 'No, I think distance would be beneficial. It allows us our own space and helps detach us from the work if we need to. All part of treading carefully.'

They headed north and had only travelled around three hundred meters away from the church when Sarah pointed out through the window to her right.

'What's that place?' she asked.

David turned and saw a building sitting just on the side of the road, protected by a strong rendered wall which ran around its perimeter. Above the wall, David could see the top of what looked like a small church, and he realised what the building was. It was one he'd heard of, and though he couldn't recall its exact name, he knew a little about it.

'The Cemetery Church of All Saints,' Father Janosch said. 'It is surrounded by quite a large cemetery within those walls.'

'Actually, the cemetery was there first,' David added. 'They had to exhume about forty thousand bodies when building it.'

Sarah turned to him and crinkled her nose. 'What happened to the bodies? Burned?'

David laughed. 'If we get the chance, remind me to show you the underground ossuary inside. I could tell you about it, but it would be more fun to see it.'

'Fun?' Sarah asked as she raised an eyebrow. 'Why do I get the feeling it will be creepy as hell?'

'Must be your spider-sense kicking in again,' David replied. 'Because you aren't wrong.'

'We're staying just a little farther down the road,' Father Janosch said. 'A small house that is leased out as a holiday cottage.' After a few more minutes, he then said something to the driver in Czech and the car slowly pulled up to the side of the road.

The street they were on was lined on one side with single-storey bungalows with white, cream, and yellow renders, along with the oh-so-familiar orange and red roof tiles. The opposite side of the road had a section of grass verge, and beyond it was a hedgerow that looked to act as boundary protection to a garden.

Father Janosch got out, and David and Sarah followed suit. The house they stood outside of looked quaint and basic, though David felt it would suit their needs perfectly. In fact, considering some of the places he had stayed during investigations in the past—both before and during his work for the Church—it would be a luxury.

They unloaded their luggage from the boot of the taxi and placed the bags on the narrow footpath. As soon as Luca had paid the fare, the driver gave a small smile and nod, then drove away without a word.

The bungalow was perhaps the only building on the street that stood out against the others simply because of the colours used. The external face wasn't rendered, instead a block wall painted white, and the roof was a sleek grey, the tiles clearly newer than those on neighbouring properties.

Father Janosch knocked on the white front door, and the group waited for a few moments. The door opened and they saw an old woman standing on the other side. She was wearing a headscarf and had a puffy face lined with deep wrinkles.

'Father Janosch?' she asked with a smile that showed only gums behind her lips.

'Yes,' he confirmed and extended his hand. 'Arianna, I take it?'

She nodded and her smile widened even more, allowing the many wrinkles to pull and deepen even farther. Despite her obvious age, the hair that snaked out from beneath the headscarf was jet black. She wore a shawl with golden tassels at the edges, and a long, navy blue skirt that stopped just above her feet.

'Yes, Father,' She then stepped away from the door, allowing them to enter. 'Please, come in, come in.'

David followed Father Janosch and Sarah inside and was immediately hit with a strong floral smell. Flower-filled vases were littered around the living room area: a mix of lilies, roses, tulips, and more. The floor was tiled a terracotta colour, and there was a low, white sofa, as well as a couple of matching chairs. A fireplace with a thick, timber mantel dominated one wall, and a dining table was set to the back of the room. There were four doors off the central space, and the ceiling above was vaulted, with some roof windows giving a view up to the sky.

'I hope it is to your liking?' Arianna asked in perfect English, laced with a strong accent. 'Everything is in working order, beds are made and clean, and the cabinets are stocked with food.'

'Very kind,' Father Janosch said. 'This is perfect. And very clean as well. We really appreciate it.'

'I am pleased to hear that, Father.' She looked to David and Sarah. 'You and your friends here have a nice stay in Kutná Hora. It's a beautiful town. And be sure to visit our cathedrals. They are the most spectacular in the world.'

David held back a smirk. *If she only knew why we are here.*

Arianna handed Father Janosch a key and moved towards the door. 'I will leave you in peace now. If you need anything, Father, you have my number.'

'I do indeed,' he replied and saw her out. 'Are you driving home?' he asked.

She shook her head. 'Only a short walk. About thirty minutes.'

Father Janosch stopped short. 'Nonsense, let me call you a taxi or something. I didn't realise you'd be walking so far.'

She waved her hand at him. 'Bah, I am old, not crippled. I like to walk. A nice day for it, too.'

David looked out of the window and saw the skies were still grey and threatening rain.

'Please,' he cut in, 'let us call you a ride.'

'It is fine,' their host insisted. 'I walk here, I walk back. It keeps me fit.'

She stepped outside. David knew to argue further would be pointless—her mind was made up. He suspected she was not the kind of person to be easily swayed.

Arianna gave them all a wave. 'Goodbye and keep safe.' With that, she walked away.

Father Janosch chuckled and shook his head. 'Charming lady,' he said. 'But very stubborn, it seems.'

'She will get soaked if the heavens open up,' Sarah stated.

'I agree, but I think she knows that. Anyway, we have work to do. Let's get unpacked, and then we can make our way over to the cathedral. It should only be a five-minute walk.'

There were three separate bedrooms, all accessed off the central living room, as well as a kitchen which was next door to the room Sarah had chosen. There was also a small back garden, which was enclosed by a high, close-boarded fence and giving of privacy. It was a comfortable place to stay.

Not bad at all, David thought to himself.

But he was eager to get started. He unpacked his clothes as quickly as he could, hanging up his shirts, t-shirts, and jeans in the old wooden cupboard in his room, and packing his underwear away in the chest of drawers that gave off a strong, musty smell of old wood.

The double bed that dominated his room looked comfortable, and the mattress seemed soft, but he didn't want to lie down to test it. He could feel a creeping fatigue due to his early start that day, and also the lack of sleep from the Chillingham Castle investigation. To lie down now would just invite exhaustion to take over. Better to keep moving and keep active.

There was work to do.

When finished, David walked back into the living area.

Sarah was already there, sitting on the sofa. She looked up and smiled at him. She had changed into a pair of heelless boots, black trousers, and thick, wool jumper. Father Janosch had not yet emerged from his room.

While there was a space beside Sarah on the sofa, David instead chose to take one of the chairs while they waited for the priest.

'Didn't expect to end up in another country so soon after finishing with Chillingham Castle,' Sarah said with a smile. 'Things have certainly taken a turn, huh?'

'I'll say,' David agreed. However, he didn't really know what to say after that to carry the conversation on. So they stayed silent.

Finally, Father Janosch emerged from his room. 'Well, then,' he said to them, 'shall we go?'

9

Luca and the others stood before the Cathedral of Assumption of Our Lady and Saint John the Baptist. Being so close to the entrance door—and looking up at the towering structure looming over them—gave the priest a slight sensation of vertigo.

The high entrance door was covered by a stone-enclosed porch with arched, open sides. Winged, angelic statues clung to the support posts of the entrance structure, bidding welcome to guests of the cathedral.

The door ahead was open, and inside Father Janosch could just make out the breathtaking nave.

He turned to Sarah and noticed her skin had paled a little.

'Feeling anything?' he asked.

She narrowed her eyes but didn't look back at him, instead staring ahead to the cathedral. 'Actually... yeah, I do.'

'What?' he asked.

'I feel nauseous,' Sarah replied. 'It came over me as soon as we approached.'

That was both concerning and also encouraging. It

meant they were likely on to something, though Luca wasn't quite sure how he felt about that.

'Anything like what you felt at Perron Manor?' David asked.

Sarah shook her head. 'Completely different. That wasn't nausea, and this is nowhere near as intense. More, I don't know how to term it... sickly.'

'I don't follow,' David replied. 'It feels *sickly*?'

'Best word I can think to describe it,' Sarah answered with a shrug.

'Continue to be mindful about how you feel,' Luca told her, 'and let us know if anything changes. If you are picking up something already, then we need to be cautious.' He took a breath. 'Let's go.'

They stepped inside and Luca looked up. His focus immediately turned to the vaulted ceiling, stories high and so stunning it immediately drew the eye. Arched, transverse rib support structures swooped over them high above, and the expanses of ceiling between each rib were decorated with intricate patterns. The effect of the ceiling reminded Luca of a ribcage.

The floor consisted of small white tiles, shaped like diamonds, which were punctuated intermittently with black tiles. Because of the height and length of the nave, the space actually seemed narrow, when in reality it could have easily accommodated ten people or more standing side by side across it.

A run of tall, open archways punctuated the walls on either side of the central nave, which gave extra floor space, though many of the openings were blocked with free-standing notice boards or pieces of art. Ahead, towards the far end was the choir as well as a grand altar with its surrounding chancel. Huge windows hugged the walls of the choir, spilling light into an area that was already bright and airy thanks to the light cream colour of the walls, ceiling, and the many other windows along the walls of the nave.

Luca saw two large paintings on either side of the steps up to the altar, each with grand and regal display cases formed from glass and gold. The paintings, he knew, were of two Saints—Felix and Vincent—and the display cases contained their remains.

Tall, unlit candles were spaced around the nave—scores of them. Clusters of white ones were placed in small alcoves in the walls, while thin red candles were held in holders that stood as tall as Sarah.

There were about a dozen people inside the nave, milling around in small groups and taking in their surroundings. Thankfully, Luca and his friends hadn't interrupted a service of any kind.

He could see only one person who stood out as someone of the cloth: a woman dressed in an all-black habit and headpiece. She looked to be in her thirties, and had dark eyes, strong jawline, and a big smile that she wore as she walked over.

'Father Janosch?' the nun asked as she reached them.

'Yes,' he answered and returned her smile. His clerical collar was on show, so Luca assumed the lady had spotted it. No doubt she had been expecting them and put two and two together.

'I'm Sister Maria Annuncita,' she said. Though she had an obvious accent, her English was very clear. 'But Sister Maria will suffice. Some people struggle with my surname.'

Sister Maria was relatively tall, taller than he and his friends. 'These are my colleagues,' Luca said. He motioned to David first. 'This is David Ritter, who is somewhat of an expert on the paranormal.' Then he turned to Sarah. 'And this is Sarah Pearson. She is... how best to describe it... able to pick up on any demonic presence.'

Sister Maria's brow crinkled before her eyes widened in recognition. 'Oh, you mean she has the gift?' the nun asked as she looked to Sarah.

'Well,' Sarah replied with a hint of embarrassment, 'I wouldn't say it's a 'gift,' exactly. I'm still getting to grips with it.'

But Sister Maria let a large smile form over her mouth, showing dimples at either side. 'Well, it may be useful to us, given what is happening here.' Her expression darkened somewhat and her eyes fell to the floor. 'Things are getting worse with Father Hus, I'm afraid. I... I fear for his soul.'

'Can you tell us what happened?' Luca asked. 'I read the file we were given, but I'd like your version of events as well. I believe you were one of the first to see Father Hus in his present condition?'

Sister Maria nodded. 'Yes, though his condition comes and goes. I can tell you everything, but would you also like to see him? I think that would help.'

Luca hesitated for a moment before agreeing. 'Yes, that would be useful.'

'Follow me,' Sister Maria replied and turned on her heels. Luca, David, and Sarah fell in beside the nun as they began to walk, cutting through one of the open archways and then towards a door close to the choir.

'I first saw Father Hus in his possessed state about four days ago. However, in truth, I think things started before that.'

'How so?' David asked.

'Some of the other priests and nuns had reported odd behaviour from him. He would often get angry with people, when normally he is the most patient and understanding man I know. Also, when one of our locals spoke with Father Hus about a problem she was having, Father Hus... well, his response was shocking.'

'What happened?' Sarah asked.

But Sister Maria shook her head. 'I would rather not repeat what he said to that poor lady—it was vile. But I am certain it was *not* Father Hus speaking. Not really.'

They reached the thick wooden door, which Sister Maria opened. A sign sat above the door with a white background and red writing. The 'keep out' warning was displayed in both Czech and English.

Sister Maria led them into a long corridor with an angled ceiling above, white plaster walls, and a tiled floor. A row of windows punctured the wall to their left, looking out onto the main high street.

'The area back here is for those that work for the Church,' she explained. 'As is the wing on the opposite side. In Kutná alone, there is the Cathedral of Assumption, but also the Church of All Saints, and another cathedral, Saint Barbara's Cathedral. Then there are the churches in the surrounding towns and villages. The two rear extensions here are owned by the Church and used for basic accommodation to clergy people who need it.'

'There must be a lot of people here,' David said. 'These wings look big. That's a lot of room.'

'They are large, yes,' Sister Maria confirmed. 'Though not full. Most rooms are empty. I think there are about twenty to thirty people living here, if my memory is correct.'

'You were going to tell us about the first time you found Father Hus in a possessed state,' Luca prodded, wanting to keep the conversation on track. He wasn't certain the priest *was* possessed as yet, but that had been the language Sister Maria had used.

'Yes, four days ago,' she began. 'I had been looking for Father Hus, but it soon became clear no one knew where he was. I started to grow worried. A little while later, we received a call from the Church of All Saints—'

'The church close to here?' Luca asked.

'That's right. Apparently, our missing Father was there, down in the ossuary—he'd frightened some tourists. I ran over as quickly as I could.'

Once the group reached the end of the corridor, they turned through another door and entered into a stairwell, with bare stone walls and a strong-looking timber staircase. The treads were carpeted a deep burgundy colour, and the spindles and handrails looked to be stained oak. Sister Maria led them up the stairs as she continued her story.

'When I got there, the ossuary had been closed off to the public, and I was told Father Hus was down there alone but refusing to come out. Apparently, he had also struck a tourist. A child, no less.'

'Jesus Christ,' Sarah exclaimed. She quickly blushed, realising her location and company. 'Sorry,' she added.

Sister Maria chuckled. 'It's quite alright. I understand your shock.'

'I bet that would have caused a commotion,' Sarah said.

'I believe so,' the nun replied. 'The child's mother was very angry. The priests and sisters at the church quickly closed the ossuary to visitors.'

'So was Father Hus down there when you arrived?' Luca asked as he drew in a deep breath. The stairs were taking their toll.

'He was,' Sister Maria answered. Luca could detect the uncomfortable tone in her voice. 'When I got there, it was quiet, but I soon saw Father Hus kneeling on the floor of the ossuary. His appearance shocked me.'

'Had he changed somehow?' David asked. 'Physically, I mean?'

'It wasn't that,' the nun replied, shaking her head. 'He... was completely naked. And he was...' she trailed off and Luca saw the woman's cheeks deepen a shade of red.

'Go on,' Luca urged.

They stopped on the landing at the top, one storey up. Sister Maria was fidgeting with her fingers, looking off ahead and deep in thought.

'I believe the term is, 'pleasuring himself,'' she finally said.

It took a moment for the statement to sink in. When it did, Luca's eyes widened. 'He was *what?*'

'Please don't ask me to say it again. I think you know what I mean. He was doing that while kneeling in front of one of the skull displays.'

Before Luca could probe the issue farther, Sarah cut in.

'Excuse me?' she asked in obvious shock. 'Did you just say *skull* displays?'

David spoke next. 'Remember when I told you that the Church of All Saints had a certain 'feature' that would surprise you?'

'And you're telling me the feature is... what? Skulls in display cases?'

'Not quite,' David went on. 'The church was built on a cemetery, and they exhumed forty thousand bodies to build it.'

'Yeah, I remember you saying that.'

'Well... can you remember asking what happened to the bodies?'

Luca saw Sarah's jaw drop.

'They put them on display?!'

'Yes. Their bones are displayed as decorations around the ossuary. It's quite fascinating.'

Sarah turned to Luca, searching for confirmation. He smiled and nodded. 'It's true,' Luca said. 'That's why it is often referred to as the *bone church*.'

'That's... that's sick!' Sarah blurted out. 'How could anyone do that?'

David chuckled. 'I agree, but it was a different time back then. I know how this will sound, but supposedly the place is strangely beautiful to look at.'

'I kind of doubt that,' Sarah shot back.

'Anyway,' Luca interrupted, turning to Sister Maria. 'You say he was looking at one skull in particular?'

She nodded. 'Yes. He was transfixed by it, touching it with his... free hand.'

Luca and his team fell into a moment's silence as they tried to process the information. It was certainly strange behaviour, especially coupled with his previous actions, but was it enough to prove possession?

'Is there any way to know who the skull belonged to?' Sarah asked. 'If he was focusing on only one, then that specific one might be important.'

Sister Maria shook her head. 'I don't believe so, no. I don't think there are any records.'

Sarah let out a disgusted snort. 'Figures. Dig up the bodies and showcase them like ornaments, but without even the decency of keeping their names and identities intact.'

'I see what you're getting at, though,' Luca said. 'Shame there is no way of knowing.'

However, Sarah's eyes narrowed. 'There may be a way,' she replied.

'How?' David asked.

'We ask the priest,' she replied. 'If he really is possessed, perhaps he will tell us.'

'Yes, well,' Luca began, 'if Father Hus truly *is* possessed, then expect much of what he says to be lies mixed in with the truth. It will be hard to know if anything he says has any validity.' He turned again to Sister Maria. 'What happened next?'

'I tried to speak with him,' the nun answered, 'but he wouldn't respond. He just continued to stare ahead, and... you know... carrying on. He did turn to look at me at one point, but just smiled and kept going. I think his aim was to disgust me, which he succeeded in doing.'

'Then what?' David asked.

'I insisted he stop. I raised my voice, told him what was happening was an affront to God. It was then he responded. He said what he was doing there was nothing compared to what was to come. I was scared. I hadn't known Father Hus to suffer from mental illness, but at the time I wasn't sure if it was some kind of breakdown. I tried to be assertive and hoist him to his feet, hoping to snap my friend out of whatever had taken hold of him.'

'And?' Luca asked after the nun fell silent.

She again looked to the ground, hands gripped together at her midriff. She took a breath. 'He grabbed my wrist and... sped up what he was doing. He shuddered and then... you know. I got some of *it* on the base of my habit. Stained it. At the time I couldn't believe it—honestly I still can't.'

'That's horrible,' Sarah said.

Sister Maria still didn't look up. 'He just started laughing. So I ran for help. When I returned with others, Father Hus was sitting on the floor, but he was different. Subdued and confused. He didn't know what was happening. We helped him up, dressed him, and brought him back to the cathedral, to a bedroom up here. Just so he could rest and recuperate. A doctor was called, obviously, but Father Hus started to seem like his normal self, though he was extremely embarrassed after we told him what had happened.'

'He didn't remember on his own?' Sarah asked.

'No,' Sister Maria confirmed. 'After he found out, he could scarcely look at me. He asked to be allowed to stay at the cathedral. Father Hus actually has a home a little outside of town. He doesn't live here, though some of us do. But there was enough room, and we thought it would be good for him to be around others.'

'Did it work?' David asked.

Sister Maria scrunched her face up. 'That night did not go well. After midnight, some of us were woken by strange noises. Howling and wailing coming from his room. I heard it myself. In all honesty... it didn't sound human.'

'Why was he howling?' Luca questioned. 'Was he hurt?'

The nun shrugged. 'A few of us went to his room and knocked, but Father Hus didn't answer. In fact, it went quiet. But I do remember the smell. It was foul, seeping out from the room. So... we went inside.' She took a breath as she recounted her tale. 'Father Hus was naked again. I knew he was in a possessed state again, and not just because he had shed his clothes, but by the expression on his face. He looked like an animal. And, like an animal, he had smeared...' Sister Maria closed her eyes as her expression turned to one of disgust, 'excrement around his room.'

Luca grimaced.

'That explains the smell you mentioned,' Sarah offered.

But Sister Maria shook her head. 'No, not quite. *Some* of

it, maybe, but there was something else there as well. Sulphuric. Like something was rotten.'

At that, Luca cast a glance at both David and Sarah. *Demonic.* He looked back to Sister Maria. 'Do go on.'

'After we entered, Father Hus started shouting at us angrily in Latin. Saying things like 'the doors will be opened,' and 'nothing has been stopped.' He was filled with hate. He suddenly attacked us, pinning one of the other priests to the ground. We managed to subdue Father Hus and lock him in his room again. Since then, he has seemed to go through phases of being himself, but then being over-come with whatever is controlling him.'

Luca noted the way Sister Maria phrased her statement —*whatever is controlling him.* 'So you are firmly of the belief that this isn't something like a break down?' He had guessed that anyway from the way the sister spoke, but still wanted to ask the question.

She shook her head. 'No, I believe it is possession. Not that I'm overly familiar with such things, but his actions make me think it could be nothing else. And... there is more. Things in the cathedral have been a little strange these last few days. Things have happened that we can't explain.'

'Such as?' David asked.

'Strange sounds. Strange smells. Not just from Father Hus' room, but from different areas of the cathedral. There are other things, too—such as sightings of a monk who watches people from the shadows. But there are no monks here at the Cathedral of Assumption. One nun was even thrown from her bed in the night.'

Luca turned to David. 'A haunting as well as a possession?'

'If true, they're obviously linked,' David replied.

'Do you feel anything?' Luca asked Sarah.

'The same as when we got here,' she answered. 'I'm still nauseous. Though now that we're on this floor, there is something else as well. A cold sensation in my gut.'

Luca nodded. 'Okay. How is the nausea? Are you okay to continue?'

'Yes,' Sarah stated firmly. 'I can handle it.'

'Is that what you feel when there are spirits close by?' Sister Maria asked.

Sarah shrugged her shoulders. 'I'm not one-hundred-percent certain as yet. As I said, I'm still getting to grips with everything.'

'But it all lends credence that we are dealing with something paranormal,' Luca added. 'Not that we didn't believe what you were telling us, Sister. But we have to be thorough, as I'm sure you understand.'

'Of course,' she replied. 'I don't take offence. I'm just glad you are here. The last few days have been a little scary. I've felt a little lost and out of my depth. Even after I was informed you were coming to help, the waiting was... difficult.'

'So you were just told to sit tight until we got here?' Sarah asked.

Sister Maria nodded. 'Yes. I was instructed to keep Father Hus in his room, but make sure he was safe and looked after. Well... that isn't strictly true. Initially, some doctors and psychologists were going to come out, but then we got a call to say the plans had changed and that you and your team would be coming instead.'

'Has Father Hus said anything else when in his possessed state?' Luca asked.

'A great many things,' Sister Maria confirmed. 'All hateful, spiteful, and intended to make us uncomfortable.'

'Such is in keeping with demonic forces,' Luca agreed. 'However, we were told that he asked to meet with someone specifically.'

'Yes,' Sister Maria replied and turned to Sarah. 'He kept saying he wanted to speak with a woman named Sarah Pearson. So he obviously knows you.'

'Though I'm not sure how,' Sarah replied.

'And the house Father Hus spoke of... something Manor?'

'Perron Manor,' David said.

'Is that your house, Sarah?'

Sarah took a moment before replying. 'Sort of, though I haven't been back in a while.'

'I see. Did something happen there?'

'Long story,' Sarah replied.

'But it is troubling Father Hus is aware of that house, and of Sarah,' Luca said. 'I take it the doctors and psychiatrists were called off after you reported the mention of Sarah and the house?'

'That's right. Does something have a grudge against you, Sarah?'

'I hope not,' Sarah replied. 'But who knows.'

A brief silence descended on them. Everything had been said that needed to be. 'Well then,' Luca began. 'Shall we go and see Father Hus?'

'Of course,' Sister Maria replied. 'Follow me.'

She led the group from the landing area, through another door, and out into a corridor. It was clear that the area, like the corridor below, was situated in one of the newer sections of the cathedral; the windows were more squat and square, the walls had a clean plaster finish, and the ceilings above were horizontal and plain. Yet again a row of windows lined one side of the corridor, looking out, and on the other side were the doors to the bedrooms. A small, elderly nun in a habit similar to Sister Maria's was headed the other way. She smiled at the group, and at Sister Maria, but said nothing as she passed.

They carried on down the hallway, eventually stopping at a door with the gold number 56 set against the plain white-painted wood. Luca wrinkled his nose at the smell that immediately assaulted him.

'He's in here,' Sister Maria said. She drew out a key and placed it in the lock. Luca could see the hesitation on her face before the nun unlocked the door. 'Not too many people come up here if they don't need to,' she went on. 'They tend to stay away, so it is usually isolated.'

Luca and the others then heard a loud chuckle from the other side of the door.

'Are my guests here?' a deep voice called out. Like Sister Maria, the accent was clearly Czech, but the English was crystal clear. And there was something else, too: an animalistic quality to his tone, making it almost guttural. 'Sarah, my dear, that *is* you, isn't it?' He laughed again.

Luca turned to Sarah, who had her jaw clenched. Her top lip was curled up.

'Be calm,' he whispered to her. 'If we go in now, it will only be for a short while. Understood?'

She looked back at him and nodded.

'Don't keep me waiting, Sarah,' the voice called. 'We have a lot to talk about.'

Luca took a breath. 'Ready?' he asked the others. They all nodded. 'Let's go.'

10

SARAH HELD HER BREATH, mentally preparing herself for battle. Father Janosch had his hand on the doorknob.

Sister Maria had earlier mentioned the smell coming from the room, and now they were all assaulted by it. The odor was foul and reeked of shit, but was infused with a distinct sulphuric scent, exactly as Sister Maria had described it.

Father Janosch turned the handle and pushed the door open.

The room inside was dark. The thick curtains were drawn, blocking out most natural light and making the room feel heavy and stuffy. It was sparsely decorated, with only a four-poster bed, dresser, chair, and bedside cabinet. Most of the furniture was damaged, however, with the drawers of the dresser all removed and lying smashed on the floor. The chair was missing two of its legs and lay on its side. The covers of the bed lay strewn on the floor as well, and even with the lack of light Sarah could see the streaks of brown on them.

Father Hus sat on his bed, cross-legged, in an almost

meditative pose. He was completely naked.

The priest was a pale man of average build and looked to be in his fifties. His heavily grey hair was messy, but showed remnants of a side-parting. A few days' worth of stubble lined the bottom of his face, sitting just below a rather wide nose. His jawline carried the softness of a man of middle-age, as did his body; his chest was starting to sag, and he had a plump gut—though it would be unfair to call him completely out of shape.

A mat of damp, silvery-black hair covered the man's broad chest, and his skin also glistened with a lather of sweat. The sweat didn't make sense to Sarah, however, since the room was ice-cold, or close to it.

She noticed that the remains of a crucifix had also been scattered around the dark blue carpet, as were the remnants of a meal, the plate smashed into pieces.

Father Hus wore a sneer on his face as the group took tepid steps inside and fanned out close to the door. Sister Maria stood next to Father Janosch, with Sarah and David on the other side of him.

'Quite the cavalry,' Father Hus said in a gravelly voice. His attention quickly fell on Sarah, however. 'I'm glad you came. Very obedient of you. I am pleased.'

'I couldn't give a f—'

'We won't be goaded by you,' Father Janosch said as he stepped forward, cutting Sarah off. 'We're just here to assess the situation, then we are leaving the country and you won't see us again.'

Father Hus threw his head back and let out a bellowing, mocking laugh. 'Priests aren't supposed to lie, Father,' he said. His laughing slowly stopped. 'And yet lies, thievery... grooming of the young. Is that not the modus operandi of people like you?'

'Hold your tongue!' Father Janosch snapped. 'We aren't here to listen to you insult and mock us.'

'No,' Father Hus agreed, 'you are here to find out why I asked for Sarah Pearson, and why I mentioned Perron Manor. You want to know if there is anything you need to worry about.' Father Hus then slowly stepped off from his bed and rose to his full height. Sarah noticed scratch marks across his inner thighs, which were a deep, angry red. 'Well, I can answer that. There is *much* for you to worry about.' He turned to face Sarah, allowing her to take in his naked form, clearly enjoying making her uncomfortable. She felt her nose begin to run a little and was forced to sniff. 'I have a message for you, little bird,' he said.

'We don't want to hear it,' Father Janosch insisted and began to turn away, stopping at Sarah. His brow furrowed. 'Sarah, David, Sister Maria, let's go,' he suddenly said. 'We can come back later.'

But Sarah didn't want to run away, nervous as she was. She sniffed again. 'No, I want to hear what he has to say.'

'Later,' Father Janosch insisted and grabbed her by the arm. Sarah turned to him and saw a fresh look of fear on his face. 'We have to go now!' His voice had an air of panic to it.

His stare was making her uncomfortable, and she shrugged him off, but she quickly realised the priest wasn't looking into her eyes—he was staring a little farther down her face. That was when she felt something running from her nose to her lip.

What the hell?

She instinctively wiped her nose with her arm, and when she looked at her sleeve Sarah saw it was streaked with blood. She also saw drops of blood falling down onto her chest.

Father Hus chuckled again and smiled—wide enough so

that Sarah could see his gums, which looked to be darker than they should be. Not quite black, but certainly a deep purple.

'Let's go, Sarah,' Father Janosch insisted again. He placed a hand on her shoulder and tried to move her. Sarah, however, didn't take her eyes off Hus.

'What are you?' she demanded. Father Janosch clearly wanted to run, but a nosebleed was hardly enough to justify fleeing. Not to Sarah. *Don't let the enemy dictate the play.* 'Are you a demon?'

Father Hus slowly shook his head. 'Just a holy man.'

'Bullshit,' Sarah shot back. 'You may have taken the body of a priest, but we both know you're neither human nor holy.'

'I used to be both,' he replied. 'I gave my life to your God —until I was shunned and threatened with death. They were going to wall me up and leave me to rot. It wasn't your dear Lord who saved me back then, though. I had to turn to... something else for help.'

'Walled up?' David asked with a hint of recognition. He took a small step forward. Father Hus turned towards him.

'Have you figured it out?'

David shook his head. 'It can't be.'

Father Hus ran a tongue over his bottom lip. He then bit into that lip, hard enough to draw blood.

'Tell me your name,' Sarah demanded. She felt her nosebleed get worse, running freely now.

But Father Hus just pointed at David. '*He* already knows it.'

Again, David shook his head. 'No. If it were true, I don't think you'd be speaking English so well. I doubt Herman would have known the language.'

'I didn't,' the man replied. 'But Father Hus does, and I know everything *he* knows.'

'Let's go,' Father Janosch insisted, this time much more forcefully. He grabbed hold of Sarah again and tried to escort her from the room. Sarah finally allowed herself to be led. The cold feeling in her gut was growing stronger.

While she wasn't exactly happy about running, Sarah had to admit it didn't feel like they were in any kind of control with Father Hus. Maybe a respite was needed.

Sarah allowed Sister Maria to leave the room first—the nun looked pale and shaken. David stepped outside next.

'Don't you want to know why I called you here, Sarah?' Father Hus yelled after them just as Sarah crossed the threshold to the corridor. She turned around, but Father Janosch suddenly stepped in the way.

'Ignore him,' Janosch said. 'We can come back later when we are more prepared.'

'Go. Run along like a little lapdog, wench. I'll see you back here when you have the courage to hear the truth.'

Father Janosch spun his head around. 'We will return when we are good and ready,' he shot back. He then slammed the door shut behind them, taking deep breaths, and looked up to Sister Maria. 'Is there anywhere we can go to gather our thoughts?'

She nodded as she locked the door again. Sarah noticed the woman's hands were shaking. 'Yes. There are some meeting rooms over in the other wing. We should head over there and put some space between ourselves and Father Hus.' She slipped the iron key into a pocket hidden within her habit.

'That sounds like a good idea,' Father Janosch agreed. 'I think we have a lot to talk about.'

11

SISTER MARIA LED David and the others down to the ground floor and then over to the farthest wing of the building, only stopping on the way to let Sarah get cleaned up. While walking, as if to keep her mind occupied, Sister Maria gave them a brief overview of the cathedral's layout.

The main section, the oldest, was the nave and choir, where the public was allowed to visit. That was where all services and ceremonies were carried out. The two rear wings, situated to the back of the original structure, were restricted from the public. Those wings mainly consisted of accommodation and areas of operation for the Church's private use. There was no symmetry to the layout of the more recent additions, with the wing closest to the high street practically a straight run, but the wing on the opposite side of the choir resembling a squared figure eight, looping back on itself.

It was clear from Sister Maria's tone that she didn't hold the new sections in the same reverence as the original building. That was understandable, as the design and materials used didn't have the same majesty or traditional cathedral aesthetics to them. They did, however, provide a lot of additional space, being bigger than the main cathedral in terms of footprint by a good margin, and were probably larger than most hotels.

Sister Maria led them to a meeting room that looked out over the cathedral car park. David had noticed many more priests and nuns of the Church roaming the halls of this side of the cathedral than had been up near to Father Hus' room. Seeing more people was both welcoming and comforting. It helped David realise they weren't alone and that this was still an operating building.

That meant the situation hadn't yet been deemed dangerous enough to lock everything down.

Hopefully, their time at the Cathedral of Assumption would be relatively uneventful when compared to Perron Manor. After seeing two of his friends die back in that house, David wasn't sure he had the bravery in him to deal with that kind of situation again.

Then why are you here?

He knew the answer to that. Like Father Janosch, after what David had seen, he couldn't turn his back on what needed to be done. Plus, the work still drove him, lighting a passion deep inside that he knew needed to be followed.

What was the alternative? Going back to a day job of fixing computers and tending to company servers?

The meeting room was much less 'business-like' than he had expected. The walls were papered with patterns of creams and royal reds, with crests of gold embossed throughout. Some detailing work had been added to the flat ceilings above, adding coving and intricate borders around the chandelier lighting fitting. The boardroom-style table in the middle had a walnut finish, though David suspected that was just a veneer over chipboard, rather than genuine wood. A number of reed diffusers had been lit around the room, lending a strong smell of jasmine that—at least to him—was rather overpowering.

A high window sat in the far wall, allowing a generous amount of natural light into the room.

Once everyone was seated around the table, with Father Janosch at the head, they got down to business. Sarah spoke first.

'I feel like we are running away,' she said. 'We were in the room with Father Hus for less than five minutes.' She still had a small amount of dried blood around her nose, which she'd missed when cleaning herself up.

'I understand that,' Father Janosch replied, 'but we are just finding our feet here. After seeing Father Hus, we are at least now able to determine the possession is genuine, though certain things have troubled me.'

'The nosebleed?' David asked. Father Janosch nodded.

'That could have been a coincidence,' Sarah threw in. 'Nosebleeds happen. They don't always mean anything.'

'In this case, I think it *does* mean something,' Father Janosch argued. 'I noted the look of surprise on your face when you realised what was happening, Sarah. It *wasn't* a coincidence.'

Instead of arguing back, Sarah hesitated, then finally nodded in agreement. 'Yeah, I guess I agree with you.'

'And that's why I pulled us out. We need to be careful here and make sure you aren't susceptible. We're not in any immediate rush. What happened back there was just an opening exchange to feel out our opponent. But we must make sure *we* dictate the pace and do things on our own terms.'

'Did you feel anything up there?' David asked Sarah.

'Yeah,' she answered. 'The cold in my gut. Same as with

our other investigations, just before we saw a... you know. It was a little stronger here, to be sure, but...'

'But nothing like Perron Manor,' David finished.

She nodded. 'Not even close.'

'Which means we are also confident this place isn't a—' David cut himself off and turned his eyes to Sister Maria, suddenly unsure about how much he should say. He sincerely doubted the nun would be aware of Devil's Door-ways and things of that nature.

'No, we aren't dealing with that,' Sarah confirmed, without the need for David to continue.

'With what?' Sister Maria asked. David turned to Father Janosch for assistance.

'Let's just say,' the priest began, 'things here aren't as bad as they could have been.'

'Really?' Sister Maria replied. 'I fail to see how they could be worse. My friend is a prisoner in his own body while some other entity controls it and desecrates his good name. I can't imagine a worse kind of hell.'

'Speaking of which,' Sarah said to David, 'just who or what *is* the entity inside of him, anyway? It gave a name... Hector?'

'Herman,' David said, correcting her.

'That seemed to ring a bell with you. Do you know who that is?'

David paused for a moment before answering. 'Poten-tially. It was the comment about being 'walled up' that got me thinking. It was strange—a weird coincidence, especially given the conversation we had earlier about the *Codex Gigas*.'

Sarah frowned and narrowed her eyes. 'Wait, is that the weird Bible thing you mentioned back in the taxi, the one that was kept here for a little while?'

'Right,' David replied. 'See, there is a legend surrounding the *Codex Gigas* and how it came to be. The story goes that a monk who went by the name of Herman the Recluse was to be walled up alive for a transgression, though what exactly that was, I have no idea.'

'So that's how Herman died?' Sister Maria asked. 'He was walled up?'

'I'm not certain,' David explained. 'The monk was desperate, and supposedly promised his brothers that if he was spared, he would produce the most complete word of God known to man—the most comprehensive Bible the world had ever seen. And he would do it in a single night. Apparently, Herman was a noted scribe. Even so, back then tomes like that took years and years to produce, and it was likely he was just trying to buy time. Still, the other monks agreed, doubting Herman could complete his impossible task.'

'Don't tell me he finished it,' Sarah exclaimed.

David nodded. 'If the legend is true, then yes. However, he didn't do it alone. Deep into the night, knowing he would fail and fearing for his life, the monk begged for help—not from God, but from the Devil himself.'

Sarah scoffed. 'Well, that was a dumb fucking move.' Sister Maria shifted uncomfortably in her seat, and Sarah added, 'Sorry, Sister. My mouth tends to run away with me.'

'It is fine,' the nun replied with a tight-lipped smile.

'Dumb move or not,' David went on, 'Herman felt abandoned by God, so he was desperate.'

'And the Devil showed up, I take it?' Sarah asked.

'Yes. The Bible was completed in a single night, in 1229 if I remember correctly.'

Sarah shook her head in disbelief. 'Forget for one moment that it's an impossibility, why the hell would the

Devil help write the word of God? I'm pretty sure he isn't the Lord's biggest fan.'

'That's the interesting part,' David went on. 'The book actually contains a full-page drawing of the Devil. No other Bible in existence has that, but this one did. Well, *does,* actually. The book does exist and is on display in the National Library of Sweden. The picture of the Devil is there for anyone to see.'

'Okay,' Sarah responded. 'So the Devil got his picture in a book. It's hardly a big win. Not in the grand scheme of things. And hold up, if the book does exist, does that mean the story is true?'

David laughed. 'It doesn't mean anything, really. The book is real, but there is no evidence of exactly *when* it was written, or by *whom.* Experts can only really agree that, judging by the handwriting, it was indeed written by one individual, but likely would have taken twenty years to finish. So no one really knows where the story of Herman and his deal with the Devil comes from. However, there is more to the tale: the missing pages.'

'The missing pages?' Sarah asked.

'Again, this part is factual. Pages have been torn from the *Codex Gigas.* It isn't clear when, but the tear marks of thirteen pages are visible. According to legend, those thirteen missing pages contained what was called *The Devil's Prayer.*'

'I've heard about that,' Sister Maria added. 'As well as laying claim to Herman's soul as part of the deal, the other stipulation was the inclusion of this 'prayer' in the Bible. Though I don't know what the prayer is about.'

'Me either,' David responded. 'Regardless, the pages were torn out and their whereabouts are unknown. Experts think those pages simply contained the monastic rules of the Benedictines.'

'The Benedictines?' Sarah asked.

Sister Maria chipped in again. 'The Order of Saint Benedictine is a religious order.'

Sarah widened her eyes a little. 'Are they like a cult offshoot of the Church or something?'

Sister Maria frowned. 'No. Why would you think that?'

'Because we know they were going to wall up someone still alive. Not very Catholic, is it?'

'Things were a lot different back then, Sarah,' David said. 'But the Benedictines still exist today, and they are a genuine order. There isn't anything nefarious about them.'

'So what's the connection with this place?' Sarah asked. 'Was the book actually written here?'

David shook his head. 'Not as I understand it, no. It *was* supposedly written in the Czech Republic, not too far from here. However, the cathedral it was written in was destroyed a long time ago. The *Codex Gigas* has travelled around quite a bit, and had a short spell here in 1295 before being shipped off again.'

'So, I have to ask the obvious question,' Sarah went on. 'Why would the ghost of a long-dead monk, who made a deal with the Devil, possess someone *here*? If the book wasn't written here, and has been kept in a few different locations, what's so special about this cathedral?'

David didn't have an answer to that. There wasn't much in the way of actual evidence regarding Herman the Recluse, so it was unclear if he ever made it as far as Kutná Hora, or if he'd even existed at all. Besides, if the book was indeed written in 1229, and didn't end up in the Cathedral of Assumption until 1295, then there was little chance Herman had still been alive at that point.

'I'm not sure what else to say,' David replied. 'That's

about as much as I know. If there is a link to be made, I'm unaware of it.'

He turned his attention to Father Janosch and noticed the priest's brow was furrowed. Luca stared down to the desk before him, seemingly lost in thought. 'Everything okay, Father?' David asked.

Father Janosch shook his head and looked up. 'I think so. Just a lot to take in.' There was something about his expression that gave David pause. However, before he had the opportunity to press Father Janosch further, they were interrupted by three loud and sudden knocks on the door, as if someone were pounding it from the other side. David jumped, as did Sister Maria.

'Yes?' the nun called out. No answer. She got to her feet and addressed the others. 'Apologies, I'm not sure what the urgency is.'

David watched her as Sister Maria strode over to the door and opened it. He craned his neck and saw the corridor outside was empty.

Sister Maria dipped her head outside of the room and looked both left and right. She then turned back to look at the others with a confused frown.

'No one there?' Sarah asked. Sister Maria shook her head. 'There were three knocks,' she said to Father Janosch, who nodded.

'Paranormal activity?' David asked.

'Back at Perron Manor,' Sarah said to Sister Maria, 'the knocking we heard always came in threes as well.'

'No doubt mocking the Holy Trinity,' Father Janosch added. 'Has this kind of thing happened much since Father Hus became possessed?'

'Truthfully... yes,' Sister Maria confirmed. 'I've heard the knocking myself a few times now, but never so loud.'

Father Janosch turned his head to Sarah. 'Are you picking up on anything?'

She paused, narrowed her eyes, and then shook her head. 'I still feel nauseous, and that seems to vary in intensity, but it's been constant since we arrived here. There's nothing else. The cold I felt upstairs with Father Hus isn't there anymore.'

David noticed that Sister Maria looked uneasy. Even though she was just a few feet away from them, her being near the door on her own while the others were seated at the table made David feel uncomfortable as well—like she was too far away from them.

'Come sit down, Sister,' he said to her.

She smiled, closed the door, and quickly padded back over to the table. No one spoke, and they all waited for something else to happen. David noticed a familiar feeling of anticipation dance its way up his spine, making his hands tingle. Was the knocking isolated, or would it lead to other things?

After a few minutes of silence, Sarah spoke.

'What do we do now?' she asked.

Father Janosch considered that for a moment. 'Well, let's try to determine where we stand. I think it is highly likely Father Hus is possessed, though we still have to bear in mind it isn't yet a certainty. His behaviour certainly alludes to that, and Sarah's feeling of sickness, cold, as well as the nosebleed back everything up. However, there is a remote chance that it is all explainable and Father Hus is actually just mentally unwell.'

'But the knocking...' Sister Maria added, pointing to the door.

Father Janosch nodded and held up his hands. 'Again, I *do* think that Father Hus is possessed, but we need to make sure we don't get ahead of ourselves before we have all the facts.'

'If so, it's also likely we know who is possessing Father Hus,' David suggested.

'But we don't know *why*,' Sarah said.

David twisted in his seat to face Sister Maria. 'Sister, would it be possible to visit the ossuary where you found Father Hus, so we can see the skull he was looking at?'

'You think there could be something there?' Father Janosch asked.

David shrugged. 'Maybe. It would be good to get a sense of where he was, and why he was there. There has to be a reason, and Sarah might be able to pick up on something that we can't. Perhaps the location itself is of interest.'

Father Janosch's eyes widened a little and he nodded his agreement. 'That makes sense. There is plenty we could be doing here at the cathedral, but I think we need to first gather as much information as we can.' He turned to Sister Maria as well. 'Is it possible to visit the church?'

'Yes,' she said. 'Visitors are allowed again after the incident with Father Hus. Just be aware that photography and videos are not permitted, however, so if you need to run any private investigations, we would need to get permission and likely do it when the ossuary is closed.'

'I understand that,' Father Janosch replied. 'For now, though, let's just have a look around and see what we can see... or feel,' he added, smiling at Sarah.

'Spider-senses at the ready,' David playfully said to her. Sarah smiled in response. For a moment, David was able to forget why things were so uncomfortable between them, but only for a moment. He shuffled in his seat and looked away.

'I have a few duties to attend to,' Sister Maria stated. 'But if you want to go over straight away, I can call ahead and tell the church to expect you.'

'Would it be possible for you to come with us?' Father Janosch asked. 'We have no problem waiting for you to finish. I just want to get an idea of exactly where he was standing and what he was doing, down to the last detail.'

Sister Maria hesitated, then nodded. 'I understand. It's just... I don't really like it down there. Though, if we must...' she trailed off. Then her eyes widened. 'I have an idea,' she said. 'Father Novák!'

'Who is Father Novák?' David asked.

'He is the warden over at the church. He took me down to the ossuary to get Father Hus. I'm sure he could help if you wish to go over there now.'

Father Janosch looked over to Sarah, then to David. 'What do you think?'

'Might as well,' David said, 'especially while daylight is on our side. We can always come back here afterward. It isn't like we have a mapped-out plan of action to work with, anyway.'

Father Janosch looked to Sarah, and she simply shrugged and nodded.

'Okay, then,' Father Janosch said, 'that sounds like a plan. Sister Maria, if you could speak to Father Novák and arrange for us to go over there to meet with him, that would be appreciated.'

'I will set it up immediately,' she replied.

The group started to get to their feet, but Sister Maria raised a hand. 'You may as well wait here while I make the call. That is...' She looked over to the door again. 'If you are okay doing so after the knocking.'

'No, it's fine,' Father Janosch replied. 'We'll be okay here.

If we have to wait somewhere, this is as good a place as any. We might even see some more activity.'

Sister Maria still had her eyes on the door. 'Well... only if you are sure?'

'Really, it's okay,' David confirmed. 'We're used to this kind of thing.'

However, that wasn't strictly true. He'd found that experiencing supernatural phenomenon wasn't something he had ever gotten totally used to.

Sister Maria gave a smile. 'I will be back shortly, after I make the call.' Father Janosch walked her to the door and closed it behind her as she left. The priest then moved back over to the other two and raised his eyebrows.

'Eventful,' he said. 'Thoughts?'

Sarah didn't offer anything, so David gave his opinion. 'I think it's highly likely this whole thing is genuine, but we need more information to try and figure out what's really going on. At the moment, we're just fumbling in the dark.'

'I agree,' Father Janosch replied.

'Wait,' Sarah suddenly said and brought a hand to her stomach. 'I think I feel...'

The creak of the door caused her to trail off. All three turned to see the door to the room drift open, slowly swinging inwards.

'Didn't Sister Maria close that on the way out?' David asked.

The hairs on the back of his arm begin to stand on end and he knew that something was nearby. Though Sarah wasn't fully in command of her new senses yet, in the short time they'd worked together since Perron Manor, David had never known her to be wrong.

'Who's there?' Father Janosch asked, his voice loud

enough to reach out into the hallway. David didn't expect any response, of cour—

'*Saaaarahhh.*'

The voice was little more than a distorted and hoarse whisper. The sound of it caused a shiver to creep up David's spine. Sarah looked pale.

The door then *slammed* shut, hard enough to make them all jump. The sound continued reverberating around the room for a few seconds afterwards.

'Keep calm,' Father Janosch stressed, though his own voice sounded anything but.

David realised his fists were balled, pressing so tightly into his palms his nails dug into the skin.

They waited. And waited.

Another sound caused David to jolt again, though this one was a dull thud on glass from behind. They spun around and looked to the window. There was nothing there to see beyond the glass and the view of the car park outside.

'Something wants our attention,' Sarah eventually said.

'Or it's testing the waters,' Father Janosch suggested. 'Feeling us out.'

The bang on the window came again and David could see the slight shake of the glass in the frame.

Another bang.

That was soon followed by a scratching sound. It was faint at first, but grew louder and more high pitched: the unmistakable sound of something sharp cutting against the glass. David took a step forward and saw three scratch marks form on the window, dragging down from the centre of the pane and reaching to the sill.

We should be capturing this.

He quickly took out his phone, annoyed it had taken

him so long to spring into action. David quickly flipped to his camera app and began to record.

He felt Sarah lean in beside him. She exhaled a strong breath onto the window, misting up the glass, but also making the scratch marks stand out more.

Good thinking!

'Three marks,' Father Janosch noted.

'Demonic?' David asked.

'*Yessssss,*' came a voice from behind.

They spun around and realised that the door to the room was once again open, though this time just an inch or so, and they were able to see out through the small gap.

However, this time the corridor beyond was blocked by someone standing on the other side of the door, staring at them with wide, manic eyes.

With his heart in his throat, David took in the details of the strange man in an instant: the pale, mottled-grey skin of his face, decayed teeth and black gums within his open mouth, and dark brown robes that looked to be made from hessian.

Whoever the man was, he had no hair on his head, and the flesh of the scalp was thin. In some areas, the bone of the skull showed through.

Black liquid ran down from the man's wide, milky-white eyes, like dark tears staining his cheeks.

The robes were streaked with muck and what appeared to be old blood. His feet were bare, toenails missing, the skin black and rotted. Because the door wasn't fully open, David could only see part of the horrifying man.

'Who are you?' Father Janosch demanded.

A horrible smile crept over the cracked lips of the stranger. The laugh that followed was cruel and mocking, and that was the only response he gave before the door was pulled shut again.

David looked to the others, unsure as to what to do next. His feet were planted to the ground and moving seemed like a Herculean effort. All he could do was raise his phone.

It wasn't lost on David that, given the robes of their visitor, the man was likely a monk—or at least had been a monk in a former life.

'What do we do?' David asked.

Father Janosch looked shaken and offered no response. Sarah jumped into action and immediately charged over to the door.

'Wait!' David shouted, but Sarah didn't listen.

Sarah opened the door and quickly as she did, her hands balled into fists.

Nothing.

She then stepped out into the hallway and looked around. Sarah was certainly brave, but even from this distance David could see how wide her eyes were.

But then, wasn't that what bravery really was? Acting courageous *despite* being scared? Then, David realised he was still stuck and rooted to the spot.

'Anything?' Father Janosch asked.

Sarah came back into the room, leaving the door open. She shook her head. 'Whatever it was, it's gone now. I'm not sensing anything anymore, either, other than the nausea.'

'There can be no doubt now,' Father Janosch stated. 'There is activity here.'

'Did you get it on video?' Sarah asked David, who still had his phone in his hand.

He looked down to it and nodded. 'I think so,' he replied.

They gathered around David's phone as he played the footage back. It showed the scratches appearing in the window. After that, the ghostly voice uttering the drawn-out word 'yes,' was faint but audible. The video then showed the camera whip around to the door.

The monk was visible, even if his features weren't overly clear. David chastised himself for not having the where-withal to have zoomed in—he'd been too preoccupied with what was happening. But the fact that a man was standing directly outside of the room, peering in, was obvious.

They now had evidence, and they weren't even a full day into the investigation.

'Do we still go to the ossuary?' Sarah asked. 'I mean, it doesn't seem right leaving Sister Maria and the others here in potential danger.'

Father Janosch folded his arms across his chest, then brought up his left hand and ran his thumb over his bottom lip as he thought. 'We'll speak to her about it,' he eventually replied. 'My feeling is if the people here have been dealing with this kind of thing for a few days anyway, then us going to the Church of All Saints for a little while shouldn't be an issue.'

Approaching footsteps echoed down the corridor outside. All eyes quickly turned to the open door. David felt himself again tense up.

What now?

However, it was Sister Maria who came into view. She stepped inside through the doorway, then paused.

'Is everything okay?' she asked.

'There has been a small... incident,' Father Janosch told her. He then recounted what happened, from the scratches on the window to the visit from the monk. Sister Maria looked visibly shocked.

'You said before that other people have seen this monk?' David asked her.

'Yes, apparently.'

'Could it be Herman?' Janosch asked to no one in particular.

'I thought Herman was inside Father Hus?' Sarah questioned. 'Can he be in two places at once?'

They both looked to David for answers, but he didn't have any. 'I'm not certain,' he admitted. 'Other than what happened at Perron Manor, I've never dealt with a possession before. I don't think it's possible, but I can't say for certain.' David then hesitated as a thought popped into his head. 'Sister Maria,' he said as he turned to her, 'didn't you say Father Hus seemed to drift between being in a state of possession and being normal?'

'That's right,' she confirmed.

'That could be the explanation,' David suggested. 'The monk could manifest when it isn't possessing Father Hus.'

'But how can the spirit just keep hopping back into Hus whenever it wants?' Sarah questioned. 'If a ghost leaves a person, isn't the possession over?'

David shrugged. 'I honestly don't know, Sarah. This is all a little beyond me. Much of what I know is just theory.'

She nodded her understanding.

Father Janosch came to a decision. 'Let's go up and talk again with Father Hus, see how he's doing.'

'What about the ossuary?' Sister Maria asked. 'Father Novák is expecting you.'

'Don't worry,' Father Janosch replied. 'I don't think the discussion with Father Hus will take long. But it would be good to determine if he has been released by the spirit that had him, temporary though it might be.'

As Sister Maria led them back up to speak with Father Hus, a knot formed in David's stomach. He couldn't help but feel considerably out of his depth.

12

LUCA WAS FLANKED BY SARAH, David, and Sister Maria. After taking a deep breath, he unlocked the door before him and pushed it open, not sure what to expect.

Light from the corridor outside seeped into the room, and Luca quickly saw Father Hus sitting at the front of the bed, legs pulled up to his chest and a blanket wrapped over his shoulders. The man looked up with red, tear-streaked eyes, and in that instant, Luca knew that the spirit that had previously possessed the man was no longer in charge —for now.

'Father Hus,' Luca began, 'are you okay?'

The poor man burst into tears, his shoulders shaking beneath the thin blanket that partially hid his nudity. Sister Maria broke rank before Luca could stop her and ran over to her sobbing friend. She knelt beside him and brought his head to her chest, cradling it, and began to soothe him. Her words—spoken in Czech—were gentle and warm.

'*It will be okay, my dear friend. It will all be okay.*'

The stench of excrement was still powerful, and Father

Hus looked greatly dishevelled. Luca couldn't imagine what kind of hell the man was going through.

Luca took a few steps farther into the room and knelt down alongside Sister Maria, close to Father Hus. He felt Sarah and David standing close behind him.

'Father,' Luca began. He laid a supportive hand on the priest's shoulder. 'Can we speak with you? I know you must be feeling scared, but we are here to help.'

'Why is this happening?' the terrified priest asked. Luca's heart broke for him.

'I'm not sure,' Luca replied honestly. 'But we will help you through it.'

Father Hus brought his head up from Sister Maria's embrace. Luca noticed that his gums still looked a dark, unnatural purple, just as they had during their last meeting—a clear and obvious sign of the possession he was battling. His face scrunched up into an expression that Luca couldn't quite read—something between pain and anger. 'There is no way to help me,' Father Hus said. His tone was cold. 'I am damned.'

The defeat evident in Father Hus' voice took Luca aback.

Luca shook his head. 'No, you are not. Don't think that way, Father, because that will just make things easier for this evil. You must fight it.'

'I can't,' Father Hus said, shaking his head. 'Look at me. I am a mess. I am broken. I know that thing will be back for me, and there's nothing I can do to stop it.'

'There *is* something you can do,' Luca stressed. 'Keep fighting it, however you can. And tell us everything you know.'

Father Hus' eyes narrowed and his head tilted to the side. 'Know? About what?'

'About what happened to you. Tell us when you think it

started, what you're aware of when the entity has control of you... the connection it has could also be a two-way thing. Could be that you can tell us much more about this entity than we would otherwise know. Think, Father, is there anything more you can remember?'

Luca quickly looked over to David to instruct him to record what the priest was going to say. However, he saw that David already had his phone out.

Good man.

Luca turned back to Father Hus.

'I... don't really remember anything,' the priest said, eyes staring off into nothing. His pupils flicked left and right slightly, as if he was searching his mind for answers. 'Everything seemed normal until recently,' Father Hus eventually said. 'I can't think of what the catalyst for all of this was. A few days ago, though, I started periodically losing my concentration, and people told me I was being a little distant. Not on purpose, but stretches of time would go by and I couldn't really remember doing anything. Then, I was told that I'd been short and irritable, yet I couldn't remember any of the incidents.'

'Okay,' Luca replied. 'That's good. It gives us something to go on. What about being at the ossuary, do you remember that?'

Father Hus again shook his head. 'No, not at all. I don't even know how I got there. I just remember being back here, in this room, after it had all happened. Sister Maria had to tell me what I'd done. I was frightened after hearing it. Thought I was ill. My father was afflicted by dementia, you see, and I just thought...'

'I understand,' Luca told him.

Father Hus went on. 'After that, I kept losing more time. I would always wake up in here, in this room again, and each time I'd be told about what I'd done, the vile things I'd said, but I have no memory of it. I insisted I be locked away in here so I could do no harm to others until help arrived. Sister Maria,' he looked up to her, 'has been an angel, caring for me when I am not deserving of such kindness.'

'Of *course* you deserve it,' Sister Maria told him, still kneeling by his side with an arm draped over him. 'None of this is your fault. You aren't to blame.'

'She's right,' Luca insisted. 'Listen to her.'

Sister Maria took another look around the room, and her nose crinkled. Slowly, a disgusted expression formed on her face. 'We need to put you in a different room,' she said. 'This place isn't even fit for a beast.'

Luca couldn't disagree with that. The smell was vile.

'You need clothes, water, and some warm food,' the nun went on. 'And we need to get you cleaned up.'

She stood and tried to help Father Hus up as well, but he appeared reluctant. However, the nun would not let him give up so easily, and hooked both arms around Hus' waist and heaved, giving the priest the support to get to his feet. He turned to her and offered a kind smile. However, Luca noted that kindness didn't quite stretch to his eyes, which seemed a little... off.

'I don't know how to thank you,' Father Hus said and embraced Sister Maria in a sudden hug.

Luca then felt a hand grab his forearm. He turned to see Sarah looking at him, wide-eyed, and she put a hand to her gut. He quickly looked back to Father Hus and Sister Maria, and saw the priest had pulled his head away.

The priest now had a sneer on his face.

'Now how about a nice, good fuck to show my gratitude, Sister!'

Father Hus suddenly grabbed Sister Maria's head with

both hands and forced her face towards his own. His tongue snaked from between his dry lips and up the nun's cheek. She screwed her eyes shut in shock and let out a cry.

Luca hesitated. The sudden change in Father Hus had taken him—had taken all of them—completely by surprise, and his feet felt like they were rooted to the spot. He could only watch as Father Hus fell forward onto Sister Maria, his weight bearing down on the woman. The two dropped to the floor with him atop her. Sister Maria suddenly started fighting back, like a switch had been flicked that triggered her survival response. She thrust a hand up in an attempt to push his head away as Father Hus again tried to force his tongue onto her.

'You'll enjoy it, bitch,' Father Hus seethed in a cruel and hateful voice. 'See what you've been missing out on all these years.'

Thankfully, however, Sarah wasn't as frozen as Luca and David had been, and she sprinted forward. The former-military woman launched herself at Father Hus, shoulder first, and there was a dull slap of impact as her body collided with his naked chest. With a grunt, Father Hus fell backwards, sprawling to the floor. Luca then found the strength to move and he quickly helped Sarah get Sister Maria to her feet while Father Hus scrambled to his own.

Sister Maria was shaking, close to tears, as Sarah, David, and Luca gathered around her and shepherded her back to the door.

'Stay a while,' Father Hus said with a chuckle. Luca felt sick when he looked back over to the naked man, who stood completely upright, with an erection on full display. He began to caress himself as Luca led the others back through the door.

'At least let that one stay!' he shouted, pointing at Sarah.

The priest ran a fat tongue over his bottom lip. 'Ohhhh, the fun I could have with you, little girl.'

'Ignore him,' Luca said to her, seeing Sarah's teeth clench together in a snarl. 'He's trying to goad you.'

'It's working,' Sarah shot back. Thankfully, however, she didn't do anything stupid, and instead concentrated on getting the now sobbing Sister Maria out into the corridor.

'Come, Sarah, stop running away,' Father Hus called. 'You've travelled all this way to talk to me, but you just blindly follow your master's orders and flee when he snaps his fingers. Is this what you have become, a scared little lap dog? Don't you want to know what I have to tell you?'

But Luca slammed the door shut between them, then locked it. 'Poisonous ghoul,' he spat.

Sarah was glaring at the door. Her jaw looked tense. Luca gently touched her elbow. Her head whipped around to face him. 'You must ignore him,' Luca said. 'Don't let the entity toy with you.'

It took a few moments, but Luca finally saw her jaw relax. She took a breath before nodding in agreement.

'I'm okay,' she said. Both then turned their attention to Sister Maria, who was trying to get her crying under control.

'Are you okay?' David asked her.

'I am fine,' she stated firmly as she wiped away some tears. She then straightened her stance and pushed back her shoulders, standing tall. Luca admired her for showing strength, but it was obvious the incident had shaken her. How could it not have?

'Let us walk you back to your room,' David offered.

Sister Maria just shook her head. Her jaw trembled, but there was a determination in her eyes. 'No, thank you. I... have duties I must attend to.'

'Are you sure you are up to it?' Luca asked.

'Of course,' she replied. 'I have God on my side, and I know Father Hus' actions were not his own. It was the monster that controls him.'

'Is that the first time he has attacked anyone like that?' Luca questioned.

Sister Maria nodded. 'To that extent, yes, though there was the incident where he struck the child, of course.'

'This was different, though,' Sarah added. 'What he tried to do to you...'

'It was likely in an effort to disgust and repulse us,' Luca stated. 'Demonic forces often resort to the most base acts to get under our skin.'

After a few moments of no one speaking, David broke the silence. 'What now?'

'Go to the ossuary,' Sister Maria instructed. She turned to Luca and looked him dead in the eye. 'I'll be fine here. Get whatever information you need, then return and help rid Father Hus of this evil. Please.'

Luca paused for a moment, then nodded once.

13

'THIS PLACE IS FUCKING RIDICULOUS,' Sarah exclaimed.

Bones of the dead were displayed like decorations around her, laid out proudly across the walls and ceiling of the ossuary. Whoever had designed and assembled this shrine of the macabre had done so with no consideration for the dead's dignity.

The other people present in the basement area of the church—tourists with cameras around their necks and faces buried in tour books—spun around at Sarah's outburst.

'Perhaps don't shout that so loud,' Father Novák sternly suggested. He had met them at the entrance of the Church of All Saints and brought them straight down to the ossuary. He seemed friendly enough, and was a man who looked to be in his mid-fifties, with thinning, grey-black hair swept over in a tight side parting. His square face sported deep-set eyes and a wide, thin mouth. The man was short and broad, dressed in a grey suit jacket with a black shirt beneath—clerical collar on show.

'Sorry,' Sarah said. Her cheeks flushed red for a moment.

Soon, however, the crowd of ten tourists all went back to their business.

Sarah heard Father Janosch chuckle beside her. 'We really need to help you develop some kind of inner filter, Sarah,' he joked.

'Noted,' she replied, still taking in her surroundings.

The ossuary wasn't as big as she had been expecting, and in truth it was a similar size to the basement back in Perron Manor. Even though most of the ossuary was below ground, the area did have the benefit of natural light thanks to a handful of windows. A portion of the ground outside was set back from the building, with a retaining wall allowing a walkway around some of the perimeter. It was along this walkway, carved into the earth, that the daylight was allowed to spill in.

The largest window sat directly ahead of the group, and was central to the wall, immediately drawing the eye of those that descended into the basement. The window was set within a tight alcove where a shrine had been set up, one that contained a large statue of Jesus hanging on the cross.

Four equally spaced display units—shaped like cones— sat central to the room. Each of those was adorned with horizontal circular plates, which in turn held grinning human skulls. The rings of skulls were evenly spaced up the display units, like grotesque decorations on a Christmas tree.

There was also an array of skeleton parts on the walls, laid out in intricate patterns, including a large and carefully designed crest. However, the ceiling was the most striking feature.

More bones and skulls followed sweeping support arches, like streamers, meeting at a centre point in the middle of the room, where a large chandelier hung. The chandelier was not made from brass or crystal; instead, every part of it was formed from human parts—from the upturned arms that arched upwards and held the light fittings on top of skulls, to the central bowl at the bottom, and even the vertical support structure fixed to the ceiling and covered in the remains of the dead.

With its stone-coloured walls and grey-tiled floor, the room seemed washed out and devoid of colour, and that was only exacerbated by the osseous adornments that so disgusted Sarah. The flickering of candlelight around the room only helped to convey a macabre aesthetic.

'Can you tell me exactly where you and Sister Maria found Father Hus after the area was cleared out?' Father Janosch asked.

Father Novák nodded and walked to one of the four cone-shaped displays, the one farthest from them to the left. Of the rings of skulls that circled the fixture, the priest pointed to the third one up. The skull his finger touched looked towards the back window and the statue of the crucifixion.

Sarah and David followed Father Janosch closer to inspect the skull. It looked like all of the other ones in the room, and Sarah couldn't pick up on any deformities or irregularities that made it stand out as different. Father Janosch turned to her.

'Getting anything?'

'No,' she replied and shook her head. Since leaving the cathedral, Sarah hadn't picked up on any sensations at all, but was at least relieved she no longer felt sick.

That, it seemed, was reserved for the cathedral, though she wasn't sure why.

'Is it true Father Hus is under the possession of a demon?' Father Novák asked in a hushed whisper.

'We aren't certain,' Father Janosch whispered back. 'But we're looking into it.'

'Will he be okay?' Father Novák went on to ask.

Father Janosch turned to face him and offered a polite smile. 'I will do everything I can to make sure he will be. I promise.'

'I can scarcely believe what's happening to him,' the priest said with more than a hint of sadness. 'I saw him only a few weeks before. He and Sister Maria were down here showing a new nun around. He seemed so normal then.'

No one said anything in reply. Sarah wanted to, but she couldn't find the words.

Their attention then turned back to the skull, but it was clear to Sarah they would get very little from it. Whether it previously belonged to the entity hounding Father Hus, or if it was just a random object his possessed self had momentarily been obsessed with, she doubted they would ever know. After looking around the rest of the ossuary, and finding little of interest, Sarah began to feel the trip had been a wasted one. At least they could say they were being thorough in their investigation.

She was just about to suggest to the others that they had seen enough, when something caught her attention. Her eyes followed the line of one of the ceiling arches down to where it met the wall. The arch had a row of skulls fixed to it, each packed tightly to the next, but at its outermost extents Sarah noticed a gap—a space where a skull should have obviously been. Sarah moved closer and saw that an old nail was driven into the support structure, and around the nail were small fragments of bone.

A skull had been removed.

She pointed to it and looked over to Father Novák. 'A skull is missing here. Know anything about it?' she asked.

The priest came over and looked up. His eyes widened in surprise.

'When did that happen?' he asked, more to himself than anyone else.

'You weren't aware of it?' she asked him.

He shook his head sternly, then looked around. 'Maybe one of the tourists stole it?'

But Sarah had a different suspicion. 'Is the area monitored?' she asked. However, she already knew the answer, having already seen a video camera in the room. It was tucked away in one of the corners.

'Yes,' he answered, pointing to it. 'But we don't always check the footage. Not unless we feel there is a need to.'

'I think we have a need now,' Sarah told him. 'I want to see the footage from when Father Hus was here.'

He shuffled uncomfortably. 'We have already looked at that,' he said. 'But Father Hus used one of his discarded socks to cover the lens. The camera picked up very little of interest.'

'So Father Hus was left alone for a while that night?'

Father Novák nodded. 'Yes. After we cleared out the area, there was a period of time where he was unsupervised while we made sure everyone was safe. That was when he covered the camera.'

Sarah then walked back over to the skull Father Hus had supposedly been so enamoured with.

'Can I pick this up to inspect it?'

Father Novák frowned and shook his head. 'No, they must not be handled.'

David and Father Janosch stood close. 'What are you thinking, Sarah?' David asked.

Sarah squatted down and studied the skull, as well as those around it. A smile formed on her lips.

'Look inside,' she said, 'through the eye sockets. The craniums on most are intact. But see, the one Hus was looking at has some damage to the back. A small hole.'

The others looked inside and saw it too.

'He replaced it with the one up there,' David exclaimed, pointing to the gap in the ceiling support arch. 'So that means...'

Sarah nodded. 'Yes. He stole the skull.'

14

THE GROUP REQUESTED to see the footage from the ossuary anyway, but there was nothing to see other than Hus covering the camera to hide his movements.

Afterward, they returned to the meeting room in the cathedral. Sister Maria joined them.

'It just doesn't make sense,' David said. 'If Father Hus stole the skull, what did he do with it? And how the hell did he get it out of the ossuary if he was *naked?*'

'As yet, I have no idea,' Father Janosch answered. He looked over to Sister Maria, who sat at the table opposite him. 'I don't suppose you saw a skull on his person when you found him?'

Sister Maria shook her head. 'I'm afraid not. He had absolutely nothing on him when I arrived. I don't see where he could have hidden it. If he did remove a skull from its place, then he certainly didn't take it with him when we brought him back here.'

'And the staff at the Church of All Saints insist he never left the ossuary until help arrived,' David added. 'So he didn't sneak it out beforehand.'

'That can mean only one thing,' Sarah said. 'The skull is still down there.'

'The most likely scenario,' Father Janosch confirmed. 'Though, why swap it with another in the first place if the plan wasn't to take it?'

'So *where* has he hidden it?' David added.

Father Luca directed his next question to Sister Maria. 'Has anything happened in our absence?'

'No,' Sister Maria replied. 'Though, no one has been up to see Father Hus since he...' She looked down to the desk with a hint of shame, one that David felt was completely unjustified. None of what had happened was her fault. 'Attacked me,' she finished in a soft voice. The nun then looked back up. 'But I am really worried about him. The conditions in his room are horrific, and we can't get him to eat food or drink water. If we don't help him soon, I fear for his life.'

'We will act as quickly as we can,' Father Janosch reassured her. 'However, it might be a good idea to move him to a different room, somewhere cleaner, and get him some food. We can do it the next time he is... himself.'

'We've tried that,' Sister Maria said. 'But every time we act, the spirit takes him again. It's like it leaves him and waits around for another chance to toy with us.'

Father Janosch took a slow breath 'I understand, but we need to keep trying.'

'Of course,' Sister Maria said. 'And we will. I just... lose hope sometimes.' However, as soon as those words had crossed her lips, the nun straightened her posture and pulled back her shoulders. 'But I know I must be stronger than that for Father Hus. And I will be.'

'So what's next?' David asked. 'Other than speaking with Father Hus again, I'm not sure what else we can do now.

Unless we feel that carrying out some investigative sessions would help?'

'Sessions?' Sister Maria asked.

'Things like vigils, séances, or EVP readings,' David explained. 'Techniques we use to capture evidence of the paranormal, or even draw it out.'

'I see. Would that help? I mean, you already know where the spirit is, don't you? In Father Hus. Is there any point in running these sessions?'

Sister Maria had a point. And if that *was* the case, was it time for them to call in outside help? After all, they'd determined the cathedral wasn't a Devil's Doorway. Was there anything left now other than an exorcism?

Father Janosch spoke up, giving an answer to David's internal questions. 'There is still much to figure out,' he said. 'But the main thing we need to uncover is *why* Father Hus demanded to see Sarah, and how he knew about the events of Perron Manor. If the spirit in possession of him is indeed Herman, then what is the link?'

'Wait,' Sister Maria cut in. 'I thought you were here to help Father Hus?'

'We are,' Father Janosch was quick to add. 'But we need to get to the bottom of *all* of this as well. There is a wider issue here. I have no doubt unravelling the mystery is also the key to freeing Father Hus.'

'What about an exorcism?' Sister Maria asked. 'If it was successful, wouldn't that bring the matter to a close? Are you not able to just sanction that? Surely you have enough evidence? And can't you just perform it yourselves?'

David saw Father Janosch shift uncomfortably at the barrage of questions. 'I'd need the instruction to come from the Church,' the priest replied. 'In all likelihood, it would be someone else who would carry it out. Our speciality is more... building a case.'

There was an air of frustration around Sister Maria now. David supposed he couldn't blame her, considering the circumstances; even the most patient and understanding of people were pushed to their breaking point when dealing with the forces of evil.

'Am I to assume that you don't plan on actually helping Father Hus, then?' she snapped. 'I expected you and your friends to arrive here and... what is the phrase... save the day? Yet I find you were merely sent to take notes.'

She rose to her feet.

Father Janosch held up his hands. 'Sister Maria, please,' he started. However, the nun simply waved him away.

'I have duties to attend to,' she snapped. 'I was instructed to let you have full access to the cathedral, so you are obviously free to do as you please. But I cannot just sit by while you play at being detectives.' She strode towards the door. 'Call for me if you need me.'

'Sister Maria,' Father Janosch repeated. However, it was futile. She left the room and slammed the door closed behind her.

David and the others sat looking at each other in bewilderment.

'That took a turn,' Sarah said.

Father Janosch let out a long sigh. 'It did indeed.'

'She's frustrated,' David said. 'And I can't blame her. Nun or not, she's seeing her friend suffer. If she was expecting us to fix all this straight away, then of course she's going to be disappointed. All she sees is us spinning our wheels.'

'Well, that isn't completely fair,' Father Janosch retorted. 'We're only just getting started. We haven't even had a full day at this yet, and we've already uncovered quite a bit.'

'I suppose,' David replied, 'but are we *actually* in a position to act? I mean, is there really any more good we can do here?'

'What are you suggesting?' Sarah asked.

'Report back,' David stated. 'Tell them what we know, and then get an exorcism in motion, as Sister Maria suggested. I mean, is there really any reason to delay the process any longer?'

'Yes,' Father Janosch insisted. 'Of course there is. Just as I said to Sister Maria, we still haven't uncovered the reason Sarah's name was used, or how the spirit knew of her. Given her role in all of this, do I really have to explain why that is important to figure out?'

David took a breath, then shook his head. 'I guess not. But the longer we wait, the more Father Hus continues to suffer. That just doesn't feel right.'

'Then we will work as fast as we can,' Father Janosch stated. He stood. 'For now, I want us to get aquatinted with the cathedral a little more. Sister Maria has said we have free rein here, so let's take advantage of that and explore.'

'And after that?' Sarah questioned.

Father Janosch paused. 'We call it a day.'

David couldn't believe what he'd just heard. 'What?! I thought you said we would work quickly.'

'Yes, but we also need to work smartly. To give Father Hus another audience today would be playing into the entity's hands. It knows we are here now, so we should make it wait for us, and only speak to it on our own terms. Plus, I think we need to report back on what we have found. I'm keen to find out more of the monk, Herman the Recluse, and I may have a contact who can help with that.'

15

THE CATHEDRAL OF ASSUMPTION was far too big to fully explore. The newer sections to the back just seemed like rooms-upon-rooms-upon-rooms, all accessed off long corridors—much like the layouts of modern chain hotels.

Some of the rooms offered accommodation and living areas, though a lot of them seemed to be empty. There were also meeting rooms, offices, and smaller chapels of worship, all presumably just for use by the residents. On the ground floor, there was even a kitchen and small canteen.

During their walk-around, which Luca led, the group saw many more nuns and priests passing them in the halls. The larger section to the right-hand side of the main nave was a lot more populated. That made sense considering its bigger size, and also because Father Hus was locked up on the opposite side, which people were obviously avoiding. Father Janosch couldn't imagine people would be happy sleeping close to the possessed priest.

The self-guided tour, while interesting, was relatively uneventful. Early evening was setting in with the clouds darkening outside. Part of Luca wanted to stay longer.

During investigations, especially the one at Perron Manor, things tended to happen more at night, which could well be the case at the Cathedral of Assumption too. However, the nosebleed Sarah had suffered worried him. It wasn't just a coincidence—he refused to believe that. Father Hus had caused it.

Luca already worried about Sarah being susceptible, since she'd been possessed at Perron Manor, so he was determined to proceed with caution, remembering the words of the Southern American member of the Council: '*tread carefully, Father Janosch.*' Better, for tonight at least, to let things settle, and also check in with the Council to update them. Luca was satisfied the cathedral was not a doorway to hell, and as such their immediate worry had been placated.

As they travelled down another long corridor on their way back to the central nave and choir, they passed a small, frail nun dressed in a light grey habit. Her face was close to skeletal, were it not for the sagging skin around her cheeks. A small amount of white curls peeked out just beneath the headpiece of her outfit, and she carried rosary beads and crucifix within her gnarled and wrinkled hands. Her movements were slow and steady, and Luca guessed she was easily in her late eighties, or even nineties. The group had passed her once before earlier, when she had smiled politely at them, not questioning why they were wandering the halls. In fact, no one had questioned that.

As their paths crossed, the old lady smiled again, though this time she spoke.

'Lost?' she asked.

Luca and the others stopped and turned to face the nun. 'Excuse me?' he asked with a gentle, friendly tone.

'Are... you... lost?' she asked in a strong Czech accent.

Each word was slow and considered, like she was not completely comfortable with the English language. Still, it was clear she could speak it, at least to some degree. The fact she knew to use it with Luca and the others meant she was aware of who they were.

'No,' Luca replied, 'just looking around your beautiful cathedral.'

She smiled. 'You... are here to help? Help Father Hus, yes?'

Word had clearly gotten around.

'We are going to try,' he stated.

'Please do,' she said. 'Father Hus is a good man. He does not deserve what is happening. The things he says now... it is not really him. You understand?'

Luca nodded. 'I do. We will do everything we can, Sister...?' He trailed off, hoping she would pick up on his cue.

'Sister Agatha,' the nun replied.

'Have you spoken with Father Hus much since all this started?' David asked her.

Sister Agatha gave a smile, though it was a distinctly sad one. 'A little. But, after last time... it was too much to bear.'

'What happened last time?' David followed up.

The sad smile only deepened. 'He said... he said would take my eyes from me.' The old lady brought a bent finger up to one of her pale blue eyes. 'My dear mother always used to say our eyes are windows to our soul. Something I believe dearly. So the thought of that happening...'

'Jesus,' Sarah uttered. However, Luca wished she could have chosen a more appropriate word. Sister Agatha quickly crossed herself and kissed the rosary beads she was carrying. 'Sorry,' Sarah added with a frown. 'I keep doing that.'

'Will you be staying here? In the cathedral?' Sister Agatha went on to ask.

'No,' Luca replied. 'We are booked in at a small guest house in town. In fact, we were just leaving for the day.'

'So soon?' the nun asked in surprise. Luca could feel David bristle beside him. However, before Luca could add anything else, a sound from a room near to them drew their attention.

The noise was loud, like someone had thrown something. Then it happened again, and again, quickly building into a crescendo. Luca saw Sister Agatha tense up and bring a hand to her mouth. As quickly as it had started, though, the noise suddenly ceased.

After a moment of stunned silence, Luca pointed to the source of the sound and asked, 'Sister, what is that room?'

The poor old woman's eyes were wide, her mouth agape, as she stared at the door a few metres down. She swallowed. 'A chapel,' she replied. 'Though it's small.'

Luca turned to David. 'Have your camera ready.'

David pulled out his phone, and Luca slowly led them towards the door. Sister Agatha began to edge closer with them. 'You don't need to come, Sister,' Luca said. 'We can handle it.'

'Are you sure?' she asked.

He gave a firm nod. 'Of course. Please, go about your business.'

The nun looked genuinely relieved. 'Bless you. Be careful. Things like this'—she pointed to the door—'the noises, happening a lot these last days. Everyone is worried.'

'We'll get to the bottom of it,' David said. 'I promise.'

Luca felt himself tense up. David's vow had come from a good place, no question, but it wasn't something they could one-hundred-percent deliver on. So much of what was happening was outside of their control. Surely Perron Manor had taught them that. That was why Luca had been careful not to over-commit to anything and raise hopes unnecessarily. He wanted Father Hus safe and free of this evil as much as anyone, but could he guarantee that would happen? Luca knew well enough that exorcisms were often dangerous for the subject and didn't always end well.

David's answer, however, seemed to satisfy Sister Agatha; after a smile and a nod, she walked away at a steady pace, checking back over her shoulder periodically.

Luca turned his attention back to the white-painted door, and he again slowly started forward. As they drew nearer, Luca saw a small sign fixed to the door. *Kapel.*

He pressed his ear to the door and listened in, trying to pick up on if anything was still happening inside. David and Sarah flanked him.

'Anything?' Sarah asked in a hushed voice.

Luca shook his head. 'It's quiet.'

He knew they would have to go inside and check, but Luca hesitated. It occurred to him that the noises had started as soon as he'd told Sister Agatha they would be leaving for the night. If whatever happened inside was paranormal in nature, was that in retaliation to them leaving?

If so, was it intended to scare them away quicker, or goad them to stay longer?

There was only one way to find out. Luca pushed the door inward, allowing it to swing open. The room was dark, but the light from the corridor spilled inside, allowing sight enough to see the carnage within, mirroring what they had seen up in Father Hus' room.

Chairs were strewn around the area, some broken, and the small altar at the back of the room was on its side, splintered down the centre. Lying in the middle of the room, framed perfectly by the stream of light that fell in from the hallway, was a broken crucifix. The golden mould of Jesus was free from the wooden backing, its arms were missing, and something was wrong with its face. Luca carefully leaned inside the room and flicked on the light.

The wallpaper inside was a dull green with subtle golden patterns to it. One of the side walls had a distinct claw mark cut through the paper; three jagged lines arced down to the ground. Luca noted there were no windows at all in the room, and only one door in and out.

'How the hell did this happen?' Sarah asked as they all stepped inside. The room felt abnormally cold, especially compared to the corridor outside.

Luca walked to the mould of Jesus and realised what was wrong with the face. He bent down and lifted the small statue up in his hand. He could feel David looking on over his shoulder.

'The eyes,' David said. 'They've been scratched out.'

Deep black gouges covered the small area where each eye should have been, stretching down to the cheeks and up to the hairline.

Luca looked up to Sarah. 'You picking up on anything?' he asked.

'No. Other than feeling sick, but that's just a constant in this place. I still don't know what it means.'

Luca turned back to the small statue of Jesus in his hand.

The door to the room suddenly slammed shut. Luca had just enough time to look up before the light-fitting above them blew out, plunging them into darkness.

16

SARAH'S VISION took a few moments to adjust to the sudden darkness. The sliver of light creeping in under the door was the only reason she was able to orient herself at all.

'What happened?' she heard David ask in a panicked tone.

Sarah had instinctively tensed up the second the door had slammed, and now had a cold sensation creeping its way up her back—nothing to do with her new senses, merely from the fear that gripped her.

'Keep calm,' she ordered, trying her best to sound in control. Thinking quickly, Sarah drew out her phone and tapped the screen, then flicked on the flashlight application to cut through the dark. She quickly whipped the phone around, this way and that, making sure nothing was in the room with them. All she could see was the devastation in the room.

The beam from David's phone soon joined Sarah's, giving them more visibility, and Sarah made her way quickly over towards the door, her hand finding the light switch first. She tried it, but nothing happened. Sarah shone her light to the door and grabbed the handle.

It isn't going to open, she told herself, sure they were trapped inside. However, she was wrong. The handle turned, and she was easily able to pull the door open without any issues.

David and Luca were already on their feet.

'Let's go,' she said to them and waved them out. Sarah let both go out in front of her, and she took up the rear. However, just as she was about to cross the threshold, something grabbed her arm.

Before she had the chance to turn and look, Sarah immediately felt an intense cold emanate from the strong grip on her forearm. Whipping her head around, she let out a yelp as she stared into the darkness beside her. In an instant, the grip was released.

'What is it?' David asked.

Sarah looked down to her arm and saw three distinct red welts. The skin around the red marks stung and throbbed. Panic was starting to take hold and Sarah's eyes flicked back up. She heard a breath from the unnaturally thick darkness in front of her. Light from the hallway should have pushed back the shadows farther, but the dark seemed to resist. A sulphurous smell flowed over her, and a feeling of radiating cold hit her as well. Two yellow orbs glinted before her, floating about a foot higher than Sarah's head.

Something was there, standing close to her, hidden by the black.

'Sarah!' Luca called from outside. 'What can you see?'

That was enough to prompt Sarah into action, giving her strength enough to snap out of the fear that held her. She quickly brought her phone around and shone the light out ahead.

All she saw was the wall at the far end of the room. In an instant, the feeling of cold around her—which had been like a frosty blanket—suddenly seeped away to nothing, as did the smell.

She eventually let out a breath that Sarah hadn't even realised she'd been holding. She quickly strode out of the room, all the way over to the other side of the corridor. When there, she spun around and pressed her back into the wall behind her, staring wide-eyed at the open doorway.

'What is it?' Father Janosch asked as he quickly approached her. The priest laid a hand on her shoulder and looked back to the door as well. 'What did you see?'

'I...' Sarah wasn't sure how to answer. She hadn't actually *seen* a whole lot, but the brief experience had left her shaken.

Deep down, she knew what had been in there with her.

Sarah felt Father Janosch take hold of her arm and lift it up. 'Three marks,' he said. Now that they were all out in the light, the angry red streaks across were easier to see. When he turned her forearm over, they saw another mark, this one a thumb-like appendage that crossed over the tips of the other welts.

'A demon...' Father Janosch uttered.

That had been Sarah's suspicion as well, especially after seeing the glinting yellow eyes. Her mind quickly jumped back to the meeting room earlier, where they had all watched three scratches form on the glass.

Her experiences at Perron Manor had shown that the hands of demons—at least the ones she'd seen—had three long fingers on them, making them look more like claws.

David edged closer to the room again, then thrust his torchlight inside and looked around. His tense body soon visibly relaxed. 'The room's empty now,' he said, and came back over to them. The worry he carried on his face was obvious. 'So,' he went on, 'it looks like we aren't actually dealing with the ghost of Herman. That looks to have been a deception. It is a demon possessing Father Hus.'

'Perhaps,' Father Janosch said. 'Or perhaps not. I feel there is more to this.'

David pointed to the marks on Sarah's arm. 'That's demonic, no question.'

'I agree,' the priest replied. 'Which makes things more serious. However, we can't get ahead of ourselves.'

'We also can't leave now,' David insisted. 'They need us *here*.'

Father Janosch shook his head. 'I understand your urgency, but we still need to gather our thoughts. This development only serves to complicate things. I need to seek advice from the Council.'

David shook his head, exasperated. Sarah could feel frustration radiate from him.

'I can't believe—'

Father Janosch cut him off. 'David!' the priest snapped. 'We have our instructions here. I sympathise with how you are feeling, but you as well as anyone know what is at stake with these investigations. We proceed with caution. That is final.'

Sarah saw David grit his teeth together and make as if to argue further, but Father Janosch turned and started to walk down the corridor, leaving them both behind. Sarah and David shared a look.

He nodded down to her arm. 'Are you okay? Does that hurt?'

Sarah rubbed it. In truth it stung a little, though nothing too severe. 'It's fine,' she answered. 'I'm just a little freaked out more than anything.'

She cast her eyes up to the open doorway again, and David's gaze followed. 'Feels like we're running away,' he said.

'I know. But Father Janosch just wants to make sure no one else gets hurt. I can understand that.'

David didn't respond. Up ahead, Father Janosch stopped and turned around. 'Are you two coming?' he asked.

'Shouldn't we tell someone about this?' David called over to him and pointed to the open door.

'We will,' Father Janosch replied. 'I want to find Sister Maria again before we go, and then we'll explain what happened here. But our work for the day isn't finished when we leave. There is someone else I want us to talk to.'

17

THE GROUP HAD CAUGHT up with Sister Maria again before leaving the cathedral to update her on what had happened. Sister Maria had appreciated the update, though Sarah thought the woman looked a little worried. The nun was still cold with them, however, and clearly unhappy with the lack of action they had taken thus far.

Sarah, David, and Father Janosch retreated back to the guest house and gathered around the small dining table in the living area. Father Janosch placed his tablet on the table, with the screen facing out towards them. Sarah took a sip of her hot, hazelnut coffee, enjoying its warmth, as the priest set up the call on his device.

David had gotten the fire in the living room going, and it kicked out wave after wave of welcome heat. With night now fully set in, the crackling of the fire, the flickering flames, and the hot coffee Sarah had brewed for them all made the room feel cosy and relaxed. A bit of relaxation was something they could all do with after a long and stressful day.

The tablet rang, and the call connected, revealing the face of a woman: Reverend Quinn. According to Father

Janosch, the woman was supposedly an expert and scholar in matters of Catholic history.

A friendly, toothy smile crossed the reverend's face, and she wore dark-rimmed glasses, with her hair hung in a simple bob. Sarah noticed the first signs of grey showing through from the roots.

'Hi, everyone,' Reverend Quinn said with a big wave.

'Hello, Reverend,' Father Janosch replied, speaking a little too loudly, as if he didn't trust the microphone to pick up his voice. He gave a wave of his own. 'Thank you for taking the time to talk with us.'

'No problem at all,' she replied. 'I'm glad I can be of service. I assume your friends here are Ms. Pearson and Mr. Ritter?'

Sarah smiled and waved back. 'Hi there.'

'I hope we aren't keeping you from anything important?' Father Janosch asked.

Reverend Quinn shook her head and laughed. 'Not at all. This is my priority now, as you know. And it means I get to focus on what I enjoy, so I definitely can't complain.'

The quality of the stream was, for the most part, stable, but her speech would occasionally stutter and slow down.

'How can I help?' she asked.

'Well, where to start?' Father Janosch began. 'Today has been... eventful, to say the least. We managed to speak with Father Hus and the information he gave us was interesting... if true.' Father Janosch then relayed the events of the day to Reverend Quinn and brought her up to speed.

When finished, the reverend shook her head in disbelief. 'It's still hard to get my head around the fact that these things exist.'

'Ghosts and demons?' David asked.

She nodded. 'Yes. Until recently, I thought that it was all just stories and folklore.'

'I hear that,' Sarah added, recalling how difficult it had been for her to come to terms with the same thing.

'What I wanted to ask you about,' Father Janosch began, 'was this Herman the Recluse character, and the *Codex Gigas*. Are you aware of the book?'

'I am. I also have an understanding of the legends surrounding it, but had always put those down as being, well...'

'Stories and folklore,' Sarah suggested with a smile.

Reverend Quinn chuckled. 'Right.'

'Well, those legends may now be pertinent,' Father Janosch said. 'I would appreciate you gathering all the information on that book, and Herman, that you can get. David tells us the *Codex Gigas* spent a short amount of time at the Cathedral of Assumption, so anything you can dig up would be helpful. We think there may be a link somewhere that ties all of this together.'

'That's no problem. I'll look into it and get back to you as soon as I can. It seems strange that the book would tie Herman to the cathedral, though. I get that he is supposed to have written it, but it was over sixty years before its arrival at Kutná Hora. The chances of Herman still being alive at that time are slim, unless he was *really* young when he'd written it.'

'And if the church didn't decide to just wall him up anyway,' Sarah added. 'Seems like the kind of thing they'd do, from what I've heard.' She felt Father Janosch cast her a frown, but she ignored it. She understood he was a priest, so he wasn't exactly happy about her slights towards his church, but what did he expect? The revelations that had come about since the group arrived in Kutná Hora, as well as in that horrible ossuary, hardly painted the Church in a good light.

'I'll find out what I can,' Reverend Quinn promised. 'Though I don't think there will be too much to learn about Herman. From what I understand, no one is really sure if he actually existed. Actually...' she said, then paused in thought. 'I may know someone who can help. Someone who really is an expert in this kind of thing specifically, focused on the Czech Republic. I'll contact them, but obviously won't fully share with them what it's really about.'

'Well, anything you uncover will be of assistance, I've no doubt' Father Janosch said.

'Is that all you needed from me?' she asked. 'I should be able to get back to you pretty quickly on that.'

'Actually,' David cut in, 'there is something else. Could you research any reported demonic activity in this area? Not sure if that is your speciality, but it would be good to know if there is a history of that kind of thing here that we may have overlooked. Whether that be the cathedral, the Church of All Saints, or in the town itself.'

'I'll look into it,' the reverend replied. She then bit her bottom lip before continuing. 'So, are you going to inform the Council what we've spoken about, Father?'

'I will,' Father Janosch replied.

'Okay,' Reverend Quinn said. 'I'll have to do the same as well.'

'Of course, that is no problem.'

Sarah noticed a slight look of relief wash over the woman. 'Good,' she said. 'I just find the whole thing a little weird. I mean, I don't even know who—' but she caught herself. Sarah could guess what the woman was going to say: *I don't even know who the Council are.* 'Well,' Reverend

Quinn went on, 'I'll get to work on my assignment. Should I call or email with my findings?'

'Email first,' Father Janosch confirmed. 'Then I can follow up with you if needed.'

'No problem. Unless you need anything else, I'll let you guys get some rest. Sounds like you need it after the day you've had.'

'Thank you, Reverend,' Father Janosch said. 'We really appreciate this.'

Sarah and David said their goodbyes as well, and the call was disconnected.

'What now?' David asked.

Father Janosch stood to his feet. 'Well, I need to make a call to Bishop Turnbull, which I'll do in my room. I may be a little while.'

Sarah made a scoffing sound. 'That is ridiculous. Why on earth are we not allowed to hear what you're talking about?'

'I can't help the way things are, Sarah,' Father Janosch replied.

'You *can*, actually,' she told him. 'Just make the call in this room, and let us hear what is decided. Forgo the secrecy. After all, *we're* the ones out here putting our neck on the line.'

Father Janosch let out a sigh, which triggered a ripple of frustration in Sarah. She was hardly being irrational, yet he was making her feel like she was an annoyance. 'As I said,' Father Janosch replied, 'it's just the way things are. I keep trying for more transparency, I really do, but I can't force the Council to talk to you directly.'

Sarah folded her arms over her chest and shook her head. She then looked away, but said no more. Father

Janosch padded over to his room and closed the door behind himself.

'This whole thing feels wrong,' David said.

Sarah turned to him. 'Yeah, I agree. I *hate* being kept in the dark.'

'Not just that, but running away from the cathedral when people there need our help. We should be staying there tonight. It's not like space is an issue.'

'Well, maybe we'll make more progress tomorrow.'

David shrugged his shoulders. The brief conversation then faltered, with neither person saying anything else. Sarah got to her feet and walked over to the sofa, then dropped down into it and exhaled, leaning her head back into the soft cushion behind her. Her bones ached, and she felt exhausted; she hadn't fully recovered from the Chillingham Castle investigation, yet had been launched straight into another.

'Do you regret deciding to work with the Church?' she asked.

His response was not immediate. 'I'm... not sure. I won't lie, the money is good, and I'm doing what I love for a living as well. I get to indulge in my passion and feel like I have a chance at making a difference. But the way everything is being run... it doesn't sit well with me.' He then turned in his chair and looked over to her. 'What about you?'

'Same, I guess. I wouldn't call this a passion, exactly, but it *has* given me a bit of direction. A bit of purpose. It was something I needed after losing Chloe.'

David looked down to his feet. 'I guess I understand that. How are you doing, anyway? You know, with what happened to Chloe?'

'Still processing it, to be honest,' Sarah replied. 'It keeps hitting me in waves. If I'm busy, I can keep it out of my head, but suddenly I'll remember that my sister is dead. Then I remember *how* she died. Before I know it, I start crying.' David remained silent, so Sarah lifted her head and looked back over to him. 'Don't worry,' she said with a smile, 'I'm not going to start crying now.'

'It's fine if you do,' he said. 'I sometimes forget how much you've been through. I just find it hard to look past... you know.'

'What I did?'

'I know it wasn't really you, the same way that it wasn't really Father Hus that attacked Sister Maria. I just... I'm struggling with it.'

'Yeah, I get that,' Sarah replied, trying—and failing—to hide the sadness in her voice. She didn't expect David to ever forgive her for what happened that night in Perron Manor. She certainly wasn't planning on forgiving herself for it. 'But know that I hate myself for what I did. It *was* my fault, because I dragged everyone out there. I'm truly sorry. And I'm sorry you have to keep seeing me to be reminded of it all as well. In that respect, I do wish I could just walk away. But I know the Church won't make that easy.'

David stood up and walked over to her. However, he sat down on the chair adjacent, rather than the spare space beside her.

'You're probably right. You have gifts that will certainly help them.'

'Gifts I didn't ask for.'

'No, but you have them nonetheless,' he said. 'And you also know the dangers out there in the world now. Not just ghosts and demons, but...'

'Doorways straight to Hell,' Sarah finished.

'Exactly. I suppose, ultimately, that's what we need to

keep reminding ourselves of. The importance of what we're doing.'

'But I still don't even know how to control these 'gifts,' or how to use them effectively.'

David could only offer a shrug. 'Then learn. Think of it like riding a bike: when you're eight, it's the scariest thing in the world, and you have no idea how you'll do it, but you push through, learn the intricacies, and it becomes second nature.'

Sarah cocked an eyebrow at him. '*Eight?*' she asked.

David chuckled. 'I was a late starter. Bikes terrified me.'

'I suppose you're right. It'll just take time.'

'Speak to Ann when we get back,' David suggested. 'She might be able to help. After all, she has her own talents, though they're not as potent as your own.'

Sarah held her tongue. Ann was a lot of things, but a medium or psychic wasn't one of them, despite what the woman claimed. At least, not in Sarah's view.

Surely David still isn't that gullible?

Instead, Sarah chose a different tack. 'To be honest, I doubt I'll be able to get Ann to talk to me about anything. She can't stand the sight of me.'

'Give her time,' David said. He offered a smile. 'Just... give us all a little time.'

Sarah's eyes met his. At first, she thought she'd misheard him. But no, he *had* offered her the first signs of hope that they—at least, *he*—would be able to move past the horror she'd inflicted on them. It made her heart swell a little.

'Something else I've been meaning to ask,' David continued. Sarah got the impression it was as much to move past the heartfelt comment as it was to ask a genuine question. Sarah didn't deal with emotional conversations very well, but David was worse by far. He went on, 'We've never really spoken about what we learned at Perron Manor. You know, about your parents?'

'About my father not being my real dad, you mean?'

He nodded. 'Yes. How are you handling that?'

'I'm not,' she replied honestly. 'I'm not giving it any headspace. It's not like losing Chloe, which I have to deal with because she isn't around anymore. I can't exactly ignore that. But finding out my actual father was a possessed maniac who wanted to help bring about the end of the world is... it's just too much to comprehend. That's why I don't like that I have these 'gifts,' as you call them, because they came from *him* and what he did. I'm forever tied to that, and I hate it. So... I ignore it. Otherwise, I think I'd go crazy.'

It broke Sarah's heart to think that her dear Dad wasn't her biological father. Had he even known? Had her mother cheated willingly, or had she been controlled somehow? Sarah knew how easily that could happen at Perron Manor.

Either way, it still meant that Sarah was... what? What did that make her, exactly? The descendant of some kind of mongrel bloodline.

A *tainted* bloodline.

David picked at the nails on one of his hands without looking up. 'Then for what it's worth, I am sorry if I've made things worse for you with how I've been acting.'

Sarah held a hand up. 'Don't apologise,' she said. 'Seriously. You have nothing to say sorry for. I—'

The door to Father Janosch's room opened and the priest walked back inside the living area. Both Sarah and David looked over to him.

'How did it go?' David asked.

'As well as can be expected,' Father Janosch replied. 'You may be happy with the outcome, David. The Council has decided that, with the risk of a Devil's Doorway gone, we are to step up our efforts and find out *why* Sarah was called out here. Once we've done that, the Church will arrange for an exorcism to be carried out on Father Hus. I get the feeling there was some disagreement on that, though. But they've ultimately decided this issue must be resolved as soon as possible. And that means staying at the cathedral, too, if necessary.'

Sarah cast a glance over to David, who seemed pleased.

Father Janosch continued. 'For tonight, we rest up. But in the morning we pack up our things and take up residence in the cathedral.'

'Is that a good idea?' Sarah asked.

Father Janosch shook his head and sighed. 'It's what has been decided. So, let's just get this resolved as quickly as we can.'

18

SISTER AGATHA PADDED her way back to her room, returning from a nice, hot shower in the large bathroom on her wing. She had a toiletry-bag in hand and was dressed in a night-gown with a thick, green dressing gown over the top.

The Cathedral of Assumption was basic in its living accommodation—no en-suites like at her last assignment—but she loved the place dearly, in spite of the recent developments with poor Father Hus. The building reminded her of the rectories and dormitories she used to stay in during her early twenties when she had just started on her path with her Lord.

The nun's slippered feet sank into the carpet with each step, and her exposed ankles felt the cold air around them. She moved as fast as she could, trying to retain as much of the heat from the shower as possible. Even though it was a relatively short trek back to her room, Sister Agatha always felt much more relaxed after her shower, enjoying the warmth that seeped into her old bones. It made finding sleep much easier.

Upon reaching her door, she tucked the light-blue,

cotton toiletry-bag beneath one arm and put her hand on the doorknob... but stopped.

For a brief moment, she was sure she heard a whispering come from the other side.

She moved her head closer and listened. Nothing.

It's just a trick of the mind.

Sister Agatha turned the handle and pushed the door open. She then leaned inside and flicked on the light switch. The room was empty.

As it should be.

After stepping within and slotting the chain across the door to lock it, she put away her toiletry-bag and hung up her robe, before clicking on the nightlight next to her bed. She then walked back over and turned off the room's main light. As she did, she heard a gentle knocking on her door.

Tap, tap, tap.

She paused. 'Hello?'

No response.

She listened for a moment, then questioned if she'd heard anything at all. The tapping had been so light that maybe she'd mistook it for something else—the water pipes in the wall, perhaps.

Eventually, she put it from her mind and walked back over to her bed and sat down. She drew her feet from her slippers and tucked her legs under the blankets before lying down. It had been a long day. Pleasant, but long.

She was feeling her age.

After letting out a yawn, she rolled over and switched off her nightlight, then finally returned to her back and looked up in the dark. She closed her eyes and silently recited a prayer to herself, one of her nightly rituals. It wasn't a formal prayer and wasn't written in any Bible. It was personal and completely her own.

When finished, the nun noticed the room was colder than normal, but the thought of getting up again to check the old, cast-iron radiator in the room seemed like too much effort now that she was comfortable.

The room had in it a single window, but the thick, dark curtain that had been drawn across was enough to block out any distraction from the moon or streetlights outside.

The nun took a deep, soothing breath and exhaled slowly in an effort to further relax herself. She looked forward to some well-earned rest.

However, a tug on the sheets caused her to snap her eyes open. She peered down to the edge of the bed in confusion. The sensation of the sheet moving across her shins had to have been caused by *something*. The nun continued to stare, just able to make out the bottom of her bed, but she could see nothing else through the darkness.

Sister Agatha waited for close to a minute, simply staring down the bed, waiting for an explanation of what she'd felt. Soon, she began doubting herself again. Another minute passed and still nothing.

It's in your head, you old fool, she thought to herself. *What's happening with Father Hus is making you paranoid.*

The nun then settled her head back against the pillow and again closed her eyes.

More time passed.

Just as she was about to slip into unconsciousness, she noticed movement again: a shift in the covers down by her feet.

This time, though, Sister Agatha didn't even have the chance to open her eyes before she felt a cold grip clamp tightly around her ankle.

Cold fingertips pressed into her skin.

Instinctively, Sister Agatha let out a cry. She sat up as

quickly as she could, kicking out her legs. The moment she did, though, she no longer felt any resistance—the hold was gone.

Sister Agatha quickly switched on her nightlight and looked back down the length of the bed. There was no one there. However, there was no way she could put down what had happened to her mind playing tricks on her. She was certain she'd felt something. There could be no doubt about it.

Her breathing became rapid. The cold suddenly seemed more potent, prickling her exposed face and shoulders.

Then Sister Agatha heard something—a strong exhalation of breath, coming from below the end of her bed.

Her body stiffened. 'Who's there?' she asked in a trembling voice.

After receiving no response, and with her heart in her throat, Sister Agatha began to slowly crawl down the length of her bed. If something *was* there, ducking out of sight, she needed to know who—or what—it was.

The closer Sister Agatha got to the bottom of the bed the more her arms and shoulders started to shake in fear.

She eventually put a hand on the frame, held her breath, and moved her head over the bottom to look down.

Once again, nothing.

Regardless, she was filled with the overwhelming sensation of dread and knew she needed to get out of the room.

Before she had the chance to move, and while still looking down, the nun heard a shuffling sound, as well as a scratching of the floorboards.

Coming from *under* the bed.

Sister Agatha's heartrate began to quicken. Her chest felt tight. She'd heard the stories from some of the other residents over the last few weeks: of them seeing someone roaming the halls at night, and of the strange noises and knockings... The nun could only imagine what was now hiding out of sight in her room with her.

You have to run, she commanded herself. However, the door looked so far away, and stepping off her bed to the floor seemed dangerous.

Yet what else could she do? If she made it out into the hall, Sister Agatha could run to one of her neighbours for help.

Problem was, the nearest occupied room was four doors down.

That meant screaming would likely be futile. Plus, Sister Agatha didn't know if she had the breath in her lungs anyway, with her chest feeling so tight.

Then, the mattress jumped.

Some unknown force from beneath the bed pushed so hard as to lift a portion of the mattress, even with the nun on it.

She let out another cry.

Run! Sister Agatha commanded herself.

She quickly swung her legs over the edge of the bed, gritted her teeth together, and planted her feet on the floor —fully expecting something to grab her exposed ankles.

Thankfully nothing did, and she raced over to the door, looking back over her shoulder while she moved. The light from the nightstand gave some illumination around her low bed, but the area beneath was cloaked in darkness. If something *was* under there, she certainly couldn't see it.

When she reached the door, Sister Agatha began to fumble with the chain, eventually sliding it clear. Before she grabbed the handle, however, she again heard three quick taps coming from the other side.

Knock, knock, knock.

She paused. Was it outside now? As if to answer her question, the knocking repeated itself another three times.

There were no peepholes on the doors, so Sister Agatha had no way to look outside. Unless...

Thinking quickly, she began to bend down. The doors had a generous gap beneath them, so she figured she could peer out and at least get an idea if anything was in the corridor, blocking her way.

As she lowered herself to the ground, she heard yet another sound, this one a long scratching that ran down the door and matched her movements.

However, she didn't stop. Once the side of her head was pressed to the floor, she peeked under the door... and screamed. There was a face staring back.

In that brief moment before she moved, Sister Agatha had taken everything in.

It was a man, though definitely not alive. His flesh was mottled and grey, like that of a corpse, and his wide eyes were milky white. In some areas his flesh had grown so thin that she could actually see the bone underneath, specifically on his cheeks and the top of his scalp.

His mouth had been wide open as well, as if in a silent roar, gums black and teeth yellow and broken.

Still on her back, Sister Agatha continued to scramble away from the door.

Please, God, no!

A humourless cackle behind her stopped the nun in her tracks. She quickly rolled to her front and looked towards her bed, to the source of the sound.

Beneath it, through the unnaturally heavy darkness, Sister Agatha saw two glinting objects. She squinted, trying to clear her vision, and realised they were eyes: pale and without any features—no pupil or irises.

It was then the horrible man from outside broke out of the shadows with a roar. He came crawling from beneath the bed with inhuman speed, moving with the quickness of a scuttling spider.

Sister Agatha had no chance to move as the terrifying man—dressed in a heavy, itchy-looking dark robe—quickly mounted her. She felt his weight atop her, and the stink of rotted and fetid meat filled the air. His cold hands found her throat and his mouth pulled back into a hate-filled grin.

'*Sissssteeeeer,*' he wheezed.

The utter terror the nun felt locked her body up in fright. She couldn't even find the strength within her to scream and was barely even aware she had emptied her bladder.

The grip around her neck was firm, though not quite enough to crush her throat. Even through the madness of the situation, Sister Agatha was aware she was merely being held down.

'*I'm... going... to... take... your... eyeeeeees,*' the monk said in a pain-filled whisper. He began to laugh. Then, his icy-cold hands worked up over her face until his thumbs were over her eyes.

Suddenly, Sister Agatha found the ability to scream... and scream she did. The cry that erupted came from the very pit of her stomach. She cried out as loud and for as long as she could. With her eyes closed, Sister Agatha felt his thumbs start to press down. She screamed and screamed and screamed, knowing this was the end.

Time seemed to slow down. She didn't know how long she lay like that, trapped under him with his thumbs resting on top of her eyelids, but it seemed like an eternity.

In an instant, the pressure on top of her was gone. Sister Agatha could feel someone shaking her by the shoulders.

She opened her eyes and realised the room was drenched in light. The monk was nowhere to be seen, but one of her neighbours—Sister Amelia—was kneeling over her, looking concerned.

'Are you okay?' the woman asked in a panicked voice. 'I was passing and heard you screaming!'

Sister Agatha broke down sobbing.

19

Luca didn't like the orders they had been given.

The events at Perron Manor had obviously scared the Council. Hell, it had scared Luca. But the way these men were reacting was far too aggressive, in his view.

Too reckless.

At least, the way *some* on the Council were reacting. Luca didn't think they were unanimous in their views on the best way forward.

After a quick but delicious breakfast at a local cafe, the trio headed back over to the Cathedral of Assumption, this time with their bags in tow. Bishop Turnbull had made the necessary arrangements after his call last night, but Luca had still considered calling ahead to speak with Sister Maria, just to inform her. In the end, he'd decided against it. Her attitude towards them had soured quite quickly the previous day. Luca could understand the stress and worry she was going through—that *everyone* at the cathedral was going through—but her sudden change had been unexpected. To him, at least.

David had suggested that Sister Maria just wanted the

problem resolved as soon as possible, to ensure her friend was free of the hell he was going through.

The trio turned a corner and the Cathedral of Assumption came into sight up ahead. As they moved closer, Luca turned to Sarah.

'How are you feeling? Anything?'

Sarah narrowed her eyes and gave a slow nod. 'I'm starting to feel a little sick again,' she said. 'It's getting stronger the closer we get.'

'That is something we need to figure out as well,' David said. 'The sickness isn't something we've noticed before. It is new to Kutná Hora?'

'That's right,' Sarah said. 'To the cathedral, specifically.'

'Well then, it clearly signifies something.'

'Demonic forces?' Luca suggested.

'Possibly' David replied, 'though Perron Manor was full of demons.' He again looked to Sarah. 'Did you ever feel anything like this at the Manor?'

Sarah shook her head. 'No, but everything was just too overwhelming there, like my senses were overloaded. It was hard to pinpoint anything.'

'That could have been the presence of the Devil's Doorway,' Luca said. 'And its connection had been strengthened because of the ritual. Something that powerful... is it any wonder you were overloaded?'

'That makes sense,' David said.

'It is all speculation at the moment, though,' Luca stated as they walked up the cobbled pathway to the building's entrance. 'Let's figure out what's going on here and focus on that.'

'For what it's worth, those 'sensitivities' are getting stronger,' Sarah said as she brought a hand up to her stomach again. She nodded to the cathedral. 'The closer we get, the sicker I feel.'

Luca stopped. 'Are you sure you're okay working in there?' He pointed to the building. 'If you are feeling ill...'

Sarah shook her head and raised her hand. 'No, it's fine. Honestly. It isn't debilitating or anything. It's just... not pleasant. But I'm okay to carry on. Don't worry about me.'

'Okay,' Luca replied. 'But the second that changes, I want you to let me know. We still have to be mindful that you could be susceptible to possession. With you feeling like this, and the nosebleed yesterday...'

They stopped at the door of the cathedral, and Sarah quickly turned to face him. 'I appreciate your concern, Luca, but I'll tell you if I'm not okay to continue. Until then, we have work to do.'

Luca sighed. He appreciated that Sarah wasn't the type to welcome or elicit sympathy, and wanted to always be strong, but this was more important than her stubborn pride.

Keep calm. He scratched at his chest. As he did, his fingers pressed against the small crucifix he wore around his neck, and Luca felt the cold bite of the small, golden cross press against his skin.

'Fine,' he said, and looked over to David. 'But we both keep an eye on her.' David nodded. Luca then said to Sarah, 'People who are possessed aren't usually forthright about admitting it. Please think about that if you start to notice a change. Trying to be brave and handle everything on your own will only put everyone here in danger.'

He didn't give Sarah the chance to argue further, instead heading straight through the open door and into the cathedral's impressive nave.

Groups of tourists wandered the large space inside.

Some were seated in the pews at the far end, heads bowed in silent reflection. Luca also noticed an elderly nun he recognised speaking to a small group of people.

Sister Agatha.

She looked up and met Luca's stare. A small smile crossed her face and she waved. She said something to the people she was with, gave a small and almost apologetic bow, then walked over to greet Luca.

'Good morning,' she said. 'I am pleased to see you.' However, Luca noticed the nun seemed much more subdued than the previous day.

'You too, Sister. How are things here? Did anything else happen last night?'

Sister Agatha paused for a moment. 'Yes, actually. I... experienced something in my room,' she said.

'What?' David asked.

'I saw the monk that has been roaming our halls. He attacked me.'

'Oh my word,' Luca replied in shock. He placed a hand on the nun's shoulder. 'Are you okay?'

She offered another smile and nodded her head. 'In truth, I am shaken. But by the grace of God I will recover. Though this morning I asked to leave the cathedral until things return to normal, so tomorrow I will be going away for a little while.' *She must be really scared,* Luca thought to himself. He didn't blame her for going. The nun took in a deep breath and continued, forcing a more upbeat tone into her words. 'I understand you are staying here now?' She motioned down to the bags in their hands. Word had clearly gotten around.

'That's right. Hopefully we can help expedite matters here.'

'Can you tell us more about what happened last night?' David asked.

Luca noticed the look of discomfort that crossed over Sister Agatha's face again, and he held up a hand. 'We can discuss that later,' he said. 'Is there a place we can unpack?'

'Sister Maria will know,' the nun replied. 'I will get her for you. Wait here, please.'

Not five minutes later, she returned with Sister Maria. Luca offered the younger woman a polite smile, which she returned. He tried to gauge her expression, to see if her attitude had softened since the last time they'd spoken. However, she was difficult to read.

'Bishop Turnbull called me last night,' Sister Maria said. 'We have some rooms set up for you all to stay in. I have put you in the opposite wing to Father Hus, of course. I assume that's okay?'

'Absolutely,' Luca said. He was happy that there would at least be *some* distance between them and the possessed priest. Or, more specifically, between Hus and Sarah.

'Follow me,' Sister Maria added.

She led them through to the left-hand wing of the building, then up to the first floor. The three rooms chosen were all next to each other.

'I trust these will be okay?' Sister Maria said as they stood in the corridor. 'The beds have been freshly made, and there is a kettle in each room with some refreshments. No televisions, however.'

'That's fine,' Luca said. 'We aren't here to watch TV.'

She gave another polite smile. 'I will let you all get unpacked, then. Have you eaten?'

'We have,' Sarah confirmed.

'When we are settled,' Luca began, 'I think it would be

good for us to go and see Father Hus again. Could you arrange for that?'

Sister Maria nodded, and there was a glint in her eye. 'Of course. Am I to assume things are speeding up?'

That should have been obvious, given they were now staying at the cathedral. Still, Luca sensed opportunity to appease the nun's anxieties.

'Yes. I spoke with Bishop Turnbull myself last night. Our orders are now to get the information we need as quickly as possible. Once we have that, I will report back, and then the Church will sanction an exorcism. Once sanctioned, I am sure they will act quickly.'

'So the end is in sight?' Sister Maria asked as she brought her hands together and lifted them up to her chin. The hopeful expression that crossed her face was unmistakable. She just wanted reassurance, a promise that her friend would be okay, but Luca didn't want to commit to something he couldn't absolutely deliver on. He cast a sideways glance to David, who gave him a subtle nod.

'Hopefully, yes,' Luca eventually said. 'The Church now wants this resolved quickly, so they have let us off the leash a little, so to speak.'

That was technically true, though Luca hadn't exactly been pushing for that. Caution would have been his preferred method.

Sister Maria's face lit up with a huge smile. 'I am relieved to hear that, Father,' she said. She then took a deep breath. 'I'm sorry for being short with you yesterday. My frustrations got the better of me, and I shouldn't have allowed that to happen.'

'Quite alright,' David replied. 'It's perfectly understandable.'

Sister Maria gave a nod of appreciation. 'So, should I

return for you in, say, thirty minutes? Will that give you enough time to get ready?'

'Fifteen is plenty,' David answered. Luca had to keep from stepping in and telling David to slow down and use restraint. There was no need to rush.

'We will see you in fifteen minutes, Sister,' Luca confirmed.

The trio was left alone to unpack in their respective rooms. Thankfully, the accommodations were comfortable, if a little basic. In Luca's room, the single bed had been pushed against the side wall. The light-blue sheets looked to be thick cotton, though there was no duvet, and the single pillow was plain white.

Luca looked down at the floor that squeaked underfoot as he took a step forward. Exposed timber floorboards were only partially covered by a pale-blue rug in the centre of the room. The walls were all plain white plaster, though slightly cracked, and their colour was dulled. A narrow wardrobe and a dresser sat either side of a window along the wall opposite him. In addition, a painting of the Virgin Mary hung on the wall opposite the bed. The room felt musty and smelled of old wood, and it was lit by a single chandelier fixture in the centre of the low, flat ceiling. Just next to the door was a small table containing a kettle and a tray full of instant coffee sachets, tea bags, sugar, and a carton of dry milk.

Not the Ritz, but Luca would hardly be roughing it.

It didn't take him long to unpack his belongings, and within ten minutes he was back out in the corridor along with Sarah and David, awaiting Sister Maria.

'How do you envision the discussion with Father Hus going?' David asked.

Luca just shook his head and shrugged in response. 'I

honestly have no idea. We know what we need to find out, but I'm not certain on the best method to extract that information. We could try being direct, or we could try something a little more subtle.'

Sarah spoke next. 'I think the direct approach would be best. I mean, think about it, the last time we were in that room, Father Hus was *eager* to tell us why he wanted us here. It was only us leaving that stopped him. I don't think it's going to be a problem getting him to talk.'

'Yes,' Luca agreed, 'but how will we know if he's being truthful with us?'

'We don't,' Sarah admitted. 'But we need to hear him out, anyway. We can determine for ourselves if we believe him or not. Unless someone has a better idea?'

Luca looked over to David, who just shook his head. 'Afraid I can't think of anything,' David said.

Luca took a breath. 'The direct approach it is. However, I'll take the lead. I think Father Hus will again try to goad you, Sarah, and shift the focus away from himself and onto you. I don't want that to happen.'

'Understood,' Sarah said. 'I'll try not to give him anything.'

'It's important you don't,' Luca stressed. 'Remember what I said before, about what's at stake.'

'More than just my ego, right?'

Luca nodded. He felt a little bad for making the comment, even though it was true. 'Yes. And Father Hus will try and make you dance to his tune. We need to rise above it all.'

'No problem,' Sarah replied. She then smiled. 'I'll be like a fucking Zen warrior.'

Luca laughed. He didn't appreciate the cursing, but was

certainly a fan of her enthusiasm. He just hoped she stuck to her word.

Soon, Sister Maria returned. 'Are you all ready to go?' she asked.

Luca looked to his two colleagues, who nodded their assent. He then turned his eyes back to Sister Maria. 'Yes,' he said. 'We are ready.'

20

'GLAD YOU ALL COULD RETURN,' Father Hus said. 'Nice to see you finally found the courage.' His voice dripped with malice.

Sarah took a breath and held it. *Don't react. Keep calm.*

The room was roughly as they'd left it before—namely, a disaster area. It was clear Father Hus wasn't afraid to relieve himself wherever he felt like it. The stench in the room had only increased since their last visit, and Sarah was finding it difficult not to gag. The terrible smell was only exacerbated by the nausea she was already dealing with. In addition to that, the icy-cold sensation in her gut was back as well. All told, Sarah was feeling pretty terrible but did her best to hold it together, standing straight and showing no signs of weakness.

David, however, wasn't faring as well. She could see him in her periphery, periodically retching, with fingers pressed over his mouth.

Sarah also noticed the buzzing of flies and could see the small black dots zip around some spoiled food on the floor.

However, she was also savvy enough to realise it was all

part of the act: theatrics by the spirit to disgust and repulse them.

Sister Maria had wanted to come inside with them, but Luca had insisted she leave them to it, since Father Hus would likely target her again. So, it was just the three of them, along with the sneering priest—who stood in front of his bed in all his naked glory.

He looked paler now, skin an ashy grey, and wet with a sheen of sweat. His eyes were sunken, with severe purple bags beneath them, and his grey hair was a wild mess.

'Don't expect us to stay for long,' Father Janosch replied. 'We have a few more questions, and then we will be gone.'

The other priest laughed and shook his head. 'Don't fool yourself, Father. None of you are going to escape this alive.'

Sarah saw Father Janosch's posture tense up. He quickly caught himself, however, and pushed on. 'Why did you demand to see us? Why did you call us out here?'

'I didn't,' Father Hus replied. 'I demanded to see *her*.' He pointed at Sarah. As he did, she noticed the nail on his finger had been torn off, showing the red and exposed bed beneath, speckled with dried blood. Sarah had to fight from letting a shudder ripple through her body.

Don't show him any weakness.

Father Janosch carried on. 'Okay, then why did you call *Sarah* out here? Speak, demon.'

Another chuckle. 'I already told you, Father. I'm no demon, just a spurned man of God who has seen the light. Or rather, the dark.' The priest focused his eyes—which looked distinctly more clouded than their last meeting—onto Sarah. 'So, little bird, are you ready to hear what I have to tell you?'

'Make it quick,' Sarah responded and tilted her head up.

Father Hus ran a dry tongue over his bottom lip.

'We... still... have... Chloe.'

Sarah's blood ran cold. Her mouth fell open and her body seized up. His words had felt like a physical blow.

That can't be true!

'No,' was all she could say, but her voice was weak, confused, and distant.

'Oh yes,' Father Hus replied, and then gave a mocking chuckle. 'And let me tell you... that bitch is suffering. The desecration of her soul and the eternal torment she is being put through, it's all exquisite.'

'You're lying,' Sarah shot back through gritted teeth. She felt a sting in her palms and realised she'd been digging her nails into her skin.

'Am I?'

'Yes!' Sarah snapped. 'We freed her. I saw what happened at Perron Manor. I saw her soul in peace. She's free!'

'You don't know *what* you saw,' Father Hus scoffed. 'It's true she isn't at that house any longer, but do you really know where she went after? Do you have the slightest idea where she went after you closed the door?' He laughed again. 'You think she went to Heaven? No such thing.'

'Lies!' It was Father Janosch's turn to snap this time.

'You bunch of fools,' Father Hus said with a sneer. 'None of you have the faintest clue how things really are. All living in ignorance. It pleases me to be the one who shatters your delusions.'

'You will shatter nothing,' Father Janosch replied. 'There are no delusions here, only your tricks and lies. They won't work. My faith is too strong.'

Father Hus paused, then put his hands behind his back, like a general addressing his troops. 'Faith,' he said, 'a funny concept. One I wasted my early life on, to a false God. To an anomaly.'

'He is the Creator,' Father Janosch argued.

'No. More lies. He did not create existence. He merely arrived in it, mutated beneath the notice of the *true* creator.'

Father Janosch laughed. 'Nonsense. The Devil was cast down by God. An angel gone bad. But the Lord existed long before Lucifer did.'

The possessed priest suddenly took a quick step towards them. 'And you believe those tales created by men to help them sleep at night? The Devil was *not* cast down; he was taken from God. Plucked from his grasp.'

Sarah looked over to Father Janosch, who shook his head in disbelief. She didn't care about any of this. She wanted to know more about Chloe.

'By whom?' Father Janosch asked with a tone of condescension.

'By the darkness, and the true god behind it—one that has existed forever. You see, darkness and chaos are the natural order of things. Your God, the light, was just a freak occurrence. A tumour to be cut away. He can't hide and protect you forever. Your existence is fading. Even now, pinpricks of the darkness tether your world to that of the true god. And the threads that bind the two realms can be traversed.'

'You're talking about Devil's Doorways,' David uttered.

Father Hus smiled. 'You're an intelligent one. Shame it will do you no good.'

'I don't believe a word of it,' Father Janosch said.

'*And I don't care,*' Father Hus replied. 'I'm just explaining how things are.'

'So where is Chloe?!' Sarah demanded. 'In this... darkness?'

Father Hus nodded. 'That's right.'

'So where do you fit in?' David asked, taking a step forward. 'Why tell us all this? Why are you *here*, specifically?'

'To deliver a message.'

'No, that isn't true,' David stated. 'There's no reason that had to be done in this cathedral. Dragging us out to a different country just to deliver a message? Why here? I don't buy it. It has to do with the book, doesn't it? The *Codex Gigas*?'

A look of distant longing fell over Father Hus. 'My greatest achievement,' he said.

'Is it true, then,' David went on to say, 'that you asked the Devil for help and he obliged, helping you write it in a single night?'

'A single night?' Father Hus replied in surprise. 'It took seven years of constant writing.'

David frowned. 'But the stories say—'

'Your stories are *wrong*,' Father Hus stated with a wave of his hand. 'Just like your Bible. Though yes, I did get help. After all, the book I created should have taken far more than seven years for a single person.'

'So the Devil wrote it for you,' Sarah said.

Father Hus shook his head. 'No. He sent another, who wrote the book *through* me.'

'And transcribed a picture of his master within its pages.'

Father Hus chuckled. 'Not a true likeness. Humanity couldn't bear seeing a true depiction of him. The image just had to be clear who it was referring to, since the idiot minds of the populace needed to be able to recognise it.'

'But why? What was the purpose of the picture?'

'To put the Devil in people's minds,' Father Hus

explained. 'But it wasn't just about the picture. There was more.'

'The missing pages,' David said with a tone of recognition.

'Yes.'

'Is it true they contained something called the Devil's Prayer?'

Father Hus nodded. 'You are well educated, boy.'

'What *is* the Devil's Prayer?'

'You should already know. Disappointing that you obviously do not.'

'I... don't understand,' he replied.

'Clearly. But the prayer was to be put out into the world. That was the whole purpose of the *Codex Gigas*.'

'A poor plan, then,' Father Janosch interrupted. 'The pages were torn out and the prayer lost forever.'

Father Hus chuckled. 'Not lost, Father. Enough people saw the pages before they were removed—that was the point. It was not the servants of your God who removed those pages, but another, one who took my work and expanded upon it, turned it into something more complete, as was always intended.'

'You're talking in riddles,' David said.

'No. You just fail to comprehend. You have all the information.'

'It was still a failure,' Father Janosch went on. 'If the aim was to spread the word of this prayer to everyone, you didn't succeed.'

Father Hus gave an exasperated sigh. 'Not everyone. Just enough people—the *right* people—for things to progress.'

Father Janosch shook his head. 'This was a waste of time. You have nothing important to tell us. All lies and misdirection. Sarah's sister is free of your master's grasp, so we won't fall for your tricks.'

'I've given you more information than you could possibly know what to do with.'

'Well,' Father Janosch went on, 'I've heard enough. I'm satisfied we can leave here now. You can just look forward to being exorcised back to the pit you came from. Goodbye.' The priest turned around and started to walk away.

Sarah, however, wasn't ready to leave. She needed to know more. Was Chloe really still suffering? Yet, before she could voice any of that, Father Hus exploded in anger.

'Do not turn your back on me, you pathetic worm!' he screamed, spittle flying from his mouth. His eyes were wide and veins bulged from the side of his neck. 'I'll kill every fucking one of you!'

Father Janosch turned back around. 'No. You won't. We're finished here.'

'If you leave now,' Father Hus replied with a snarl, 'then I will kill that old bitch Sister Agatha. I'll pluck out her eyes and feed them to her before yanking out her intestines. Then I'll fuck her writhing, dying body while the life drains from her. Her own blood will be the lubricant for her dry, aged cunt. Do you hear me?!'

'Enough!' Sarah yelled, appalled and disgusted.

Father Hus ignored her. 'And that will just be the start. Everyone here will die, and all of it will be your fault.'

'Idle threats,' Father Janosch shot back. 'You've been trapped in this room for days. If you don't even have the power to break out of here, how do you propose to kill all those people without being stopped?'

Another sneer. 'I stay here because I choose to. Because it suits me. Besides... we both know I'm not here alone.'

'What do you mean?' David asked.

'You've already felt the presence of my guardian.' He then looked to Sarah and pointed at her arm. 'And I know you've seen it, maybe even felt its touch.'

'The demon,' Sarah said as she looked down to the marks that still lined her forearm.

'Yes. It remains here with me, anchored as I am. It's not just me you need to worry about, but my friend as well. Are you willing to gamble the lives of the sheep that live here? After all, I know you are perfectly aware how... blood-thirsty... these demons can be when unleashed.' He looked to Father Janosch. 'Your friend Jamie is testament to that, is he not?'

'Let's go,' Father Janosch ordered the other two. He then moved towards the door again.

'Wait,' Sarah argued. 'I need to know more.' She turned her glare to Father Hus. 'Tell me what you know about Chloe. Are you lying? Tell me she's safe!' Anger and desperation start to bubble up from within her.

Then, she felt arms grab her shoulders. She instinctively and forcefully twisted and pushed away whoever had grabbed her. She saw a look of shock and confusion cross Father Janosch's face before he fell to the floor from the force of her shove. His head struck the exposed floorboards with a thud. Sarah let out a gasp and quickly rushed over to the fallen priest to help him up. At first, he shied away from her, before eventually taking her hand.

'I'm so sorry, Father,' she said. 'Are you okay?'

He rubbed the back of his head as he got back to his feet, eyeing her warily. 'I'll be fine,' he said.

'Fighting in the family,' Father Hus mocked. 'How delightful.'

'Let's go,' Father Janosch again said to Sarah. 'We need to regroup.'

'You do that,' Father Hus said. 'But don't go too far. Remember my promise.'

Father Janosch glared angrily at the chuckling priest, but then turned and left. David and Sarah followed behind. Before she stepped out of the room, however, Sarah cast a look back. Father Hus gave her a wink.

'Come chat anytime, Sarah. There is *lots* more I could tell you.'

21

'WELL, THAT WAS A SHIT-SHOW,' David stated as they got back to Father Janosch's room. Sarah strode past him over to a corner and stood looking away from them with her arms folded across her chest, jaw tense.

Father Janosch closed the door and took a few steps into the room, then let out a long exhale.

'Accurate description, David,' he said. 'But let's just keep our heads. There is an awful lot to unpack from that exchange.'

Sarah turned to face them. 'I can't get over the vile things he said.' She sounded furious. 'I've never heard anything so fucking depraved.'

'Depravity is what we are dealing with, unfortunately. The demonic forces revel in it, precisely because of how it makes us feel. It is a weapon they wield against us.'

'I'll wield my fist straight through his fucking head if he says anything like that again,' Sarah snapped. From the look on her face, David believed her.

'But you would only be physically hurting Father Hus,

not the agent that is controlling him,' Father Janosch explained. 'Be mindful of that.'

Sarah just shook her head and began pacing.

'Father,' David began, 'do you think there could be any truth to what Father Hus was saying?'

'Which part?'

'Well, *any* of it. The light and the dark, God not being the first, also'—he cast a subtle glance at Sarah—'what happened to the souls at Perron Manor.'

'No,' Father Janosch said firmly. 'He is merely toying with us. Trying to confuse and scare us with lies. Just ignore it.'

David nodded, but he wasn't sure he fully believed it. He had to question if Father Janosch was *truly* that convinced— or if he was just being adamant and dismissive to protect his own worldview.

'Okay,' David replied. 'So, what are our next steps? The discussion with Hus has hardly yielded answers.'

'I'll contact the Council and report back,' Father Janosch said. 'I'll tell them there is little else we can do here and request an exorcism be sanctioned.'

'We aren't leaving,' Sarah stated. Her arms were again folded over her chest and she glared at Father Janosch. 'You heard what he threatened. We can't let that happen.'

Father Janosch folded his own arms and stared at the ground for a moment. David could practically see his mind working. Eventually, the priest nodded. 'No, you're right, we should stay until backup arrives. I'm not sure how much use we will be, but it would be irresponsible to flee and leave these people here alone with those... things.'

David saw Sarah breathe a sigh of relief, and he let out one as well. The idea of staying was scary to him, knowing what was lurking here, but the thought of running away and letting people get hurt was unthinkable.

'I'll call Bishop Turnbull,' Father Janosch said. 'Start the process of—'

A chiming sound from his mobile phone drew their attention. Father Janosch pulled out his phone and tapped at the screen. 'It's an email,' he said, 'from Reverend Quinn. She has some information for us. That was fast.'

David had to agree. She had only been given her assignment the previous evening—it had been less than sixteen hours.

'What does it say?' Sarah asked.

David watched Father Janosch's eyes scan left and right as he scrolled down on his phone.

'There's quite a lot here, actually,' he replied. 'Whoever Reverend Quinn's contact is, they really came through for her.'

'How about you give us the highlights?' Sarah suggested allowing Father Janosch a few more moments to read.

'Well, it appears there may be a prior link with Herman the Recluse and the Cathedral of Assumption. Reverend Quinn's contact claims to have heard stories—though this isn't verified—that the monk travelled to Kutná Hora when the *Codex Gigas* resided at the cathedral. He would have been an old man at the time, *really* old... in his nineties, according to this.'

'*Nineties?*' David asked. 'What are the chances of someone living that long back in those days?'

'Very slight,' Father Janosch agreed. 'Which is why this contact stresses it is just a story. However, it is pertinent to us. He claims that Herman also died here and was buried in an unmarked grave after some kind of indiscretion.'

'The ossuary,' David said. 'If he was buried in the cemetery, there's a good chance his bones were in the ossuary.'

'So the skull Father Hus was found staring at,' Sarah began, 'the one he moved. Do we think that was Herman's?'

David had come to the same conclusion himself. It seemed logical, assuming the story Reverend Quinn's contact had relayed was true, though they couldn't be certain. Still, it was more than they currently had to go on, and David had learned from the *Ianua Diaboli* and Perron Manor that legends and ancient tales could frequently turn out to be true.

David watched as Father Janosch kept reading his email. The priest's face fell.

'What is it?' David asked.

'Something Reverend Quinn has said. At first she mentions what is supposed to be in the missing pages.'

'The Devil's Prayer?' David asked.

Father Janosch nodded. 'Yes, exactly.'

'But we already know that. Didn't we tell Reverend Quinn about it?'

Father Janosch shook his head. 'No, her contact told her. An oversight on our part. If we had mentioned it, the other information she gives here would have come to light sooner.' Father Janosch closed his eyes and exhaled. 'Damn it, I should make this connection myself.'

'What connection?' Sarah asked. Come on, Father, spill it.'

'The Devil's Prayer... the Reverend has seen that term before. And so have I.'

'Where?' Sarah asked.

'In the book Reverend Quinn is now studying on behalf of the Church. The one you donated to them, Sarah. *Ianua Diaboli*.

'Come again?' she asked with a frown. 'The book from Perron Manor has the Devil's Prayer in it *as well?*'

Father Janosch brought a hand up to his mouth and nodded. David noticed the colour had already drained from the older man's cheeks. 'How could I have missed this?'

'Father,' David cut in, 'just walk us through it. Where in *Ianua Diaboli* did you see it?'

Father Janosch drew in a deep breath before beginning. 'It was when we were trying to find a way to close the Devil's Doorway. One section was titled the Devil's Prayer.'

'Is it the same prayer as from the *Codex Gigas?*' Sarah asked.

'I can't be sure,' Father Janosch replied. 'If it isn't, this is all an awfully big coincidence.'

'I'm not sure I believe in coincidences anymore,' David said. 'What was the Devil's Prayer supposed to do?'

The priest looked over to him. The expression he wore was almost apologetic. 'It opens a doorway,' he stated.

David's eyes widened. Sarah's shock, however, was given voice. 'It fucking what?!'

Father Janosch sighed and nodded. 'The ritual that opened the doorway was named the Devil's Prayer.'

David suddenly felt lightheaded. He took an instinctive step back to keep his balance. 'Shit,' he uttered.

'Shit indeed,' Father Janosch agreed. 'With all the talk of the Devil's Prayer, I can't believe I didn't tie this together.'

'Well, Perron Manor was a few months ago,' Sarah said. 'And there was a lot to take in that day. I mean, you read a *ton* of stuff. It isn't so surprising that one little phrase slipped your mind.'

'But if it hadn't, we'd have been a few steps ahead already.'

'Hold on,' David cut in. 'What does this mean, exactly?

Are we suggesting the missing pages from the *Codex Gigas* are in *Ianua Diaboli?*'

'Possibly,' Father Janosch said. 'Maybe not the actual pages, but likely a copy.'

'It was the start of it,' Sarah said. Her voice was quiet, though it was laced with realisation.

David turned to her. 'What do you mean?'

'Think about it,' she said. 'Father Hus... or Herman, rather... said that a demon wrote that passage *through* him. Which means the ritual was put down on paper in order to spread it to the *right* people. Those were the words he used.'

'Okay,' David said. 'But what did you mean by 'the start of it'? I don't quite follow.'

'Well, whoever ended up with the missing pages from the *Codex Gigas*, is it really a leap to think they were the ones who wrote the *Ianua Diaboli*? Or at least started it? Maybe that was how the book from Perron Manor was created in the first place. We always wondered how the author could know so much about these doorways. There's the answer: it came from a demon. A literal written instruction in the form of a ritual.'

'Couldn't a demon have just given the knowledge directly? Did it have to go through Hus and the *Codex Gigas* in the first place?' David asked. 'Seems long-winded.'

'We can't be certain of anything,' Father Janosch said. 'The theory could have merit. We saw at Perron Manor that these events play out over many hundreds of years. The forces pulling the strings always tend to line up their pieces well in advance. Maybe Herman wasn't the right person to compile the *Codex Gigas*. Considering the amount of information in that tome, I'd be surprised if the author was just one person, anyway.'

'Herman could have been the right person at the right

time to just transcribe the prayer in the first place,' Sarah said. 'He was desperate, calling on the Devil for help, ready to turn his back on God.'

'So why was Hus even needed?' David asked. 'Why not just give the information straight to whoever ended up with the pages and completed *Codex Gigas*?' To David, the whole thing just seemed too convoluted.

'It's all conjecture anyway,' Father Janosch said. 'Could be there was a reason it happened this way. Or, it could be that we're completely wrong and off-base.'

Sarah went on, 'We have to work on the assumption the pages in the *Codex Gigas* actually *are* instructions to open a doorway to Hell. It's the only thing we have to go on. And it's the only reason the thing possessing Father Hus would be interested in us and what happened at Perron Manor. It fits.'

David thought about that. While everything was total guesswork, Sarah's suggestion did make as much sense as anything they had at present.

'Perhaps,' Father Janosch said with a nod.

'Do you need to report this to the Council as well?' Sarah asked.

'Probably,' he replied. 'But Reverend Quinn would have passed the same information on, so they likely already know.'

'I wanna get back in there and talk to Hus,' Sarah stated.

Father Janosch held up his hands. 'We still need to cool down after what just happened. The spirit in Father Hus has a talent for causing us to lose our focus rather quickly.'

'He's wrong about Chloe,' David said to Sarah. 'You know that, right?'

He saw her jaw tense. After a few moments, she shook her head and shrugged. 'But is he? How can we be sure?'

'Because he's doing what demonic forces do best,' Father

Janosch said. 'Using lies and hate to sway you from your path.'

'You said that you saw Chloe, Jenn, and Jamie after we closed the door at Perron Manor,' David went on. Sarah nodded. 'Okay,' he said, 'did they look like they were about to be dragged off to Hell?'

Sarah looked down and blinked a few times. Her eyes looked wet. But she shook her head. 'No. No, they didn't.'

'Then hold on to that,' David said.

Sarah lifted her head back up and gave a small smile. 'Thank you,' she said.

Father Janosch walked to his bed and sat down. It squeaked under his weight. 'This is all a lot to take in. I can't help but wonder about the games that are being played. How things have been lined up.'

'How so?' David asked.

'It just... reminds me of Perron Manor, where it became clear events had been set up in a certain way, and the end result was Sarah being born with her...' He looked up to her.

'Tainted bloodline?' she said with half a smile.

'I was going to use the term 'gifts' again, though I know you aren't fond of that. But it's the same again here. I just wonder what else is in store for us.'

'It doesn't matter, we'll stop it,' David said, feeling a swell of determination. 'Just like we did at Perron Manor. Don't forget that. No matter how long things had been in motion, we closed the door there. *Us*. We need to remember that.'

Father Janosch nodded in agreement. 'That is something I often think about. Are we getting help from something else? A force in the background working against the darkness?'

'The dark and the light,' Sarah stated.

'Perhaps.'

'So... you think *God* is helping us?' she went on.

Father Janosch let out a laugh. 'Who knows. It's just a feeling I've not been able to shake. Because, as much as the dominos were in place for the house, things lined up well for us, too.'

'Best not to think on that too much, Father,' Sarah suggested. 'Either it will drive you crazy trying to wrap your head around it, or you'll end up believing you're God's right-hand man. I mean, I know you're a priest, but that's still a hell of a promotion.' She offered him a mischievous smile, and he laughed.

'You may be right,' he said.

A brief silence descended over the three of them as they each struggled with what had just been revealed. Eventually, David asked the obvious question, one he felt he'd been repeating a lot since they had arrived in Kutná Hora. 'So... what now?'

Father Janosch opened his mouth, but paused. 'Honestly? I don't know.'

Three sudden and thunderous bangs on the door shocked them all, the last strike hard enough to actually splinter the door down its centre. David tensed up in shock, his body braced for... something, but he didn't know what.

'Jesus fucking Christ!' Sarah exclaimed. She quickly brought a hand to her chest in fright.

She looked over to David, who stared back wide-eyed. He had no idea what to do. Sarah, however, faced the threat head-on, just as she had before. She strode over to the door and swung it open. David could see nothing outside. Sarah stepped into the hallway and looked around, fists clenched. She turned back to them.

'Nothing.'

'You really need to stop running head-long into trouble,'

Father Janosch said. 'There is certainly a time and a place for caution.'

'And there is a time and a place where caution just fucks things up,' she replied as she came back into the room.

'Something's clearly trying to get our attention,' David said, pointing to the crack that ran down the centre of the door.

'I agree, Father Janosch said. 'It's a warning... I think we're making it mad.'

22

BISHOP TURNBULL STOOD ALONE in an office in Newcastle Cathedral, a phone pressed to his ear while he looked out of a large window to the high-street outside. Throngs of people wandered there, all going about their shopping and daily lives.

Oh, to be that ignorant, he thought to himself. Sometimes he wished the discovery of Devil's Doorways had been made in the jurisdiction of another Bishop, so he, too, could have remained blissfully in the dark.

But that wasn't how things had gone. Now *he* had a responsibility, not just to the Council of men he had only recently been made aware of, but to the world as a whole. It was a weight that felt crippling.

It was also made worse by the recent email from Reverend Quinn, potentially linking the Cathedral of Assumption in Kutná Hora to Perron Manor, something Father Janosch had recently assured them was not the case. He had been certain the cathedral was not a doorway.

That may still have been the case, but he certainly couldn't ignore the presence of the Devil's Prayer.

'Pick up your phone,' the Bishop hissed.

Eventually, the call connected.

'Bishop Turnbull,' Father Janosch said. 'I am with Sarah and David at present, so speaking will be—'

But Bishop Turnbull cut him off. 'Have you seen the email from Quinn?'

'*Reverend* Quinn? Yes, we've just read it.'

'Care to tell me what's going on?'

'What do you mean?'

'This email clearly states the cathedral is a doorway, yet you assured us it wasn't!'

'Excuse me, Bishop,' Father Janosch argued back. The Bishop picked up on a hint of anger in the usually polite and accommodating man. 'That *isn't* what the email says at all. There is a potential link between the *Codex Gigas* and the *Ianua Diaboli*, but despite that, I still don't believe the Cathedral of Assumption is a doorway. Nothing points to that; there is no history of death, and Sarah hasn't picked up on the same kind of overwhelming energy as in Perron Manor.'

'But the *Codex Gigas* spent some time at the cathedral,' Bishop Turnbull replied.

'As it did a lot of other places.'

'Regardless, this still needs to be investigated fully. The Council is worried about it.'

'I understand,' Father Janosch replied. 'We will speak to Father Hus again and see what we can uncover. But I think it is time to sanction an exorcism here—both for Father Hus and the cathedral itself. As I explained previously, it is our belief that a demon has somehow taken residence here, along with the spirit infesting Father Hus.'

Bishop Turnbull hesitated. 'But if an exorcism is successful, we lose our link to the spirit. The entity might have further information that would be useful to us.'

'There were threats made against the people who live here. It is the safest course of action. My team and I will remain here and find out what we can until help arrives, but I do think this is the only way forward. Please, you must grant and organise this exorcism. It's either that, or we evacuate everyone here. Temporarily, at least.'

Bishop Turnbull let out a sigh. Rehousing those people, even if it was only temporary, would take time and work. However, he understood Father Janosch's concern. Turnbull knew not all members of the Council would see it the same way.

'Find out what you can, Luca,' Bishop Turnbull replied. 'I will speak to the Council and try to get something arranged. However, I want to ask... have you ever performed an exorcism?'

'I...' but Father Janosch trailed off for a moment. 'You aren't suggesting *I* do it, are you?'

'Just something to consider, if you feel it necessary. After all, it's you out there in the middle of all this. *You* know the level of danger you face. The Council can only really advise from afar. If the need arose, could you do it?'

Another pause. 'Possibly.'

'Then please consider it,' Bishop Turnbull said. 'I'll update you on what the Council decide, of course, but it would be a good idea to brush up on what you need to. I trust you to make the right decision. And I'll back you on that, should I need to.'

'Back me? Is this not direct instruction from the Council?'

'*I'm* telling you to use your judgement. The priorities of the Council might lie in drawing out as much information as you can, even if there is a price to be paid. So, unofficially, I'm telling you the request for an exorcism will likely be ignored. Officially, I'm instructing you to do what you think is best.'

There was a pause. 'Understood.'

While the scale of the threat the Council was facing couldn't be overstated, Bishop Turnbull couldn't, in good conscience, allow innocent people to be hurt... or worse. He hadn't joined the Church to sanction or accept things like collateral damage. Thankfully, at least two of the Council members would likely agree with him on that. In fact, it had been the American who had privately suggested the idea of Luca himself performing an exorcism if needed, so they could bring the matter to a close.

Other members of the Council, however...

'Best of luck, Father,' Bishop Turnbull said. 'Find out what you can and work quickly. Do what is needed to protect both yourself and the others there.'

Bishop Turnbull ended the call and again stared out of the window. He watched the people outside with something approaching envy as they carried on with their lives in blissful ignorance.

23

Luca and his team found Sister Maria and let her know that an official request had been made to carry out an exorcism. He didn't, however, let on about just *who* might be performing it.

The thought of doing so scared him. Luca had been through an ordeal many years ago, alongside a much more experienced priest, where an exorcism had gone horribly wrong.

Zsámbék Church. A place that had haunted him for a long, long time.

But this isn't Zsámbék. I'm older and wiser now.

Luca spent the rest of the day alone in his room, studying. One of the many books he had brought with him was one that dealt with the rites required for an exorcism. The document was called *Exorcisms and Related Supplications*, or *De Exorcismis et Supplicationibus Quibusdam* in its original Latin. Luca took it on every investigation now, along with his Bible, and it detailed the required steps, rites, and prayers that were to be used. It was thin, only eighty-four pages, and the cover was a bright red with an image of Jesus embossed in gold at the centre.

The document was split into four sections, the first being *The Rite of Major Exorcism*, which outlined the formal ceremony. The second was sub-divided into multiple parts and listed other various texts that could be used if the priest felt they were needed. These texts were made up of psalms, prayers, and even some Gospel readings. The third section was actually the first of two appendices, and it provided steps to be used if the congregation of a church were to be involved in proceedings. The last part, and the second appendix, included prayers a priest could use privately in their personal struggle against the darkness. Luca recited a few of them aloud to himself as he studied.

Sarah and David had gone to look around the cathedral, speak to the residents, and try to get as many testimonies of incidents over the last few days as they could. Regardless of what happened next, Luca knew they still needed to conduct a thorough investigation. The records they gathered could be vital, for both the future and the immediate threat. Still, he had told them what Bishop Turnbull had suggested, and asked if they would be willing to assist him if needed. They both agreed, but Luca still didn't know if it was such a good idea getting Sarah involved. He had no idea how she would react, or if she could potentially be a weak link because of her connection to the other side.

Luca had another call scheduled with Reverend Quinn soon, which Sarah and David were also due to sit in on. After that, they were going to interview Father Hus once more. This time, Luca hoped they would be armed with a little more knowledge.

He lifted his tired eyes and saw that dusk was already setting in. The studying was intense, but good for sharpening his memory. In all honesty, however, he hoped the Council would see sense and come through, so this burden could be passed to someone more capable.

As Luca was deep into his third reading of *Exorcisms and Related Supplications*, there was a knock on his door. After setting the book down, he stood up from his bed, feeling his knees crack a bit.

'Coming,' he said and walked over to the door. He opened it, fully expecting to see Sarah and David standing outside.

Luca glanced in both directions, but no one was there.

'Hello?' he called, feeling a growing sensation of dread work its way up his spine.

When there was no response, Luca again closed his door. Sarah had warned against him staying on his own, studying or not, but the priest had been stubborn, insisting he would be fine. Now he was regretting that decision.

Hold it together, Luca, he said to himself. *The presence is just trying to scare you. It can't hurt you.* Regardless, he wrapped two fingers around the base of the small, gold crucifix he wore around his neck beneath his shirt and clenched it tightly for comfort.

Was the knocking in a set of three?

He tried to remember, but couldn't. However, moments later—and before he'd had a chance to walk back to his bed —he heard something else: a light tapping on the door.

One. Two. Three.

Luca gritted his teeth together and quickly pulled the door open yet again. Nothing. The hairs on the back of his arm began to stand on end and he wanted to scream out into the hallways that he wasn't scared of whatever was there.

Even if it was a lie.

It's toying with you. Don't let it win.

He remained standing out in the corridor, one hand still clutching the crucifix. Waiting.

Then he heard something else, a sound to his far right. It was quite distant, but growing louder. Voices. And... footsteps. Luca braced himself, then quickly realised he recognised the voices. David and Sarah turned the corner up ahead and came into view.

Though he tried to hide it from them as they approached, Luca let out a small sigh of relief. As they got closer, Sarah shot him a confused frown.

'Why are you standing out here?' she asked.

Luca let go of his crucifix. 'Something was trying to get my attention,' he said, knowing that keeping information from them would accomplish nothing. 'Knocking on my door to scare me.'

Sarah's smile said it all. 'Told you that you shouldn't have stayed here alone.'

'You did indeed,' he admitted with a chuckle. 'I suppose you were correct.'

'Anything else happen?' David asked. 'Or just the knocking?'

Luca shook his head. 'Just the knocking. Other than that, my studies have been uninterrupted.'

'Are you confident you can do what's needed?' David asked.

Luca scrunched up his face. 'I'm confident I know the steps. Putting it into practice is... a little more difficult. I've learned that there are no certainties with this kind of thing.'

Sarah patted him on the arm. 'You've got this, Father,' she said with a smile. 'I know you do.'

He nodded his appreciation and couldn't keep his own smile from his lips. 'Thank you, Sarah, I appreciate the vote of confidence. You should both be aware, the instruction to carry out the exorcism ourselves hasn't come from the Council. I get the feeling they won't be unanimous in their decision about sanctioning one.'

'Why?' Sarah asked.

'They want to know all they can. The spirit that possessed Father Hus is a resource to be used.'

'Where did the order come from, then?' Sarah asked.

'Bishop Turnbull,' Luca replied. 'He advised me in confidence of the situation, and what might need to be done. He said it was our call to make and he would back us, though the Council may not be best pleased.'

'Wow,' David began. 'Going against the Council, now. Are you now officially rebelling?'

'Well, technically I am only following what my Bishop said. It was all his suggestion.'

'And here I thought he was just the Council's mouthpiece.'

'I thought that, too,' Luca admitted. 'But who knows what is really going on there.'

'When are we doing this, then?' David asked.

Luca raised his eyebrows. 'Hmmmm?'

'The call to Reverend Quinn. That's soon, right?'

The priest checked his watch. 'Heavens, I didn't realise the time. Yes, we should be starting shortly. I suppose we can do it in my room. I'll set the tablet on the night stand, but we'll all have to just stand around it, I'm afraid, since there aren't any chairs.'

'That's fine,' Sarah replied. 'If my legs get tired, David will get on all fours and offer himself up as seat for me, being the gentleman that he is.' She wore a mischievous smile and prodded David in the ribs.

He laughed and shook his head. 'With *my* back? Not likely. Your legs will have to stay tired.'

They're being a little more friendly, Luca thought to himself.

He wasn't sure if the two of them had privately spoken and cleared the air, or if it was just a natural progression from David in coming to terms with what happened. Either way, their banter was nice to see.

'Let's get started,' the priest said and led them back inside his room.

24

REVEREND QUINN'S FRIENDLY, smiling face once again filled the screen of Father Janosch's tablet. She gave her customary wave.

'Hi, everyone,' she said. Thankfully, the picture was sharp and the sound was clear.

David hadn't been sure how well the video call would work inside the thick stone walls of the cathedral, given they had been using mobile data as opposed to Wi-Fi.

However, so far, so good.

'Your email has caused quite a stir,' Father Janosch said to the Reverend.

She twisted her mouth a little. 'Yes, so I understand. Erm... sorry about that. It wasn't meant to. I just thought the link might be relevant, if it was true. My contact was keen to stress that everything he relayed was merely stories and folklore. No certainties there.'

'Well,' David began, 'we've learned not to discount things like that. It's surprising how many stories can be based on truth.'

Father Janosch leaned forward. 'Reverend,' he said,

'you've been studying the *Ianua Diaboli*. Are you familiar with the part that deals with the Devil's Prayer?'

She nodded. 'I've read it quite a few times. It's one of the worst sections of the book. Really quite vile.'

'Yes, from memory I tend to agree with you, though I've not had as much time with the book as you. I was thinking it may be useful for us all to go over the prayer and the ritual. We're going to speak with Father Hus again later, so I want to be armed with as much information as possible. If the *Ianua Diaboli* and the *Codex Gigas* are linked, I want to know as much as I can.'

'Okay,' Reverend Quinn said with a nod. 'Obviously I don't have the book with me now—it's under lock and key, as you might imagine—but I have extensive notes with me. Please give me a second.'

She disappeared from view for a few moments before returning and dropping a leather binder down onto her desk.

She again took her seat and opened up the file, flicking through the loose pages. 'I have everything here,' she said. 'Is there anything specific you need to know?'

'How does it work?' Sarah asked. 'Could you guide us through from start to finish?'

'I can,' the Reverend replied, 'though it won't make for nice listening. It's all about blood sacrifice, desecration of the human body... delightful things like that.'

Sarah chuckled. 'To be honest, I'd expect nothing less.'

'Are you already familiar with the specifics, Father?' she asked Father Janosch. 'I know you read some of the book yourself.'

'Vaguely,' he replied. 'But please go through in detail, refresh my memory, and bring my team up to speed.'

'Okay, then,' Reverend Quinn began. 'Settle in and I'll

explain the steps. There is quite a bit involved, so please bear with me. It starts with the sacrifice of what is termed 'an innocent.' At first, I was unsure as to what that meant. I was worried it was referring to a child. However, it does clarify that an innocent is actually a holy person, someone who believes in a higher power of good. Their involvement is a way to mock the God they believe in.

'There are descriptions of symbols and markings, and the sacrifice has to take place in one of these symbols: inverted pentagram, the tip of which should point south. The four elements need to be present. Air—not difficult— but also earth, fire, and water, all placed in the symbol. So a mound of soil, candles, and a bowl of water... that kind of thing.'

David was reminded of the ritual they had used at Perron Manor to close the Devil's Door—*Claude Ianua*. In that instance, the elements had been used to pull back together the Earth's dominion. He guessed this ritual was going to be the opposite—splitting the elements apart in order to open the gateway.

Reverend Quinn went on, 'There also needs to be something reflective. A mirror. Or, again, a bowl of water. This allows the otherworld to have a view into our own.'

The similarities with *Claude Ianua* kept on coming, which made sense to David, since one ritual was used to open the door, the other to close it.

'So, the innocent is killed in this symbol, their blood spilled. However, it gets worse. The method of death specifically has to cause pain. The more pain, the stronger the link. So while they are still alive, the victim is cut up and dismembered, each limb severed. These limbs are then placed around the pentagram, at each point of the star, and they have to be linked together by a... string of their innards.'

'Well, this is just a fucking delight, isn't it?' Sarah quipped. She then winced and leaned in closer to the tablet. 'Sorry for the language, Reverend.'

Thankfully, the Reverend just laughed. 'It's no problem. I did say this would be heavy stuff.'

'Is that everything?' David asked. 'Once the unfortunate holy person is killed and his parts placed around the symbol, does that open the door?'

'Not quite,' she said. 'There are a few other things to go over. The next is regarding the person doing the sacrificing.'

'Go on,' David said.

'Well, they have to give themselves over. First, incantations are spoken in order to summon the Opener of the Gate. A demon named Pazuzu.'

David felt his body tense.

'Pazuzu?' Sarah asked.

'Yes,' Reverend Quinn confirmed. 'Have you heard of him?'

'We've... encountered him,' Father Janosch confirmed. 'At Perron Manor.'

'More coincidences,' Sarah said, and cast a look over to David.

He nodded in response. 'Something is definitely going on here.'

'Interesting to note Pazuzu's title,' Father Janosch said. 'I think it is safe to assume 'Gate' is just another term for a doorway. That would tie in with the whole Seven Gates end of the world thing, so it seems Pazuzu plays a key role in that process.'

'So his presence at Perron Manor makes sense,' Sarah said.

'The demon we've been seeing here... that's likely Pazuzu as well,' David suggested.

Father Janosch nodded in agreement. 'I'm thinking the same thing.'

'So that could be what's happening here,' Sarah added. 'Maybe there isn't a doorway currently, but they are trying to create one.' She turned to Father Janosch. 'There are plenty of holy people here to use as a sacrifice.'

'Well,' Reverend Quinn cut in, 'here's the thing. The person who summons Pazuzu needs to be impure. Of unholy blood. So, specifically a person who has turned their back on the light, accepted the darkness—someone like that would qualify. There has to be a connection to the otherworld.'

'Herman the Recluse springs to mind,' Father Janosch said.

David nodded his agreement. 'Exactly. He turned his back on God and asked the Devil for help. And didn't he say that the Devil sent a demon to help? Likely Pazuzu. This is all making sense.' David felt a sinking feeling in his gut. 'So that's their play here,' he added.

'There's one last thing,' Reverend Quinn added. 'The final part calls for unholy blood to be spilled. So, I'd imagine the one who summons Pazuzu either offers up their blood, or their life is taken... something like that.'

'Would that work with Father Hus?' David asked. 'After all, he is a good man, really, just one who is possessed. Can his blood really be considered unholy?'

'I think we have to assume so,' Father Janosch said. 'It would make sense. If this ritual is completed and Father Hus spills his blood, a door could be opened.'

'Would Father Hus *have* to give his life?' David asked Reverend Quinn.

She shook her head. 'It doesn't stipulate that, just that the ritual needs unholy blood.'

'Even so,' Father Janosch said, 'I think we can assume that Herman and Pazuzu would have no qualms about killing Father Hus, whether it's required or not.'

'Agreed,' Sarah added.

David turned to Father Janosch. 'I don't think our exorcism is going to be able to wait.'

The priest looked ashen, but nodded his head. 'It would seem that way.' He then turned to the tablet again. 'Anything else we need to know about the Devil's Prayer?' he asked.

'Well, those are the broad strokes,' Reverend Quinn answered. 'I can scan in my notes and email them to you if that would help?'

'Couldn't hurt,' Father Janosch replied.

'No problem, I'll do that as soon as we finish here. I hope that's been useful. Sounds like things might be ramping up over there. Please be careful.'

'We will,' David said. However, he had no real conviction behind his words, and the knot that had formed in his stomach was worsening. He just hoped they were wrong about what was happening here.

'I think we need to speak to Father Hus now,' Father Janosch stated. 'Reverend, be sure to update Bishop Turnbull. I'll report in after we've met with our possessed priest again.'

'Good luck,' Reverend Quinn offered. David and Sarah said their goodbyes as well, and the call was ended.

Father Janosch crossed his arms over his chest. 'This is troubling,' he said.

'One thing I don't get,' David began. 'Why bring us out here? I mean, Father Hus demanded to see Sarah. He wanted her *here*. But why do that? If anything, that just makes things more difficult for them. After all, we've successfully closed one door before. Having us here surely does the demon and Father Hus no favours.'

'There might still be something we're missing,' Father Janosch replied. 'So... let's try to get some answers.'

25

'I DON'T UNDERSTAND why you can't tell me more,' Sister Maria said. 'You're scaring me.'

'We're not trying to worry you, Sister,' Luca replied, 'but please listen. We fear something may be happening, but to say any more might put you and the people that live here in danger.'

Luca and his team had sought out Sister Maria after speaking with Reverend Quinn, finding the nun in a small canteen area. Priests and nuns were seated, starting in on their evening meal, and a smell of roasted chicken permeated the air. Luca also saw Sister Agatha seated not too far away. She looked troubled—her head was down and a worried expression was nestled on her face.

The team, along with Sister Maria, stood close to the entrance door, out of earshot of the others in the hall.

'So what are you asking exactly?' Sister Maria asked. 'You say there may be an imminent threat hanging over us, but don't tell me what it is. How can we remain vigilant if I don't know what we need to be vigilant against?'

'First of all,' David began, 'is everyone in the cathedral accounted for?'

Sister Maria frowned, then turned and cast her gaze around the room. 'That is hard to answer,' she said. 'Not everyone is here in this room, but I wouldn't expect them to be, because some of the residents here eat at different times. Some may be up in their rooms, and others are attending to duties.'

Luca thought on that. If the forces they were working against were going to sacrifice someone to Pazuzu, then it needed to be done within a specific symbol. If they couldn't account for everyone's whereabouts all the time, perhaps their efforts could be better spent elsewhere.

'Maybe there is another way,' he said. 'I need you to look for something.'

'What?' she asked.

Luca chewed his lip for a second. 'This is going to sound strange, but I need you to see if any strange markings have been placed around the cathedral. Do it quietly. You... will know it when you see it.'

Sister Maria's confused frown deepened. 'What markings?'

'A pentagram.'

Now her eyes widened in shock. 'A... pentagram?' she asked in disbelief.

'I know how it sounds,' Luca said. 'But we need you to look. The pentagram will be marked out on the ground. It will be a good size, so should be easily noticeable, which means it might be in a place that is not often accessed. Is there anywhere like that you can think of?'

'Somewhere that's usually off-limits,' Sarah suggested.

'Below ground as well,' Luca added. He realised they were probably overloading Sister Maria with information, but he felt that point could be important. At Perron Manor, the ritual of *Claude Ianua* had to be carried out in the basement in order to increase its potency. He figured that the same could apply here.

'Is there a subterranean crypt here, or anything like that?' David asked. 'Anything like that.'

Sister Maria shook her head. 'Not that I am aware of. The only thing you could call a crypt in Kutná Hora would be the ossuary over at the Church of All Saints.'

Luca turned to look at both David and Sarah. *The ossuary.*

'Could that be where he plans to do it?' David asked.

'Do you think the ossuary is the door?' Sarah asked. 'Rather than Cathedral of Assumption?'

'We can't be sure,' Luca replied. 'We just don't know enough.'

'What door?' Sister Maria asked with a deep frown. He winced. In their eagerness to figure everything out, they had clearly said too much in front of her. He placed a hand on her shoulder.

'Sister, search the building and look for a pentagram. Also, search for any signs that indicate someone may have gone missing. It is critical.'

'You are scaring me, Father,' Sister Maria stated. 'I wish you would tell me more.'

'I will when we figure things out,' he promised. 'But time is of the essence. Please, Sister, I beg of you. Just trust me.'

Her brown eyes stared intently at him. Her face was unreadable. Eventually, though, Sister Maria nodded. 'I will, though I don't particularly like it.'

'Thank you,' Luca replied. 'But before you go, can we have the key to Father Hus' room? We need to go and see him again.'

'Fine,' she said, and drew out the key that she kept with her. She handed it over. 'I thought we were moving closer to resolving everything here. Has something changed?'

'Actually, yes,' he replied. 'Given recent developments, I may need to perform an exorcism myself. In which case, we would need your help.'

Surprise flashed across the nun's face. 'Really?'

'Really,' Luca confirmed. 'But first, I need you to help find that pentagram.'

'And the ossuary? You mentioned it might be important.'

'We'll look into that after we speak with Father Hus.'

'Okay,' Sister Maria said. 'I will report back with what I find. I hope it goes well with dear Father Hus. God willing, he will be free of this soon.'

Luca watched as the nun gave a polite bow, then walked away from them.

He felt Sarah step close. 'I keep thinking about the missing skull down in the ossuary,' she said. 'It's got to be connected somehow, don't you think?'

'I honestly don't know,' Luca replied. He felt frustrated. Everything was just too woolly at the moment, and there were no clear answers. 'But we can't rule it out.' He then turned to face Sarah and held her gaze. He took a breath, knowing she would not react well to what he was about to suggest.

'It... might be a good idea if you accompany Sister Maria,' he said.

Sarah did a double-take. A single eyebrow raised in confusion. 'Excuse me?'

'Well, you have seen this type of pentagram before at Perron Manor. So you could help her find it quicker. Plus, I would feel safer if you were with her to protect her.'

While both of those points were true, they were hardly the reason he had proposed the idea.

As he feared, she saw straight through what he was trying to do.

'What's going on?' she asked as she shook her head.

'It's just—'

'It's just *nothing*, Father,' she snapped. 'David saw that symbol back in Perron Manor as well. Hell, he helped you *draw* it. So why me? Do you think I'm less capable in there with Father Hus? Is that it?'

'No, not exactly, but—'

'You think I'll lose my cool, don't you? You think I'll blow it.' She quickly folded her arms over her chest.

'Sarah, remember what I told you before, about your pride,' Luca said while trying to keep his tone calm. 'It isn't just about you losing your cool. Heaven knows I lost mine the last time we spoke to the priest. But with what we know now, I'm worried about having you in that situation. David raised a good point earlier: we still don't understand why you specifically were called out here. There has to be a reason. If their plan is to open a new doorway, you could then be even more susceptible. By having you with us, we might be playing into Father Hus' hands.'

'We've spoken with him multiple times already,' Sarah said. 'And I feel fine. I'm not falling under their influence.'

'Would you know if you were?' Luca asked.

Sarah paused, then stated, 'Yes.' However, there was no conviction in her voice, and her eyes then drifted down to her feet. 'No,' she admitted.

'Exactly,' Luca said in a soft voice. 'The nosebleed, the sickness you've been feeling since you arrived here... those could all be symptoms of possession.'

'We don't know that,' David cut in.

'No,' Luca agreed, 'we don't, but we can't discount the possibility. Again, caution is needed here.'

He saw Sarah's shoulders slump. It was clear she hated the idea of running away—at least, that was how she'd likely see it—but this would be the safer option. He had considered asking her to go back to the guest house, but he figured there was zero chance of Sarah agreeing to that.

'Fine,' she said. 'I'll go help Sister Maria. Call me if you need me.'

'We will,' Luca promised. Sarah gave them a dejected look before turning and walking after Sister Maria, who was standing a few feet away, caught in discussion with a small group of priests.

'Are you sure it's a good idea,' David began, 'cutting her out like that?'

Luca watched her go. 'I'm not cutting her out, David,' he said. 'Just being sensible. She may not like it, but I'm sure she understands.' Luca then turned to face him. 'Let's find out what we can. I think we should carry out the exorcism tonight, to bring this whole thing to a close.'

'So soon?' David asked. 'Are you comfortable doing that?

Luca drew in a deep breath and nodded. 'I have to be. It needs to be done.'

The two men then left the canteen and headed back upstairs.

26

'JESUS CHRIST,' David uttered when he saw the form of the priest. He stopped short as soon as he entered the room behind Father Janosch.

The priest had changed. How that was possible in such a short space of time, David didn't know, but he had to believe what his eyes were showing him.

Father Hus was now sitting on his bed, legs stretched out before him, arms folded over his gut. He was smiling at them, black gums on show, but his teeth were now visibly yellowed and cracked.

His flesh had gone from merely being pale to a dull, ashen grey—the mottled colour broken only by lines of dark-purple veins beneath the skin. The eyes that stared back at them were milky, with the pupils and irises extremely dulled, as if covered by a film of mucus.

But it was the hair that struck David most of all—or rather, the lack of it. Clumps looked to have been torn free, leaving sporadic clusters about the scalp, and there were patches of dried blood and angry red flesh where the hair had been pulled out.

The stench in the room was still present, but now mixed with a hint of vile body odour, just to top things off. Though the atmosphere was heavy and oppressive, the temperature was freezing, and David saw his own breath hang in the air in front of him. The room was dark, as well, with no working light fittings, and the small amount of daylight that had previously seeped in through the curtains had dimmed. David remained at the doorway, propping the door open to allow the light from the corridor to wash in.

'Where's the little lady?' Father Hus asked. Like his appearance, his voice had changed as well. It was deeper, raspier, more pained, like his throat had been screamed raw.

'She's none of your concern,' Father Janosch said and took a step forward. David almost moved with him, but caught himself—he didn't want to let the door drift closed and plunge them into further darkness.

'But she is,' Father Hus replied as his smile deepened. 'You seem protective of her. Do you even know *what* she is?'

David saw Father Janosch cock his head at the question. 'What a ridiculous thing to ask. She's a person. A good person. She's one of us.'

Father Hus let out a chuckle that caused his naked gut to shake. 'She isn't one of you at all, priest. You know that. She's the daughter of darkness, of our blood. And we want her to come home.'

Don't let yourself be goaded, David thought, seeing a scowl form over the face of Father Janosch. For all his talk to Sarah about keeping calm, David had noticed the priest himself was sometimes quick to anger when dealing with Father Hus.

The possessed man had a way of getting under everyone's skin.

'Sarah is where she belongs,' Father Janosch replied. 'She stands with us. She is a servant of the light, as we are.'

Father Hus just sneered. '*Of course* she is.' His voice dripped with sarcasm.

It was then Father Janosch held up his crucifix out before him, aiming it towards the man on the bed, who winced slightly. Father Hus didn't seem pained, however, just annoyed, as if momentarily startled by a bright glare.

'You will answer our questions!' Father Janosch demanded.

'If I choose to. Though, I suspect I know what you are going to ask.'

'And what's that?' David cut in, still propping open the door.

Father Hus looked up to him. 'Ah, the doorstop speaks. I wondered if you had a use here.' Hus then turned his attention back to Father Janosch. 'You are going to ask me about the doorway, correct? If that is my plan: to open another gateway to Hell.'

Father Janosch took a small step back. 'How could you possibly know that?'

'I have eyes and ears all over this cathedral, Father. Always watching, always listening.'

'Then tell me,' Father Janosch stated. 'Is that what you intend to do here?'

Father Hus remained silent. He simply stared back at them without blinking and still wearing a mocking smile.

'Where will it happen?' David asked. 'The ossuary? Here?'

Still nothing.

'Answer!' Father Janosch snapped. He took another step forward, holding the crucifix higher.

Another wince. However, Father Hus' sneer remained. 'Only when you ask the right questions.'

David was concerned with Father Janosch inching ever closer. It wasn't like the priest on the bed was tied down or restrained; he was free to leap up and attack at any time.

'There *are* no right questions with you,' Father Janosch said. 'You will just lie and subvert the truth. I think we've given you far too much of our time already.'

'Then go,' Father Hus calmly replied.

'Wait,' David said. 'I have a different question.'

Hus again looked up to him. 'Very well, doorstop. Speak.'

'We believe you died here in Kutná Hora. As in, Herman, the spirit we are speaking to. Is that correct?'

Father Hus nodded.

David went on. 'Okay. And you died while the *Codex Gigas* was here at this cathedral?'

'Yes.'

'But... how could you have survived that long? Wouldn't you have been in your nineties?'

'I was. I was old and frail at that point, but my mind was still very much active—the demons had granted me that much.'

'The demons?' David asked. 'They were responsible for your long life.'

'They helped, certainly,' Hus said.

'So why did you return? Were you trying to get the book back?'

'No,' Father Hus said. 'The book was where it needed to be. I just tried to use its knowledge while I was here.'

Use its knowledge? Surely he means the Prayer?

Then something clicked. 'You tried to open a doorway back then,' David said.

'It wasn't easy,' Father Hus said. 'With my failing body, I didn't really have the strength I needed. I came close, though. *Oh so close.* I spent months and months in the cathedral, right under the noses of those that resided here, hiding in the shadows and getting things ready. I managed to sacrifice a nun: had my way with her, cut her up, and then summoned the demon. But before I could spill my own blood, I was stopped. The other priests found me. For men of God, they took great delight in ending my life. The violence they indulged in when killing me... you should have seen it.'

Had his way with her? David pondered on that comment for a moment. His stomach lurched. *That* was not part of the ritual, as far as he knew.

'I wish I had seen it,' Father Janosch replied. 'You deserved it for what you did.'

'Righteous vengeance, eh, priest? Anything is allowed as long as it's in the name of your God, isn't that right? You're just like the ones who killed me, looking for an excuse to allow your true darkness to show through.'

'Now you're going to try again,' David said, trying to guide the conversation back. 'You need to kill again to start the ritual once more. And Pazuzu is already here, helping you.'

But Father Hus gave a slow shake of his head. 'No. Pazuzu isn't the one roaming these halls.'

David frowned. 'Lies. Of course it is.'

'I speak the truth. So much of what I have been telling you, you two just take as lies. I told you about the true darkness at the heart of existence, but you dismissed it. Now you insist I'm lying about the demon. You could all learn so much if you simply opened your minds as well as your ears.'

'If not Pazuzu,' Father Janosch interjected, 'then who?'

'One of Pazuzu's brethren. A particularly nasty entity called Nergal.'

David felt thrown for a loop—none of this was adding up.

Nergal was a name he'd heard before, though he wasn't too familiar with that particular demon.

'But I thought Pazuzu was the Opener of the Gates?' David asked.

'That is true,' Father Hus responded. 'He is the one that opens the doorway initially, to allow the ritual to then be completed.'

'So he still needs to be summoned,' David added. That meant Nergal was just here to aid Father Hus, and Pazuzu was still to come.

However, Father Hus then confounded David further. 'No. The demon's role here was finished many years ago, after I summoned it. Besides, I do believe Pazuzu is busy at the moment.' Father Hus now bared his teeth as his smile lengthened. 'The things that demon has put into motion are glorious. Though that is for another time.'

David shook his head. 'I don't understand.' The frustration he was feeling seeped through into his voice.

'I know you don't. You're fumbling in the dark. However, I'll cast you a lifeline. Answer me this... why would I need to call on Pazuzu again?'

'You need him to complete your work,' Father Janosch answered.

'Do I?'

'Yes,' David replied. 'You said yourself, he needs to be summoned to open the gate.'

'And I told you I already summoned him.'

'Years ago,' David clarified. 'Surely the ritual would need to be performed again...' he trailed off. 'Wait, it's *still* active?'

Father Hus began to laugh. '*Very good.* There is no need to retrace my steps. What was started long ago remains in progress. There is no expiration date on these things. The realms here are already merged, and things are able to seep through, though only a little at a time. You have no idea how close the gate is to being opened. For centuries it has been tantalisingly close to us, yet not close enough to let the darkness fully through.'

Father Janosch turned to look at David, his eyes wide. 'What does all of this mean?' the priest asked.

David shook his head, at a total loss. 'I... don't know.' He directed his next question back at Father Hus: 'But the symbol you drew back then, surely it can't exist today. I refuse to believe it wasn't wiped away when those priests found you and killed you.'

'They cleaned up what they could, certainly.'

David shook his head again. 'So the pentagram isn't needed once Pazuzu is summoned? Because the only step left would be to spill your blood.'

'Spilling unholy blood is the last step, yes. I had the blade to my throat back then, right before those worms rushed me and knocked me to the ground. They dragged me up to the surface outside and cast their judgment. Shame, if they'd have killed me on the spot, my work would have been done.'

'You plan to take Father Hus' life now, to spill his blood and complete the ritual. That much is obvious,' Father Janosch went on. 'So that means you have to remake the symbol again, or... what? Just let the blood fall on the same spot, whether the pentagram is there or not?'

Father Hus shrugged. 'I think I've given you enough for now.'

'Why are you even giving us this much?' David had to ask.

'Because I enjoy seeing you fumble about,' Father Hus answered. David wasn't sure he bought that.

'You can both run along now,' Father Hus said. The sneer suddenly fell from his face. His eyes glared at them with a burning hatred. It was like a switch had been flipped, and his expression immediately changed.

'*We* will decide when we're done,' Father Janosch replied. However, no sooner had he said the words than Father Hus was up on his feet, his body rising up in one swift motion. The possessed priest stood on his bed.

David instantly tensed up. He saw Father Janosch backpedal a few steps.

Father Hus was not done, and his body lifted further up from the bed, his feet dangling in the air above the mattress. The man then held out his arms by his side, mimicking the crucifix position. He tilted his head to the side and his grin returned. He began to laugh, cackling like a madman with his horrible, yellowed teeth on display.

Father Janosch quickly scuttled backwards to join David, and they watched in horror as cuts began to form on the skin of the floating man.

Angry red lines formed across his arms and torso, opening up the flesh, causing the blood beneath to run free. Wounds bloomed in the centre of Hus' palms, which were facing out towards David and Father Janosch. Bloody holes also opened on the tops of his feet.

More cuts and scratches appeared around the crown of the priest's head. Blood trickled free beneath the hairline.

'Pathetic worms!' he bellowed. His voice had once again changed. It boomed, but was animalistic, almost demonic, and certainly not human. 'You dare to demand anything of me?!'

David struggled for breath. Absolute panic flooded through him and he felt a tight grip on his arm. He glanced down to see Father Janosch holding on to him in fright.

David took a step backwards and drew his friend with him.

'Get out!' Father Hus screamed. The loudness and intensity of the words were enough to cause a ringing in David's ears. He ran backwards, along with Father Janosch, and the pair tumbled out of the room to the floor.

David looked up, expecting to see Father Hus continue out into the hallway with them, but instead, he saw the door between them slam shut on its own as the floating man continued to laugh.

27

SARAH AND SISTER MARIA strode through the ground floor hallways of the cathedral, giving cursory glances into rooms as they passed to see if they could spot anything obviously out of place. The pentagram had to be of a good size in order to fulfil its purpose, so hiding it would be difficult. So far, they'd found nothing.

'Can I ask something?' Sister Maria went on as they continued their search. 'Why are *you* helping me look? Aren't you the one with the gifts? I would have thought you'd be needed with the others upstairs.'

Sarah felt herself bristle at the question. 'Well, it's important we find that pentagram,' she said. 'If it exists. But also, Father Janosch is worried my 'gifts,' as you call them, will be used against me. My connection makes me a bit more susceptible to these dark forces. Or, at least Father Janosch thinks so.'

'Is he right?' she asked.

Sarah took a few seconds to answer. 'Yes. I guess he is— though I don't particularly like it. It makes me feel like I have to be held back and wrapped in cotton wool.'

'Cotton wool?' Sister Maria asked in obvious confusion. Then her eyes lit up with realisation. 'Ah, you mean you are to be protected?'

'Exactly,' Sarah said. 'But I've always been one to protect *myself*. So... I struggle with the whole thing.'

They continued on for a few steps before Sister Maria asked. 'What is it like?'

'What is what like?'

'The gift you have. What does it feel like for you?'

'Oh,' Sarah said. 'It's hard to explain. I haven't really figured it all out yet. Different things have different sensations. For example, whenever I'm near Father Hus—or, rather, the spirit that possesses him—I get a cold feeling in my gut. I've had that before when encountering ghosts.'

'So you know when they are near.'

Sarah nodded. 'I think so, yes. But it isn't just that. Here in the cathedral, for example, I've been feeling nauseous all the time.'

'You feel sick?'

'Yes.'

'Is it bad?'

'It's tolerable,' Sarah answered. 'And it varies in intensity, though I can't figure out why. I'm obviously picking up on something.'

'But you don't know what?'

'No,' Sarah said with a shake of her head. 'At least, not yet. Most of this is all new to me.'

Sister Maria nodded in understanding, though she didn't offer any more questions.

They emerged into the large choir and nave area. The space was quieter than earlier in the day, with the entrance door now locked and the building closed off to the public for the day.

There were three other sisters in the room, all seated in pews while they silently prayed.

Sarah and Sister Maria scoured the tiled floor for any markings. As she walked, Sarah followed Sister Maria over towards the choir area. While standing at the base of the steps up to it, she looked up at the large altar to the back. It was a stunning display, predominantly dark wood, but carved in such a way as to look like the front of the cathedral. Miniature statues of people she didn't recognise adorned the altar, which itself sat on a stone plinth.

She looked down at the four stone steps at her feet that were lined centrally with a plush red carpet. The red carpet continued through the choir and across to the altar.

'We could go up there,' the nun suggested as she pointed to the display.

'Am I allowed?' Sarah asked.

Sister Maria nodded. 'Yes, that would be fine. It is normally reserved for members of the clergy, but you and your friends were given permission to go anywhere while here.'

However, before Sarah ascended, her eyes were drawn to two large paintings that hung either side of the steps, each depicting a different scene. One showed two men dressed in white robes feeding two other men who were clad in black. The second painting showed a group of people gathered around a baby, swooning over it. The paintwork in each was masterful.

Below both pictures were two large, identical cases. Each was predominantly glass, revealing what lay within, though the frames around the glass were intricately carved gold, giving each a regal feel.

When peering closer, Sarah saw that each contained

what looked to be life-sized sculptures, both men, though they were fashioned to look withered and mummified.

'Those are strange statues,' Sarah said, nodding to the closer one. 'Who are they depicting?'

She noticed the smile that played over Sister Maria's lips. 'They are saints: Felix and Vincent,' the nun said. 'Though they aren't statues, I'm afraid.'

It took Sarah a moment to realise what the nun meant. When she did finally catch up, however, her eyes widened. 'Wait, those are the actual men? Their *bodies?*'

Sister Maria nodded. 'Their remains, yes.'

Sarah looked back at the body in the glass case in disgust. The skin had a waxy sheen to it, not at all how she'd imagined an aged carcass would look.

'What is it with religion and displaying the bodies of people?' she asked with her nose crinkled and top lip curled. 'It's sick.'

Sister Maria tilted her head as she gazed at the body as well. 'Oh, I don't know. Death is a part of life. Something we must accept. We all rot and decay and fade away, but our souls live on. This is a reminder of that.'

'Well, it's a bit too in-your-face for my liking,' Sarah said. 'When I was in the military, I quickly learned that people who display the dead are never noble. They usually turned out to be psychopaths or fanatics. This kind of thing was always done by people to scare and intimidate the enemy.'

'You believe *this* was done to intimidate someone?' Sister Maria asked as she motioned to the case.

'I have no idea,' Sarah replied. 'But I know the person in that box now has no dignity in death. Same as the poor souls displayed down in the ossuary over at the church.'

'Well, death is a tricky subject for people,' the nun replied. 'I used to take comfort in the fact that after the body dies, we live on. I truly believed that to be true. And now, with what has happened with Father Hus, I *know* it to be true. But... it also scares me.'

Sister Maria bowed her head and began picking at her fingers.

'Why?' Sarah asked.

'Some of the things Father Hus said when possessed. Before you and your friends got here, he took a great deal of pleasure in telling me how things 'really are,' as he termed it. He says that if the souls of the dead aren't of use to the darkness, then they just rot and erode over time, just like our bodies. Eventually, we are simply a husk, lost in the afterlife, alone and scared... and fading.'

Sarah was immediately reminded of her experience in Chillingham Castle, and the ghost of the little boy.

I don't remember... anything.

Was that what they had to look forward to in death? Either existing as a mindless husk, or giving themselves over to the darkness to be used and tormented forever?

Was *that* the price of everlasting self-awareness in the afterlife?

It was a horrifying thought—one Sarah didn't want to dwell on.

'Father Hus is full of lies,' Sarah eventually said. 'Ignore him.'

'I try,' Sister Maria said. 'Although... it's hard. I just worry he's right.'

'He isn't,' Sarah stated. She had to believe that, because if he was right about it, then maybe he was right about Chloe, too.

Sarah moved up the steps to the choir area, where there was benched seating on either side of the central walkway. The floor tiles underfoot were the same greys and blacks as the main nave. She scanned the floor, looking for any signs of possible underground access.

A place below-ground would be preferable for the ritual, so there had to be something.

She carried on all the way to the altar. Three more stone steps led up to a base plinth, which the wooden display rested on. The front of the plinth kicked out a little, forming a shelf, and that was covered by a long white cloth with two potted plants sitting on top.

Sister Maria moved beside Sarah and looked around as well. The toe of her shoe clipped the step in front of her and she wobbled momentarily, trying to keep her balance. 'Clumsy of me,' the nun said with a small laugh.

Something clicked in Sarah's mind as she looked at the step. The stone was a light colour with swirls of grey. But there was something about it...

She quickly walked back to the other set of shallow steps that had led up to the choir area. They were similar to the ones farther along. Similar... but not the same. The greys were deeper, more pronounced, and the lighter areas still darker than those close at the altar. A different type of stone, perhaps? Or maybe the steps to the altar had been installed at a different time. Sarah paid more attention to the actual tiles that surrounded the altar's base plinth.

It was then she realised: *the steps to the altar are newer than the others.*

As was the associated plinth and raised floor.

Maybe that was normal. After all, it was an old building, and modifications and alterations through the years were to be expected—the two rendered wings to the back of the cathedral were proof of that. But maybe there was more to it.

Sarah knelt down at the base of the steps to the altar and checked the intersection where they met the floor. There was a mortar strip along the joint, though in some areas it had crumbled and eroded away. She moved her hand over one of the gaps and concentrated. Cold air passed over her palm.

'Is the area beneath the steps hollow?' Sarah asked Sister Maria.

'I honestly couldn't say,' Sister Maria answered. 'I know a bit of the building's history, but I'm far from an expert. Why do you ask?'

'There's a small draft under there,' Sarah replied. 'Which means the cold air is coming from somewhere.'

'An underground area?' the nun asked.

Sarah shrugged her shoulders and got to her feet. 'Maybe. It's hard to say without ripping the whole area up.'

Sister Maria's eyes went wide. 'I'm afraid I can't allow that, Sarah,' she said in horror.

Sarah chuckled. 'Don't worry, I wasn't suggesting we break through ourselves.' She looked at the area again. 'Even if it *is* a way underground, no one is getting in there without considerable effort. And clearly no one has been down recently—we'd be able to see signs like drag marks or broken mortar. So even if it is an access, no one has used it anytime recently.'

Sister Maria frowned. 'It's strange to think there is something under there,' she said. 'It would be odd to know there is a section of the cathedral we aren't aware of. And if it had been covered over, then why?'

'No idea,' Sarah said. 'But I suppose we need to keep this place in mind. If Father Hus is planning to get underground, this might be how he plans to do it.'

Sister Maria shook her head, though more in disbelief than disagreement. 'Are the possessed strong enough to move something like this?' she asked and raised her arms to the tall altar.

'I'd hope not,' Sarah replied. 'Father Hus is scary enough as he is. I don't want to even think about him having the strength of the Hulk.'

Sister Maria raised an inquisitive eyebrow. 'The Hulk?'

Sarah laughed and shook her head. 'Never mind. Come on, let's keep looking and see what else we can find.'

28

LUCA SET the items down on his bed that he would need: his copy of *Exorcisms and Related Supplications,* a flask that would need to be filled with water and blessed, his crucifix, and his Bible.

The crucifix was a large one, something he could hold out before the possessed man and hopefully keep him at bay. Luca did wear another one, however, beneath his jumper and shirt. The golden image of Jesus on that cross pressed against his skin, offering some familiar comfort.

'We need to call Sarah,' David stressed. Luca could hear the panic in his friend's voice. It was an anxiety he shared.

Seeing Father Hus look the way he did, and watching him levitate, indicated a strength and power Luca hadn't expected.

He had been blind—too comfortable and confident in what they were doing.

Too complacent.

The possessed priest had obviously been hiding the true extent of what he was capable of.

The fact-finding mission was over. There wasn't time to bring in outside help.

They needed to end things.

Luca felt a bead of sweat run from his brow to the end of his nose and fall to the bed. His hands were trembling. He took a moment and closed his eyes.

You can't do this, he thought to himself. *You aren't capable.*

'Father, we need to contact Sarah and tell her what's happened,' David repeated.

'We will,' Luca said, 'but we first need to prepare.'

'But she needs to at least *know*,' David shot back.

He was right, of course, but right now Luca needed to keep his mind focused on the job at hand. He wanted to concentrate on what he *could* control. Otherwise, fear would take over and he would unravel.

You can't do this. Remember Zsámbék Church. People are going to get hurt. They'll likely even die.

'Father?!' David said, louder this time.

Luca spun around. 'For God's sake, David, I hear you!' he shouted. 'But I need to concentrate. So just be quiet for a little while!'

David's head recoiled in shock. He took a moment before responding in a flat tone. 'Don't snap at me, Father.' He then pulled his phone from his pocket. 'I'll do it myself.'

Luca shook his head and turned his focus back to the items on his bed, trying to swallow his annoyance. Why couldn't David have just called her on his own in the first place? What need was there for the man to keep bugging him?

In an instant, he realised he'd been harsh and was taking his frustrations out on his friend.

Because you're scared, that voice inside said again. *Scared of what's to come.*

You can't do this.

Luca tried to ignore those doubts and plan through in his mind how things could go. The first problem they had was that Father Hus was in no way restrained. He was free to walk—or even *float*—about, and there was no way he'd let them simply try to perform the exorcism in front of him. That meant the first point of order was to somehow immobilise the man. Not an easy task. None of the group were exactly fighters.

Sarah is, the voice said. *She could do it. But if you take her in there, then you'll likely get her killed.*

If they were able to restrain the priest, they could then move on to the exorcism itself. Those were impossible to plan for, as they often provoked a strong reaction as the spirit was forced from the body. And in this case, they didn't just have to worry about the spirit of Herman the Recluse, they also had a demon to contend with.

'Sarah,' he heard David say into his phone. 'We need you to come back up to Father Janosch's room. There's been a development.'

Luca heard the muffled sound of Sarah's reply and David finished with, 'Okay, see you back here.'

David disconnected the call, then put his phone away before turning back to Luca. 'She's on her way,' he said.

Luca nodded. 'What do we know about the demon Father Hus mentioned? This... Nergal entity.'

David shook his head. 'I don't know a great deal,' he replied. 'But we could always consult the internet.' He once again tapped on his phone.

'Not always the most reliable source,' Luca said. 'Perhaps we ask Reverend Quinn to look into it?'

'Do we have time?' David asked with his eyes still fixed

on his screen. He made a good point. Time was something they didn't have the luxury of anymore.

'I guess not,' Luca answered. 'Find anything interesting on there?'

'Some articles mention Nergal,' David said. 'Some say he is a Mesopotamian demon, associated with pestilence. Another one here says he is the demon of pestilence, war, and death.'

'Charming,' Luca said. 'Pestilence seems to be a theme.'

David tapped on his screen a few more times before nodding. 'Yeah, looks like that's mentioned in most of the articles I'm seeing.'

'But we don't know how much stock to give those websites,' Luca added. 'Anyone could have written them. Hardly reliable sources.'

'True,' David said and put his phone away. 'But it's something, I guess. If we wanted to find out more, we'd need to delay,'—he then nodded to the items laid out on Luca's bed —'this.'

That wasn't an option.

After a few more minutes there was a knock at the door. Luca jolted a little, reminded of when a savage banging had resulted in the door being splintered. The long crack could still be seen down its centre.

'You guys in there?' he heard Sarah call from out in the hallway.

'Come in,' David shouted back. The door opened and Sarah entered, followed by Sister Maria.

'How did it go?' David asked them.

'We didn't find much,' Sarah replied. 'Though... I have a hunch. The altar down in the main nave. I think there could be something below it.'

'Come again?' David asked.

'Hard to say for certain,' Sarah replied. 'Could be nothing. I felt a draft at the base of it, as if there was a cold spot underneath. Like a void or something. Could lead somewhere. That was about all we could find, though.'

'But other than that,' Sister Maria went on, 'we didn't find anything else. Certainly no pentagram.'

'You said on the call there had been a development,' Sarah cut in. 'You sounded... panicked.'

'The latest meeting with Father Hus didn't go well,' Luca said.

'What happened?' Sarah responded, her body straightening up.

'It appears the Devil's Prayer is already in progress,' Father Janosch told her. 'And it's been that way for a long time, just waiting to be finished.' He then relayed what had happened during their session with Father Hus.

'We also briefly looked into the demon Nergal,' David added. 'Didn't find too much, just that it is a demon of pestilence and death.'

'Pestilence?' Sarah asked. 'Like... the plague and stuff?'

David nodded. 'Yeah, sickness and disease, that kind of thing.'

Luca saw Sarah frown, like her mind was piecing something together.

'What is it?' he asked her.

'Sickness. That... can't be a coincidence to the way I've been feeling while here.'

'The nausea!' David exclaimed.

'Right. It could be I've been picking up on the demon the whole time.'

'Could be,' Luca agreed. The logic in her thinking seemed to make a lot of sense. 'You said before that it seems to ebb and flow in intensity, is that right?'

Sarah nodded. 'Yeah. It's always manageable, but sometimes it lightens up a bit.'

'Then it would make sense to think it's stronger when the presence is closer to you.'

'In that case, it's been pretty damn close most of the time we've been here,' Sarah said.

'Are you still feeling it now?'

She nodded. 'Yeah. It's... pretty strong at the moment.'

Luca cast a gaze around the room. The others did the same, realising what he was thinking. 'Then it could be close right now.'

'Always watching and listening,' David said. 'Father Hus said he had eyes and ears all over this place.'

'In which case, it knows what we are planning,' Luca added and nodded down to his bed.

'Wait,' Sarah cut in upon seeing the items laid out. 'The exorcism is happening *now*?'

'It has to,' Luca replied. 'We've underestimated Father Hus. I believe he has just been toying with us the whole time, and I'm concerned if we leave things any longer, the situation will be unsalvageable. We have to put a stop to it.'

He cast a glance to Sister Maria, who had her hands clasped together, but just stared at the floor in total silence. It was clearly a lot for her to take in.

Sarah took a moment. 'Okay,' she said. 'So what's the plan? Just go over and start exor... cising? Or whatever the term is.'

Father Janosch nodded. 'Not much of a plan, I admit.'

'But better than nothing,' Sarah added. 'Do you have everything you need? If that demon is watching us now from wherever it's hiding, then we'll need to act quickly.'

Luca looked over to Sarah and began to chew at his lip. 'Sarah... I'm not sure if you should—'

'No!' Sarah snapped. 'You aren't cutting me out of this. Sorry, Father, but you need me. No disrespect to you or David, but you are going to need all the help you can get, especially if things get physical. Or do you genuinely think you can restrain Father Hus on your own?'

Luca didn't want to answer that question. Mostly because he didn't like the answer.

David had no such qualms however. 'She's right,' he said. 'We need her.'

'What about me?' Sister Maria asked. 'Anything I can do to help Father Hus, I will.'

'That is kind of you, Sister,' Luca said. 'But I couldn't ask you to get involved any further. It will be dangerous.'

'Wait!' Sarah exclaimed. Everyone turned to look at her.

'Sarah?' Luca asked as she brought a hand up to her stomach.

'The cold...' she said. 'I can feel it again, and it's getting stronger.'

Luca's eyes fell to the closed door. 'What does that mean?' he asked her. 'Is Father Hus approaching?'

'Maybe,' she said after a short pause.

'Didn't you lock him in?' Sister Maria asked.

'We did,' Luca answered. 'But I doubt a simple lock is going to be effective now. I doubt it ever was in the first place.'

The energy in the room suddenly changed. Luca could *feel* the fear and apprehension radiate from those around him as they all watched the door. Was Father Hus here? Or had the ghost left him again? Perhaps it was the vile monk in his spirit form stalking the hallway outside.

'He's approaching,' Sister Maria said.

'Can you hear him?' David asked her while tilting his head, aiming his own ear towards the door.

Sister Maria shook her head. 'No, but I can sense it.'

It took a few moments for those words to register with Luca. 'Sense it?' he asked. 'How?'

A cold, harsh smile played across her lips. 'Because I can. He's coming because I called him. It is time.'

There was a knocking on the door.

'I don't understand, Sister,' Luca said. *What the hell is she talking about?*

The woman coughed, bringing a fist up to her mouth. When she moved her hand away, Luca noticed a dark smear across it. A black liquid also trickled down her chin.

Luca felt his stomach sink.

In an instant, an odour permeated the air of the room— the stench was sulphuric, like rotten eggs.

No.

Everyone moved away from the nun whose smile now showed her teeth and blackened gums. She turned to face Luca, and he saw a yellow glint in her pupils.

'What the fuck!' Sarah yelled.

It can't be, Luca thought.

Sister Maria let out a chuckle. But the voice wasn't the one they had been used to. This time it was deep and ethereal, with a growling, echoey quality to it.

Suddenly, the door to the room exploded inwards. A shower of thick splinters rained down on them and Luca fell backwards to his bed. Father Hus stood in the now open doorway. His wide eyes were completely white, his lips were black, and his skin was horribly grey and mottled. He looked like a corpse. In his hands, Luca could see that he had a human skull held just in front of his stomach.

'What's going on?!' David screamed in sheer terror, cowering back.

With confusion growing, Luca pointed to the skull in the priest's hands. 'That's from the ossuary.'

Father Hus just laughed.

Luca then heard a growl and spun his head. He saw Sarah charge at Sister Maria. The tall woman, however, simply swung an arm, and in an instant, Sarah was thrown through the air without any contact being made. She crashed into the far wall, striking her head hard against it. The sound of her skull colliding with the solid surface was awful, and her body dropped lifelessly to the floor.

Sister Maria let out a demonic laugh. Her face had changed, twisting into a monstrous visage, with elongated teeth, burning yellow eyes, and deep purple veins criss-crossing her skin.

Luca's mind was racing, struggling to make sense of the scene unfolding around him. David dropped to the floor and pulled his knees up to his chest, wrapping his arms over his head.

'Father!' he called over to Luca in a desperate plea. But Luca had nothing to offer. No ideas sprang to mind. He was immobilised with fear. The demonic nun silently drifted over towards him.

'*Now, priest,*' it said in a hideous, inhuman growl. '*It is time to finish what was started.*'

29

PAIN. That was all Sarah knew.

Even before she was able to open her eyes, the agony that bloomed from the back of her head was all she could focus on, and it screamed angrily for her attention. She was lying on the floor, but couldn't remember much else.

She groaned and blinked open her eyes.

The surrounding room was dark. After a few moments, she realised it was Father Janosch's room... though everything was quiet. She could hear nothing. All was still.

Sarah was cold as well, unable to stop a steady shiver in her arms and jaw. However, the cold wasn't the same sensation she had grown to associate with the presence of the supernatural. There were no icy waves emanating from her stomach.

Wooden splinters and debris littered the floor. Sarah moved her eyes to look over to the entrance to the room, where what remained of the door hung limply on its hinges.

It was then, through the fog of pain, she remembered what had happened before blacking out: Sister Maria revealing just *what* she really was; Father Hus shattering the door; Sarah being flung against the wall and striking her head before blacking out.

Now... everyone was gone. She was lying alone in the dark. The only light offered was from the dim rays of the moon rolling in from the corridor outside.

She tried to speak and managed to croak out a single word. 'Hello?'

No answer. Only silence. *Where are David and Father Janosch? Did something happen to them?*

How long was I out?

The questions tumbled frantically over in her mind. Then the questions turned to Sister Maria. *Was she possessed by the demon the whole time?*

After giving it some brief thought, Sarah assumed the nun had to have been. Sarah's nausea—which at this moment was greatly reduced—had started soon after arriving at the cathedral, and the more she thought about it, the more sure she was it had been more intense the closer Sister Maria had been to her. But because the nun had almost always been around, it wasn't something Sarah had picked up on.

A panicked urgency flooded through her.

Get up! You can't just lie here. People are in danger!

If they weren't already dead.

Sarah rolled forward to her front. More pain erupted from the back of her head. She let out another unintentional groan, then brought a hand to her scalp, worming her fingers through the thicket of her hair. When her probing fingers connected with the skin of her cranium, she felt a lump. She pulled her hand away and saw dried blood smeared across her fingertips.

Great, Sarah thought. *Might be a concussion.*

She pushed herself up to her knees, and as soon as she

did her vision spun and her stomach lurched. Sarah took a moment and closed her eyes, breathing deeply while trying to steady herself.

Get it together.

When things finally settled somewhat, she pushed herself up fully to her feet. She swayed. Eventually, however, Sarah was able to get the dizziness and disorientation under control, at least enough to take a step forward.

Scanning around the room, she saw that the things Father Janosch had previously laid out on his bed had been destroyed. The flask had been crushed against the floor. The Bible and the other, thinner book with the red cover had both been torn to shreds, their remains littering the bedcovers.

Sarah quickly brought her hand to her pocket, searching for her phone, but even before she did she realised her pocket felt empty. She quickly saw the phone lying on the floor, screen cracked, and the plastic casing destroyed. She wouldn't be calling anyone for help. Sarah then checked her watch, squinting to see the face of it in the darkness.

It was a little before 3 AM. Which meant she had been unconscious for hours.

Renewed panic filled her. Was she already too late? Were David and Father Janosch dead?

Had the demon already succeeded in opening the Devil's Door?

She took another step forward, closer to the door. Her head spun again, but she pushed through and took yet another step. Sarah soon emerged out in the corridor, leaning into the door frame for support. Looking to her left, she saw no one, but when she looked to her right Sarah's breath caught in her throat.

A body lay on the floor at the end of the hallway. Even

from this distance, Sarah could see that it was an elderly woman—the skin pale, sagging, and wrinkled.

Sarah then heard a low moan coming from the fallen person.

She set off in an instant, keeping her arm out to her side, feeling her way along the wall as she moved to keep from toppling over. As Sarah got closer, she realised she recognised the woman on the ground.

Sister Agatha.

Standing over her, looking down, Sarah drew in a breath and brought her hand to her mouth.

Sarah couldn't understand how the poor nun wasn't dead, considering the lacerations that covered her battered, naked body. One arm was bent at an unnatural angle at the forearm, and a jagged edge of broken bone penetrated the skin.

Bruises covered the skin as well, both dark purples and sickly yellows.

However, it was what had happened to the nun's face that disturbed Sarah most.

Sister Agatha's eyes were gone.

Dark, ruined pits were all that was left, with the exposed flesh around them red and angry. Tears of dried blood streaked the nun's cheeks.

'Sister Agatha,' Sarah said as she knelt down next to the poor woman. The nun could only moan and whimper. Her breathing was shallow and rapid. Sarah felt helpless.

What do I do?

There was only one answer. She had to get help. She needed to contact someone and get an ambulance here as soon as possible.

'Sister Agatha,' she said again in a gentle, quiet voice.

'Please hold on, I'm going to get something to make you more comfortable.'

The nun rolled her head slightly towards Sarah's voice, and those empty pits fell directly into Sarah's line of sight, causing her to look away.

'Help... me,' the terrified nun weakly begged.

'I will,' Sarah whispered back. While time was of the essence, Sarah didn't want to just leave Sister Agatha naked on the floor, exposed to the cold in the hallway.

Standing back up to her feet, Sarah moved back down the corridor, this time to her own room. Her eyes flicked to every door that she passed on the way, fully expecting one of them to open and someone to jump out at her. Though she couldn't see any direct threat, she could practically feel unseen eyes on her.

However, with no cold sensation emanating from her stomach, and the only feeling of nausea being caused by the blow to her head, Sarah knew that neither Father Hus nor Sister Maria were close by.

As Sarah moved, it suddenly dawned on her to check the other rooms as well. Given the time of night, the other residents of the cathedral should be asleep, likely blissfully unaware of what had happened. However, of the rooms that were unlocked and able to be checked, Sarah found each was empty.

Where the hell is everyone else?

Once in her own room, Sarah quickly threw on one of her own jackets to ward off the cold, and then she gathered up the sheets from her bed, as well as the pillows. On the way back, she collected more bedding from Father Janosch's room and returned to the fallen nun. She draped both sets of covers over Sister Agatha's exposed body, careful not to put any pressure on Sister Agatha's broken arm, and gently lifted the woman's head to tuck the pillows underneath. Sarah thought about trying to reset the arm—it was something she had done before—but she had nothing to use as a splint or bandage. Besides, resetting it would cause a hell of a lot of pain to the old woman, and there was nothing on hand to alleviate that.

So this was as much as Sarah could do for now.

'I'll be as quick as I can,' she whispered and stood back up, feeling bad for having to leave the poor old woman like this. She couldn't help but look at the nun's ruined face again and to those empty eye sockets. The windows to Sister Agatha's soul had been plucked free and discarded some-where. Even if the woman survived—and Sarah wasn't confident she would—then she'd be blind for the rest of her life.

Rage swirled inside Sarah at what had been done to this defenceless old woman. She turned towards the door that led out of the hallway. With fists clenched, she took a step forward, but as she did, something wet and glistening on the floor drew her attention.

There were two objects, bloodied and mashed, each with a stringy, wet tail of red flesh behind.

She knew what they were even before taking in all the details.

Sarah balled her fists tighter and fought to keep from gagging. She then strode quickly out of the corridor, step-ping over the eyes, and did her best to ignore Sister Agatha's scared and pained cries for help as she left.

30

SARAH MOVED SLOWLY and carefully down the stairs. Each step creaked under her weight. With no other sounds to hear, those creaks were even more pronounced, as if signalling her arrival to anything that was waiting below. She wanted to call out again to try and get someone's attention, but knew whatever was listening might not be friendly.

She had no idea where the other residents of the cathedral were, or what had happened to David and Father Janosch, but Sister Agatha had been left as a message specifically for her.

As Sarah descended lower to the ground-floor, she noticed that familiar cold sensation return in her gut, faint though it was. And while her spinning head and disorientation faded the more she moved—which was a welcome relief—the sickly feeling Sarah now associated with the cathedral reared its head again.

She was walking into something. She knew it. Her time in the army had helped her develop a radar for danger, and right now, it was in overdrive.

Sarah kept climbing down, peering through the dark of the stairwell that dropped down below her. When she reached the half-landing, however, she stopped dead.

The cold suddenly increased, pushing out in strong waves and filling her up. Yet again, Sarah was reminded of her time in Chillingham Castle, when she had seen that ghost boy—the one who had seen *her* as an approaching darkness.

Sarah's eyes darted around the area, but she could see little beyond the wooden stairs and the white plaster of the walls. There were no windows in that area, and the light switch she'd tried at the top had not worked. As she glanced over the handrail, she saw darkness swallow up the steps that dropped down into it, not allowing her to see the bottom.

However, a voice came up out of the void.

'Saaaraaaah.'

Her stomach tightened in an instant and her body tensed up. The voice was quiet, little more than a whisper, but in that single word, Sarah heard so much: pain, evil, and a hollowness which made it clear the thing speaking was not among the living.

Then, another sound followed, this one much louder and equally terrifying. A loud thump, likely from a heavy foot dropping onto the first step far down below.

Then another.

And another.

Each step was spaced out a few agonising seconds before the next—something was slowly climbing up towards her.

Sarah froze. *What do I do?*

Thump... thump... thump.

She tried to focus her mind and consider her options. It soon became apparent there were only two ways to proceed.

After all, she was on a fucking stairwell, which meant she could either go up them or down them. Unless, of course, she wanted to take her chances jumping off the side.

Sure recipe for a broken ankle, Sarah.

Thump.

Come on, Sarah, she said to herself as panic began to overwhelm her. *Do something. Shit or get off the pot.*

Thump.

Another noise accompanied the heavy footsteps now. It sounded like something sliding. She looked over the side again and could see the bannister below. On it, there was a pale hand with blackened nails. It moved along the wooden bannister, sliding across the timber.

'Saaaraahhh,' the voice whispered again. The thing below her, still mostly hidden from view, was mocking her, trying to scare her. Sarah hated that it was working.

Then the hand pulled back, and disappeared. She heard a chuckle. Her heart turned to ice and her body locked up in fear again. The footsteps started again, only this time, at a much faster rate.

Thump, thump, thump.

The thing below her was now running up the stairs, sprinting towards her. Sarah back-pedalled and moved to the first step up from the half-landing. However, the footsteps were coming much too quickly—at an inhuman speed —and were now booming in their intensity.

They drew closer and closer. Sarah tried to take another step back, but her heel caught on the first step and she fell, her back hitting against the incline of the stairs. She drew her arms up in front of her in a pathetic attempt to protect herself—the footsteps drew nearer and were almost on top of her now.

However, just at the point where Sarah should have

been able to see someone emerge onto the half-landing, the sounds immediately stopped.

Sarah, with her heart still in her mouth, remained motionless, wide eyes fixed on the top step before her, still expecting something to appear. Nothing did. She sat that way for a few moments more, breathing quickly, feeling ice-cold pinpricks all over her skin.

She waited. Still nothing.

After a few moments more, Sarah let her body sink into the steps behind her... and let her head fall back.

She immediately screamed when she saw the monk standing a few steps above her, looking down. Sarah quickly scrambled forward and threw herself over to the far wall, spinning as she did to look back at the horrifying man who stood four steps up, motionless, staring at her with manic, gazing eyes.

It was the same monk they had seen downstairs the day before. He wore the same hessian robes, his skin similarly pale and waxy—thin in some places, allowing bone beneath to show through. His eyes had no pupils and were merely white, fleshy orbs that ran with black tears.

He wore a smile as well. The teeth that showed beneath were yellowed, cracked, and connected to black gums.

The man didn't move an inch, not even exhibiting a natural sway or movement of breath. He was like a photo-graph. The monk continued to stare at Sarah with his dead eyes as panic flooded her.

Sarah gritted her teeth and crab-walked away from him, over to the flight of stairs that dropped down below. He didn't move to follow.

Once she was at the top, Sarah quickly got to her feet and spun, taking two steps down in one leap. She glanced back over her shoulder to see that the monk now stood on the half-landing itself, closer to her, but was still motionless, as if he had just blinked forward somehow.

A coldness emanated from his form, rolling towards her and making the hairs on the back of her neck stand on end.

She took another step down, then another, still keeping a watchful eye on the apparition. Her body was tense and her jaw was set. If he was going to do something, she wished he would just get on with it and act. Having him merely watch her, smiling, as she crept backwards down the stairs was almost worse than having to deal with an attack.

When she was about halfway down, and the ghost was lost to the darkness above, she turned and ran down the rest of the way, going so fast that, on a couple of occasions, she almost lost her footing and fell. Luckily, she managed to make it to the bottom, jumping the last few steps. Sarah let her body fall forward into the door from the stairwell, spinning around as she did just to make sure he hadn't followed.

He had.

The monk stood only inches behind her, his face now close enough to make out every horrible detail: eyes bulging from the surrounding skin, which had sunken into the sockets, the dry, flaking edges of flesh where the skull beneath was exposed, and the dried blood that streaked the heavy-looking hessian robes, all accompanied by a sickening, fetid odour, like rotten meat.

Sarah screamed aloud again and swung open the door behind her before running through and slamming it shut. The monk continued to grin as the door was closed on him.

After taking another step back, Sarah doubled over, breathing heavily. Her head spun and it was a struggle not to vomit, the earlier knock to her head clearly still affecting her.

Keep it together. You have to keep moving!

She allowed herself a few more breaths, then stood up and turned around. There, in the main nave of the cathedral, Sarah saw death.

Everywhere.

31

She'd found the residents of the cathedral. And they were dead.

Not just dead. Desecrated. Violated. Displayed like macabre pieces of artwork. Sarah struggled to take in the sickening sight around her, and her mind immediately jumped back to the ossuary, where the dead there had been given the same kind of dishonour.

Here, however, things were much more visceral.

While the main light fittings in the area were off, it was illuminated by the flickering glow given off by the many lit candles clustered around the nave and choir.

The gentle, orange light—which only offered pockets of light and still kept most of the room in darkness—only served to make the horrors around Sarah even more unnerving. She had no idea what else was hidden in the shadows.

But what she could see terrified her enough.

Naked bodies sat slumped against the walls, heads hanging down to their chests. She could see that on many, their eyes had been removed just like Sister Agatha's had.

Some lay prone on the floor as well, and one man was positioned in the crucifixion pose, though his stomach had been pulled open, the intestines from within snaking out over to one hand, where it looped around the wrist, only to run across the man's chest and wrap around his opposite hand. A huge amount of blood pooled below him, partially dried, looking almost gelatinous in the candlelight.

Sarah cast her eyes over to the main entrance door, which was still closed, only it was now barricaded by more of the dead.

Even though she was dealing with the demonic, her mind couldn't figure out *how* those forces had arranged the bodies across the door.

They were bound together in an interlocking nightmare, tied with their own innards and intestines, forming a small wall of crumpled corpses in front of the main door. Heads were bound to arms, arms to legs, torsos to limbs... Even with everything Sarah had experienced over the last few months, she had never seen *anything* like this. With the number of bodies blocking the way, Sarah knew she couldn't hope to open the door even if she tried.

Expressions of horror were still etched on the faces of the poor souls bound together in the human wall; mouths lolled open and their eyes were wide with a vacant stare.

Lastly, Sarah looked up to one of the walls and saw one of the large, decorative crucifixes had a new addition: an elderly woman, who had been tied to the golden frame in an obvious mocking of the son of God.

There was something else Sarah noticed as well when gazing up to the choir and the altar behind it... or at least, to the place the altar had once stood.

It had been destroyed, its remains lying on the floor, as if a wrecking ball had swung through it, destroying everything it hit: the altar, the base plinth, even the raised floor and the stone steps. Rubble and debris covered the area. However, there was a perfectly formed square hole in the floor where the altar had previously stood, and it dropped down below ground and into darkness.

The way ahead was obvious, but Sarah desperately didn't want to tread it. She was being herded, that much was obvious, and she feared what was waiting.

She quickly looked to the large windows on either side of the choir areas, knowing that if needed, she could break one and get outside.

Getting free of the cathedral and running for help seemed like a good idea. Staying and going down into the void was clearly madness.

Then... she heard something. A faint cry of pain, echoing out of the hole.

David.

Whatever had caused his distressed yelling had done so to deliberately draw Sarah's attention. She knew that. It was a warning. Leave... and David dies. Father Janosch, too.

It was an obvious trap, but she couldn't run away from it.

Her nausea had worsened the lower Sarah had descended, and would no doubt further intensify should she venture below ground. The demon was waiting for her down there. The ghost of Herman, too, she guessed, especially since the cold sensation had dampened since she'd emerged from the stairwell. The ghost had clearly funnelled Sarah down where it wanted her to go.

The safest, most sensible option was to run. Surely there was nothing she could do to stop the Devil's Prayer from being completed now. The hole in the ground looked to have been formed many years ago, certainly not any time recent, so it didn't take a genius to figure out that was where the original Prayer had taken place.

And if the body of Father Hus was down there now, Sarah guessed his blood had already been spilt. Because... why would they wait?

She'd failed. They'd all failed.

Now, it seemed, the demon here wanted to torment her further by showing her what it had done to her friends.

So, yes, running was the sensible option.

However, when she took her first step, it was towards the hole.

32

THE OPENING in the floor gave access to a flight of old, uneven stone steps that sank down into the darkness. Below that was a formed passageway, clearly part of the original building, but blocked off for who knows how long.

Sarah moved steadily and carefully. The light from above was easily swallowed up by the shadows, and as she dropped farther down, her sight was cut off completely. Sarah held out a hand before her to feel for obstacles, as her other hand kept a constant touch on the stone wall beside her as she descended. The air here was cold—colder than above—and stale. Sarah shivered, both because of fear and the dropping temperature, which even her coat was unable to ward off.

She almost stumbled as her foot hit the ground beyond the last step, as she hadn't realised the flight of stone stairs had come to an end. She continued steadily forward, hands out before her, feeling her way through the dark. After a few feet, her fingers made contact with the cold, coarse surface of a wall.

To her right, she noticed something: a flicker of light

indicating the way ahead. As she continued to move, Sarah noticed that the light seemed to be coming from around another corner, but at least she had a way forward. She hesitantly pushed on. Her mind screamed at her that to continue was suicide, but her pride refused to let her leave her friends behind.

The almost total darkness was difficult to navigate, and not just physically; she was on high alert, expecting cold hands to reach out through the black and grab her at any moment. That, coupled with the increasing sensations of cold and nausea, made moving forward bring with it a sense of impending doom.

What do you hope to achieve here, Sarah? They're dead. The Prayer is complete. Now, you're going to die as well.

Despite her internal war, Sarah kept walking, taking one careful step after another, until she finally turned the corner ahead.

Now she could see more. The light, she realised, was again from candles, and the glow framed a narrow passageway ahead that opened out into a large room beyond. She could see little of that space other than what was offered from the opening, but could make out what appeared to be a stone sarcophagus. Decorative crests had been carved into the sides and the statue of a man lay on top, hands over his chest, dressed in what looked like long robes. There were golden stands close to the sarcophagus that held lit candles. The amount of light flickering through to the corridor, however, indicated there were other candles in the space beyond what she could see.

'Saaaraaahhh,' the same ghostly voice as before once again whispered from the room ahead.

Herman.

You have the opportunity. Run!

She knew she wouldn't. Besides, did she honestly believe the forces that had slaughtered everyone in the cathedral would just allow her to walk out of here of her own free will? There was no *real* opportunity to escape. All she could do was to carry on forwards and meet whatever fate waited for her.

33

SARAH ENTERED the room and gasped.

David and Father Janosch were both alive... but only barely. They were beaten and bruised, their faces bloody messes. Both men lay on the ground, tied up with their hands bound to their bent legs, which forced the pair into a foetal position. They both lay close to the centre of the large room, which Sarah quickly realised was a crypt.

There were many more sarcophagi than the one she had initially seen, all of a similar construction, though the decorative carvings and the effigies on top varied slightly from one to the next.

The room was of predominantly stone construction, with the walls mismatched blocks, the floor uneven slabs, and the ceiling a flat stone surface. The addition of the many sarcophagi helped overwhelm the aesthetic in dull, plain greys, only broken up by the orange of the candlelight.

Thick pillars ran up from the ground and held the relatively low ceiling above. Those columns had square bases and heads, with the central section being cylindrical.

Father Hus and Sister Maria were there as well. They stood between David and Father Janosch, facing Sarah, and had become even more horrific to look at. The naked priest's skin had turned an even duller grey, and the purple veins that had shown beneath the surface were now more pronounced and a deep black. In addition, sores had formed on his skin—crusty, flaky patches that wept with a dark liquid. The wrinkles across his face had deepened as well, which Sarah soon realised was due to the swelling of his flesh, making him look unnaturally bloated. Little remained of his grey hair now, only a few bloody clumps. And his milky white eyes still held their dead stare.

Sister Maria was still clothed in her black habit and accompanying headpiece. The pupils of her eyes again burned yellow, glinting in the relative dark. She looked taller than she had, and she loomed over Father Hus. She was still ghostly white, with dark areas to her cheeks and around her eyes, as well as dark veins showing from under her skin. The teeth Sarah remembered from their last encounter, long and jagged, were still bared. An unnaturally long tongue emerged from between her upper and lower set and licked along their surfaces.

'Come in, little bird,' Father Hus said. David and Father Janosch continued to moan in pain. One of David's eyes had swelled up and could no longer open, and Father Janosch's nose was clearly broken.

At least her friends weren't dead. However, Sarah struggled to see a way she could help them. Regardless, she closed her hands into fists and took a few steps farther inside. As she did, she noticed something, and her eyes drifted down to the ground close to Father Hus' feet. There was a skull.

She remembered he had been holding that skull back up in the room before she'd been knocked out. She also recalled Father Janosch's words.

Father Hus saw her looking at it and grinned. 'When I died, the demon Pazuzu bound my spirit to a part of me so that I could remain here, ready to be called on again when needed. It has been centuries of hell... of waiting in limbo. Finally, I was beckoned.'

'But you couldn't have brought it here from the ossuary,' Sarah said. 'You were naked. There's nowhere you could have hidden it.'

He cocked his head. 'Really? Use your imagination, child. If one is willing—and brave enough—there is always a place.'

She looked down to his waist. Had he really shoved the—

'No fucking way,' she exclaimed.

Father Hus tilted his head back and laughed. 'Of course not, you idiot. I don't think the poor Father would stretch that far. But... *I* wasn't the one who brought it back.'

He turned to look at Sister Maria.

'You?' Sarah asked.

'Of course,' Father Hus replied. 'Plenty of places to hide it under those robes. Everyone had their eyes on me, so it was quite easy.' He turned back to Sarah. 'My original body was buried in a cemetery where the church now stands, and then dug up and put on display by your men of God. A horrible existence.'

Sarah took another step forward. She wondered if she could keep him talking long enough for her to edge close enough to attack. She'd come to learn the possessed priest liked the sound of his own voice.

Her attempt would likely fail, especially with a demon standing close by, but at least it was *something*. She could fight and struggle, not just wait for things to happen.

'I don't understand,' she went on. 'Father Hus displayed signs of possession before he went to the ossuary—before the skull was even taken.'

Another step.

'Come on, little bird, this is a small town. The meat-sack I live in ventured to the church and ossuary fairly frequently. Sister Maria accompanied him as well, which let me bore into his soul little by little each time, until I finally had enough strength to call him back there to finish the possession.' He then prodded the skull with his toe. 'And with the anchor always close by, I have been able to use your priest as I need to.'

'So that skull was with you the whole time?'

'Under the bed,' he said with a smirk. 'No one checked —not even you.' He laughed again.

Another step. The possessed priest certainly had no problem revealing information to her now. Was he just over-confident, or was there another reason? The demon close by made no attempt to stop the priest from talking, either, and merely watched on in silence.

His explanation did leave another question, of course. If the demon inside Sister Maria was the architect of all this madness, how had the *nun* become possessed in the first place?

However, Sarah didn't want to turn any attention to that looming menace for fear of what it could trigger. She felt safer keeping her focus on Father Hus.

She looked again at the skull and wondered: if it was destroyed, would that banish the spirit of Herman back to whatever hell he had been hiding in?

Suddenly, she stopped dead in her tracks.

Sarah frowned, noticing what had been marked out on the floor, and she heard another chuckle from Father Hus.

'Finally, you spotted it,' he said.

It had been difficult to see in the poor light, but Sarah still admonished herself for missing it so completely.

The pentagram.

It wasn't formed by chalk or salt, and had instead been carved into the stone ground. The deep scratch marks looked very old, and the main circle of the symbol was about six feet in diameter, fitting neatly between the spaced-out sarcophagi. David and Janosch lay just outside of its perimeter, and Father Hus and Sister Maria stood on the edge as well, with Sarah herself a few feet away from the symbol's edge.

The lines of the intersecting star were far from neat or even, and the circle was a little lopsided, but it was still clearly a pentagram.

Father Hus looked down at the etching with pride. 'Not bad for a man in his nineties, wouldn't you say?'

'It's been here all this time?'

He nodded. 'Yes. Not as many people stayed at the cathedral back then, so I hid down here for weeks, working when I was able to, carving the symbol into the floor. When I was ready, I acted. Soooooo close,' he said and held up a hand with the thumb and forefinger about an inch apart.

'You still failed,' Sarah said, trying to goad him.

The brief flash of anger that crossed the man's face brought her some satisfaction.

'That will be put right tonight,' he shot back.

Sarah noted his words. *Will* be put right. So, they hadn't completed the ritual yet. Why?

'But after you were killed, the priests here just left all this?' she asked and kicked a foot out to the symbol.

'They removed the body and cleaned up the mess I'd made of that pathetic nun,' he said with glee. 'But you can't exactly wipe away a carving, can you? They considered doing something, but Pazuzu revealed himself to them, put the fear of... God,' he said with a sneer, 'into them. They ran, closed the area off, and insisted it was cursed: the resting place of the Devil, or something like that. I think they even considered closing the cathedral completely. In the end, the crypt was just covered over permanently, and the incident brushed under the carpet. After years of nothing else happening, the surviving priests grew confident the cathedral was safe, as long as this place was never again uncovered. So, it was deliberately forgotten about and the incident swept under the rug. Standard practice for your church.'

'It isn't my church,' Sarah shot back.

The priest's smile deepened. 'Glad to hear that. Because, despite everything that has happened, there is an actual reason I was told to bring you here.' Father Hus turned to Sister Maria, who continued to watch without blinking. He went on, 'You are wanted, child. There is a place for you, not just in this world, but *beyond* it.' He looked down to Father Janosch, who continued to squirm. 'People like *him*, and those he obeys, they don't care about you. You are merely a tool they use to try and exert their will. They are madmen who profess kindness and virtue, but are merely drunk on power.'

'And you're offering something different?' Sarah asked, letting her obvious disdain show through.

'Honesty,' he replied. 'Chaos is the natural order. If you accept it, revel in it, you become something much more. I wasn't lying when I told you about your God and just what he is... a mistake, born from a mindless dream of the true Lord over all. Sarah... your true family calls to you now. They can show you the true path.'

Sarah gazed over at the unmoving nun, who stared back at her, expressionless. The yellow eyes seemed to look into her soul, boring into her.

Did they really expect her to fall for that? It sounded like a nightmare. Chaos being the true order was as far from appealing as Sarah could imagine. Yet, the comment about the men Father Janosch obeyed certainly had some merit. And her time in the army proved that chaos had its place... She shook her head.

What am I thinking?

'Ignore them, Sarah,' Father Janosch said weakly. 'Fight it.'

The nun's stare continued and Sarah felt as if it actually cast a weight onto her, pinning her down. She shook her head again and looked away.

The susceptibility Father Janosch had always feared was brought front and centre.

'I need you to be strong,' Father Janosch went on.

Sarah nodded. 'I need you to be strong as well,' she replied. 'Because you have work to do.'

Father Hus cocked an eyebrow in surprise.

It was fortunate that neither Father Hus nor Sister Maria were inside the pentagram. To finish the Devil's Prayer, tainted blood needed to be spilled, and it was obvious Father Hus was to be the sacrifice. Which meant Sarah needed to keep him out of the circle long enough to let Father Janosch do what he needed to.

Without giving any warning, Sarah quickly launched

into a full sprint, barreling over to Father Hus, whose face dropped in surprise. With a roar, she thrust her shoulder into him, her momentum knocking the older man backwards from his feet.

The demon screeched.

34

Luca felt Sarah frantically work on the ropes that bound his legs to his hands.

His body ached and his nose burned with a fierce pain. He'd truly believed he was going to die down here. In truth, he still likely would, but he couldn't deny that his heart leapt after seeing Sarah enter the crypt.

She continued to work on the knots in the rope that held him, and it started to slacken.

He looked over to David, who still lay helpless, close to the demon that continued its screeching. The awful sound pierced the air around them with inhuman intensity.

David looked terrified.

Luca couldn't blame him. Ever since Sarah had been knocked unconscious upstairs, things had spiraled out of control. They had both been dragged by Sister Maria down to the nave. They would have screamed, of course, had her hands not been clamped around their throats so tightly they couldn't breathe.

The demon had uttered some unintelligible words, and

then the altar at the back of the choir had exploded. He and David had then been carried down to this crypt, where Father Hus had gotten to work tying them up. From there, he took glee in beating them while Sister Maria disappeared back upstairs.

Luca didn't know what happened up there, exactly, but the many screams of pain he'd heard terrified him. Then everything had grown quiet.

'Heathens!' he heard a voice shout out. Luca turned and saw that Father Hus was back on his feet, face twisted in animalistic anger.

'Come any closer and I'll rip your fucking throat out!' Sarah screamed in reply. 'If Hus dies, then *you* won't exist here anymore.'

She continued working on the ropes.

'You wouldn't dare,' he replied. However, the man looked far from certain. Judging by her tone, Luca wasn't so sure she was bluffing.

'Try me!' she seethed. Luca felt his bonds fall free and Sarah heaved him up to his feet. His legs and arms ached, and a sudden tingling erupted in his thighs as the blood started to circulate again. The sensation sapped the power in his legs, but he fought through it.

Sarah grabbed his head. 'You know what you need to do,' she said urgently. He frowned in confusion. She let out a quick sigh and shouted, 'The exorcism!'

The exorcism? How? I don't have my book or my holy water.

His thoughts were interrupted by a flash of motion and a dull thud. Sarah went sprawling to her side with Father Hus, who had tackled her, falling on top. Both hit the ground inside the pentagram.

Sarah managed to wriggle to her back as Father Hus mounted her.

'Hurry!' she screamed over at Luca.

Panic flooded through him. He couldn't do it without his book. Could he? He closed his eyes and searched his memory, trying to recall everything he'd studied earlier that day.

Concentrate!

Luca took a breath and tried to remember.

'Any time you like, Father!' Sarah yelled. He opened his eyes again to see Father Hus still on top of her, trying to rake out her eyes. Sarah, however, had hold of his forearms, just barely keeping his searching fingers away from her face.

Sister Maria was still emitting an awful sound while she watched on, but now the screeching had changed, resembling more a demonic laugh.

Remember the words!

Luca had no holy water to help, but there was little he could do about that. However, he could at least try to recite a prayer.

'Halt!' he shouted at Father Hus. However, the possessed priest ignored him. Luca quickly reached under his jumper and grasped the small, golden crucifix he wore on a chain around his neck. With a small tug, the thin chain snapped, and he pulled the effigy free, then held it out between his fingers at Father Hus. He would have much preferred his larger crucifix, but this was all he had to work with.

'I said halt!' Luca yelled again. For a brief moment, Father Hus did, and turned his eyes to Luca. Seeing the crucifix, he visibly winced. In that moment, Sarah thrust the palm of her hand up into his face, forcing his head back.

Father Janosch held his breath, fearful the blow was going to burst Hus' nose.

Don't draw his blood, Sarah!

Father Hus quickly twisted his head and managed to

find the side of Sarah's hand with his mouth. He clamped his teeth down over her skin, then shook his head savagely from side to side, like a pit-bull after it had latched on. Sarah shrieked in pain. The horrible laughter from the demon increased in intensity as the chaotic scene continued.

Sarah tried frantically to pull her hand free and ended up using her other fist to strike Father Hus on the side of the head. The blow sent him tipping to his side, taking Sarah's trapped arm with him.

He rolled away and Sarah let out another cry as she yanked her hand free. She brought it up to her chest and pushed herself up to her knees. Blood ran freely from a nasty-looking wound where the skin had been split apart. Fortunately, the chunk of flesh between the teeth marks hadn't been yanked completely free.

Father Hus grinned as blood dribbled down his chin. He spat it to the ground and licked his lips.

Sarah was scowling now, and there was a wild rage in her eyes. She set her wounded hand down to the ground and used it to push herself up.

'I'll fucking kill you,' she seethed. Her teeth were gritted together. She pulled her fingers into tight fists, causing her right hand to drip more blood.

The manic cries from the nun increased in intensity. They were also accompanied by an unexplainable booming sound that nearly shook the area they were in. It was maddening.

'Sarah, no!' Father Janosch shouted in panic. 'That's what he wants! You'll complete the Prayer!'

He desperately hoped Sarah would be able to control herself. He wasn't sure how much of her aggression was born from natural anger, and how much was a result of the unnatural influence. The terrible noises around them continued.

Luca lunged forward and put a hand on her shoulder. 'Be calm, please!'

Calmness was perhaps a lot to ask in such a situation, but he hoped that he could help talk her down from attacking, at the very least. He stepped beside her and raised the small crucifix in his hand a little higher, pushing it closer to Father Hus.

'Back, I tell you!' he shouted at the possessed priest, who now snarled and spat like an animal, moving closer to his master. The nun grinned, showing its piranha-like teeth.

Luca wanted Father Hus out of the pentagram's circle completely.

However, he had to wonder why the priest didn't just draw his own blood and be done with it. Was there something they were all missing here?

Luca's other worry was David, who still lay bound on the floor; the investigator was closer to the demon and Father Hus than to Sarah and himself. Thankfully, their colleague was at least making an effort to slowly shuffle and roll further away from the danger.

Looking Father Hus directly in the eye, Luca began to recite the Lord's Prayer, while still pointing the crucifix at the man.

'Our Father, who art in Heaven, hallowed be thy name.'

Father Hus spat again. 'Fuck you!' he growled. 'Fuck you and your God.'

Luca just continued. He took a small step forward, but was careful not to get too close.

The demon continued to watch. Was it waiting for something? Luca realised the horrible booming sounds had ceased as well.

Father Hus stood up straighter and raised his arms to his sides. 'You think you have any power here, priest?'

Just as up in Hus' room, he began to lift off the ground and his feet dangled a couple of inches from the concrete floor. With frightening speed, Father Hus suddenly shot forward, flying through the air with his arms outstretched before him. He quickly reached Sarah and grabbed her by the throat.

Luca continued to recite the Prayer in panic. He moved closer to the grappling pair as the possessed priest tried to drag Sarah back inside the pentagram with him.

After a struggle, Hus managed to overpower Sarah and force her into the circle, and then to the floor. 'Fight me, bitch,' he snarled down to her as he continued to choke her. 'If you think you can. If not, I'll choke the life from you while your pathetic friends watch.'

Luca saw Sarah's face begin to turn red as she gasped for air. Father Hus was levitating lengthways above her, forcing all of his strength down into his arms and onto her throat.

In response, Sarah brought her hands up and found Father Hus' face. She moved her thumbs over his eyes.

'Do it!' the man snarled.

Luca stopped the prayer. 'Sarah, no!'

He could see the struggle on Sarah's face. The desire to unleash all her anger was palpable. David continued to roll away from the fighting, seemingly unnoticed by everyone except Luca.

All Luca could think to do was to pull Sarah free. He stepped forward... and finally Sister Maria acted, tossing Luca back through the air with a mere sweep of her arm. He hit the ground, hard, and let out a groan of pain.

Get up, you old fool!

Luca quickly pushed himself to his elbows. Sarah's gasping was growing more severe, and Father Hus used her weakness to push his head closer to Sarah's hands, actually slotting his own throat into her grip.

'Rip and tear, little bird,' he said. 'Free yourself of this pain.'

'Don't do it!' Luca shouted.

He then caught eyes with David, who was nodding frantically over at something, trying to draw Luca's attention. Luca followed David's gestures and his eyes fell on the discarded skull. Luca had heard what Father Hus had said about that skull, and how it bound him to this place. Luca quickly scrambled over to it, grabbing it in his hands.

'Let her go!' he shouted, lifting the skull high above his head.

Father Hus looked over to Luca, snarled again, but then turned back to Sarah.

'Destroy it!' David shouted.

Could it really be so simple? With no time to debate the matter, Luca lifted the skull a little higher. The hideous form of Sister Maria screamed and raised a hand to him again. In an instant, Luca threw the skull to the ground as hard as he could.

Though he heard a crack, the object merely bounced off the hard floor and skittered forward, bumping against Sarah's head and coming to a stop near her. Luca's mouth fell.

Sarah's eyes found him. Even through her obvious pain, a frown formed. Her expression said everything: *what the fuck was that?*

Luca even heard David's groan of frustration.

'Do it, you dumb bitch!' Father Hus screamed. His face

was contorted into pure rage as he pushed the soft flesh of his throat down farther into Sarah's thumbs.

Sarah gritted her teeth more, and Luca saw her begin to squeeze.

Father Hus let out a satisfied moan. 'Good,' he said with a strained voice. 'Now rip out my throat. Do it!'

Sarah's nails began to dig in. The expression in her eyes changed as Luca watched. There wasn't just anger... there was also a kind of twisted enjoyment.

'Father!' David shouted. 'Hurry!'

That was enough to snap Luca into action. He dashed forward and raised his foot above the skull, thrusting it down as hard as he could. The demon screeched again.

Luca felt a jolt of pain in his foot on impact, even through the leather of his shoe, but he heard a crunching sound. After a brief moment of resistance, his leg slammed down even farther and his shoe made contact with the ground. The aged skull shattered and exploded outward. Luca then began to stomp on some of the larger shards, and he again held up his cross as he began to recite the Lord's Prayer.

Father Hus began to squirm and claw at the air, screeching like a wounded cat. Sarah, with her throat now free, managed to quickly roll away as Hus fell to the ground with a thump.

On his hands and knees, the priest began to violently cough and heave, eventually expelling a long stream of thick, yellow bile onto the ground. Steam rose from the disgusting pool of mucus, and it grew larger as Father Hus continued to purge.

While Luca continued his prayer, shouting it with all the conviction he could muster, he kept an eye on the demon who was roaring in fury. However, it still didn't intervene.

Knowing he had to keep the pressure up, he stepped closer to Father Hus and pushed the crucifix to the man's sweaty forehead.

Father Hus' face was contorted into pain and anger. His eyes began to change, the milky white being replaced by a cloud of something darker, until they quickly became jet black.

Luca completed his prayer, then immediately launched into the same one again.

Sarah was now back to her feet and standing beside him, thankfully calm enough to keep her hands and fists to herself.

'For thine is the Kingdom!' Luca shouted as he continued. 'The power and the glory!'

With a final purge, where the liquid spilling from his mouth became a dark grey, Father Hus pitched forward to the ground and lay still, his head to the side. The black of his eyes subsided, like water draining from a sink, and dark tears spilt down from his cheeks.

He wasn't breathing. For a moment, Luca worried the man was dead. Sister Maria stared down at the body of the priest as well, still motionless, back to just letting things play out.

What is she waiting for?

Father Hus suddenly pulled in a large gulp of air, like someone emerging from water, desperate for oxygen. He quickly drew in more breaths as he coughed and spluttered. His eyes looked their normal blue now, distinctly human, but were clouded by an expression of confusion. He looked around.

'What... where am I?'

He then saw Sister Maria and cried out in shock. Luca

grabbed hold of him and drew him back, away from the demon and out of the pentagram between them.

While it could have all been a trick, Luca felt the spirit from Father Hus had indeed been exorcised. However, there was now a bigger problem to deal with.

Sister Maria was finally moving.

35

SARAH STOOD close to Father Janosch, who in turn huddled over Father Hus. The Czech priest stared in disbelief as Sister Maria glided to the centre of the pentagram, arms down by her sides and face tilted down in an ominous glare.

David, Father Hus, and Sarah all backed up in kind. Even in the midst of all the chaos, Sarah felt bad for Father Hus. With him just snapping back to reality, he would have no idea what was happening—to see his friend like this must have been horrifying.

'What's going on?' he asked in a terrified voice. 'Sist— Sister Maria?'

Father Janosch put a protective arm around him. 'It's okay, Father.'

Hus turned to look at him with an expression that read, *how is any of this okay?*

'What do we do now?' Sarah asked. She quickly glanced down at David, who continued to frantically wriggle away across the cold, hard ground. She thought about running to untie him, but the threat of the demonic nun had her rooted to the spot.

'I have no idea,' Father Janosch replied.

'Should we run?' Sarah asked in a hushed but panicked voice. 'Father Hus was the one whose blood was tainted. Unless she counts,' Sarah said and nodded towards Sister Maria.

'Tainted?' Father Hus asked in obvious confusion.

He was ignored, however, as the other two concentrated on more important things. If a possessed Sister Maria spilt her own blood, or took her own life, would that constitute tainted blood and complete the Devil's Prayer?

Were they about to find out?

She slowly raised an arm up to her side.

'Carry on with the exorcism!' Sarah cried. It was all they had, the only card they had to play, though there wasn't an anchor to break like the skull with Father Hus.

The blood from Father Janosch's face drained, but he held up his small, almost pathetic crucifix regardless. He began to speak aloud in Latin. Sarah had no idea what he was saying, but assumed it was a prayer of some kind.

The corners of the nun's mouth merely pulled back into a grin, revealing more of her teeth. She flexed the fingers on her outstretched hand. Her arm began to shake as if struggling with something.

To Sarah's horror, David then began sliding backwards across the floor, right towards Sister Maria.

He tried to squirm and fight against the invisible force. However, he continued to be pulled closer to the demon.

Sarah was shocked at the show of power. Scared or not, though, she couldn't just let David be dragged to his death. For the second time that night, she let out a roar and charged at Sister Maria.

However, the nun reacted with blinding speed and

grabbed Sarah around the throat with a ferociously strong grip, then easily lifted her from the floor.

Sarah tried to draw in a breath, but couldn't. Sister Maria squeezed harder and Sarah was sure her throat was close to being crushed. Through blurred eyes, she saw David rise up into the air until the nun had him by the neck as well, though his bonds kept his body in a foetal position.

'Let them go!' she heard Father Janosch demand. The priest sounded terrified, and the order hadn't had any real conviction. Sarah turned her head away from the horrible sight of Sister Maria's twisted, demonic face, and was able to see Father Janosch behind her, standing upright and holding out his crucifix again. It didn't seem to have the same power over the demon as it did with the spirit of Herman. The nun didn't even wince.

Father Hus crouched near to Janosch, hugging himself in terror.

Sarah felt herself pulled closer to the demon as David squealed in pain; his cries rose in pitch, then became gargled. Sarah was forced to face the monster again, where a rotting and sulphuric smell assaulted her senses.

She could do nothing but stare into the eyes of her captor, seeing the intense yellow of the irises and the deep black of the pupils. The longer Sarah looked at them, the more she began to feel her body relax and the fight leave her. Her hands, which had been clawing at Maria's arms, fell to her side. Even David's cries of pain began to fade away.

Sarah felt something else when staring into the dark pupils as well—a certain pull, like she could dive in and swim through the welcoming blackness.

Strangely, it seemed familiar to her.

Come home, a voice said, though not one she heard with

her ears. Instead, she heard it internally. More specifically, she *felt* it.

The grip relaxed, though Sarah wasn't set down. She was simply held and allowed to gaze into those warm eyes.

Somewhere in the back of her mind, she was aware that Father Janosch was desperately shouting at her, trying to draw her attention. Sarah didn't care. His concerns would no doubt be unimportant, just as David's feeble cries for help were.

Suddenly, something struck her on the back of the head. She winced and again spun her head around. A shoe lay on the ground close to her. Sarah cast her eyes back up and saw Father Janosch, red-faced, and with his left foot wearing only a sock.

'Fight it!' he cried at her.

The jolt of pain, and the resulting anger, stirred her, causing her temporary hypnosis to waver.

Father Janosch was right. She needed to fight. That susceptibility he'd worried about had been all too evident. She'd lost control too easily.

Her gaze moved to the small crucifix Father Janosch still held aloft between two fingers. Her eyes widened and she opened the hand that was behind her back, shaking it to draw his attention. She glared at Father Janosch, hoping he would pick up on her intent—but then the squeezing around her neck suddenly resumed.

She saw a brief frown of confusion cross the priest's face, but it was quickly followed by realisation. He glanced at the crucifix, then back over at Sarah's hand.

He took aim, and threw it.

As the small object sailed through the air, the thin chain arced behind like a tail. Sarah just prayed Father Janosch's aim was true.

Her plan was one born of desperation. She had no idea if it would work, but had to try. She *had* to keep fighting. Sarah's head was forced back around just as she felt the small cross hit the skin of her palm. However, it bounced free before she was able to close her fist.

Sarah's heart leapt to her mouth. Her only chance of getting free was now falling to the floor... until her closed fist tightened around the trailing chain, which had thankfully not dropped out of reach.

Sarah quickly twisted her hand and swung the cross around in a loop, finally catching it fully, all while being once again forced to stare into the eyes of the demon.

She brought up her hand, but immediately felt the will to fight start to leave her. The draw she saw in that horrible gaze... she longed for it, to be embraced in its warmth.

'Sarah!' Father Janosch screamed again, sounding desperate.

Though she heard him, Sarah considered dropping the cross. It would be so much easier. No more fighting. No more worrying. No more missing her sister. The promise of peace that the demon's gaze offered was tantalising.

'Sarah!'

The priest again. Always demanding something of me.

Somehow, he had positioned himself in her life as the one to give her orders.

But why? What was he to her other than a sycophant who wasted his life following a false god?

A weak god.

With the last of her free will, Sarah flicked her eyes to the side. She saw David. He wasn't moving, and his head had lolled to the side.

Was he dead?

She shouldn't care about that. He wasn't important to her.

But... she did care. Something inside her ached at the sight of him, hanging there so lifeless.

Had she caused that? Just like she had caused Chloe's death?

Fight it!

It wasn't Father Janosch this time. The voice was her own.

Sarah clenched her jaw and frowned, determined to rebel. The demon seemed to recognise her resolve and opened its nightmarish mouth into a thunderous roar.

That was her chance.

She thrust her hand forward, punching her fingers into the gaping mouth, cutting her already wounded hand further. More blood spurted free and dripped down to the ground.

With a flick of her fingers, Sarah cast the small crucifix into the back of Sister Maria's throat. Sarah then quickly withdrew her hand as the demon's head dropped back, letting out another bellowing cry, this one filled with pain.

The grip on her instantly intensified. Sarah opened her mouth to let out a cry, but it was blocked by the hand around her throat. Beyond the deafening noise the demon was making, Sarah was just able to make out Farther Janosch shouting, though she realised he was once again reciting a prayer. Another voice was also demanding the demon leave the body of Sister Maria and was alternating between English and Latin.

Father Hus.

Both priests appeared at her side. Father Hus still naked but standing tall and bellowing his commands.

Eventually, just as Sarah thought she may pass out and

her throat be crushed completely, the iron grip released. She—along with David—dropped to the ground.

David remained motionless.

The two priests continued their verbal assault on the demon, who backed away from them as smoke started to drift out from its mouth. It coughed and made gagging sounds. The thin golden chain dangled from its open maw. The monster brought clawed hands up to grab it, but the duo advanced, shouting out their commands and prayers.

It seemed to be working.

The demon was down on its knees before it managed to pull the crucifix free. Its coughing continued, and the yellow eyes bulged from their sockets. Nergal began to growl something, words in Latin, and turned its head to Father Janosch. The expression was one of pure hatred.

Sarah crawled over to David and rolled him to his back. His eyes were closed, and he was breathing, but the sound of his inhaling was strained. She quickly got to work on untying his bonds, constantly casting her eyes over to the nun. Sarah had no idea if the exorcism would completely banish the demon, so she wanted to be able to get David out of there if things took a turn.

To her relief, the demon seemed to be growing weaker. The horrible noises and cries it was making were beginning to fade. Eventually, the demon dropped to the ground, lying face down, just as Sarah managed to fully untie the ropes that held her friend.

'David,' she whispered urgently. She then began to lightly tap his face. His head rolled to the side and his eyes flickered open, though they didn't appear to be focused.

Still, that was enough for Sarah.

At least he's alive.

She stood and quickly moved over next to Father

Janosch and Father Hus, and the three of them looked down on the prone nun.

The demon's eyes were wide open, but the fierce yellow in the irises was fading as the priests continued their exorcism. The nun's skin, too, was beginning to shift back to normal and lose the ghostly-white pallor. The piranha-like teeth started to disappear as well. They didn't retract, but instead they actually dissipated.

A pool of light-grey liquid spread out beneath Sister Maria's form, dripping out from her now-soaked habit, like a gallon of sweat had instantly been pushed from her body.

As the last of the yellow drained from her eyes, a final, insidious smile crossed her lips.

That smile alone caused a shudder to work its way up Sarah's spine. There was something about it, like the demon knew something they didn't. Finally, however, the yellow faded completely, and Sister Maria's eyes slowly closed.

Thankfully, the nun was still breathing, but was unconscious.

Had they done it?

Sarah was still tense, expecting something to happen, but a notion suddenly became clear to her: the nausea was gone. Completely.

She started to relax. They had actually succeeded! Both Herman and Nergal had been successfully exorcised.

David began to sit up, gripping his throat and wincing in pain. Sarah rushed back over to him and knelt down by his side.

'Are you okay?' she asked him.

He opened his mouth and took in a wheezing breath, then tried to speak, but all that came out was a strained noise. He winced in agony.

God only knew what that monster had done to his

throat. Sarah's own felt like it was on fire, but she was still able to talk, despite being in a bit of pain. She helped him up to his feet.

'Don't try and talk,' she said to him. 'It's over now. We'll get you looked at to make sure you're okay.'

He nodded, and tears began rolling from his eyes.

'What... what happened here?' Father Hus asked as he looked around in disbelief. Sarah couldn't imagine how confusing all of this was for him, but still appreciated how quickly he'd acted and instinctually helped Father Janosch in the exorcism.

It was then a groan escaped from Sister Maria. She rolled to her back. Her eyes slowly opened and settled on the others. The confusion that crossed her face was immediate. She quickly began looking around her surroundings before sitting bolt upright.

'Kde to jsem??' she asked in Czech. She looked up to Father Janosch, Sarah, and David. 'Kdo jsi?'

Father Hus quickly knelt by her side. She withdrew, flinching backwards. Sarah didn't blame her. Seeing a naked man, even one the nun knew, suddenly lunge forward would be startling.

'It's okay, Sister,' he said in a soothing tone, speaking in English. 'You are safe.' He looked up at the others as well. 'These people have helped us.'

'Helped us... with what?' she asked. 'I don't understand.' Panic rose in her voice. The poor woman seemed terrified.

'I'll explain everything to you both once we're out of here,' Father Janosch told them. 'Though... it will be a lot to take in.'

'What of everyone else?' Father Hus asked. 'Are the others here okay?'

Sarah lowered her head. 'Actually,' she cut in, 'there is something you need to brace yourself for.'

After a pause, she explained what she had seen up in the nave, of how the dead now decorated the cathedral's interior there. As she spoke, Sister Maria looked like her mind might snap, and Father Hus began to openly weep.

'Sister Agatha needs medical help,' Sarah urged. 'She was still alive when I left her, so we need to get help here. Quickly.'

'I'll make a call,' Father Janosch said. 'We need to make sure we don't create a scene. What happened here can't become public knowledge.'

Sarah frowned. 'That's pretty callous, Father,' she said. 'There's already a 'scene' upstairs. A fucking horrible one. What we *need* is an ambulance here, immediately.'

'I understand that,' Father Janosch replied. 'And we'll get one. But we also need to make sure the people of Kutná Hora don't see the inside of the cathedral. This needs to be handled quickly, but delicately. Or would you rather word got out about exactly what happened here?'

'Why *shouldn't* it?' Sarah argued.

'Think it through,' he shot back. 'Possession. A demon. Who knows how many dead... It would cause mass panic. There are some things the wider world is better off not knowing.'

Sarah wasn't sure she agreed with that—with any of the secretive bullshit. It wasn't for the Church to decide. However, she just wanted to make sure poor Sister Agatha got to a hospital.

She shook her head. 'Go and make the call. But if there isn't an ambulance here in fifteen minutes, I'll go and find one myself.'

Father Janosch hesitated, as if to argue further. Thankfully, he didn't.

'I need a phone,' he said.

'There should be one in one of the offices upstairs,' Father Hus offered. 'I can show you.'

Father Janosch nodded. 'We can get you some clothes as well,' he said.

Sarah then moved over to Sister Maria and offered the nun her hand. 'Sister, my name is Sarah. We should talk—you've got a lot to get caught up on.'

Sister Maria stared at her hand for a moment, as if it were a foreign object. She looked up to Father Hus for guidance, who gave a smile and nod of approval. She slipped her hand into Sarah's, and Sarah heaved the larger woman up to her feet.

'Now, be strong, Sister,' Sarah said. 'This is going to shock you.'

36

2 Days Later...

Sarah and David stood in the main nave of Newcastle Cathedral, milling around with the tourists, waiting for Father Janosch to return from his debriefing. Sarah had seen enough of cathedrals over the last few days to last her a lifetime.

David's throat was an explosion of purple and yellow bruising. Those colours, along with the swelling, drew confused glances from those that walked past him. The poor man still struggled to talk for extended periods, though hopefully his discomfort would be a short-term thing. At least, that's what the doctors had said.

The inside of the cathedral was no less stunning than the one in Kutná Hora. It had long, carved wooden pews for the choir, a breathtaking altar at the back, and great, sweeping stone arches that gave the space a grand and gothic aesthetic.

Sarah had wanted to accompany Father Janosch upstairs for his meeting with the Council. However, she had been predictably denied.

The way those men operated, which had already been frustrating, was now seriously starting to anger her. The Council's tactic of trying to draw out more information, rather than just exorcising the priest to begin with, had caused innocent people to die.

Many people had lost their lives at the Cathedral of Assumption, because of the Council's botched handling of the situation—though Sarah placed a lot of the blame for the events on her own shoulders as well.

Even though they had succeeded in banishing Herman and Nergal, had stopped another door from being opened, and had also found out more of the origins of the *Ianua Diaboli*, the whole investigation still felt like a failure to Sarah.

After over an hour of waiting, Father Janosch eventually emerged into the nave and joined up with Sarah and David.

'How did it go?' she asked.

'They're struggling to keep the whole thing under wraps,' Father Janosch replied.

That didn't surprise her. Though a specialist team of medical staff had been sent in by the Church, there was no way something like that could be kept a total secret. The bodies had to be removed, and someone would have likely seen that happen. A leak was inevitable.

Still, the whole episode had caused less furor than Sarah might have imagined.

Father Janosch went on, 'And they are still concerned we didn't find out *how* Sister Maria became possessed in the first place. That is a worry, since it was the catalyst for the whole thing.'

Sarah's eyes widened in surprise. 'Let me get this straight, are they saying they're *disappointed* in our performance over there?' *The arrogant pricks.* 'Because, if so, I have a few words for them on how *they* are handling things.'

'They aren't disappointed,' Father Janosch was quick to add. 'They want to understand how a nun was able to be possessed like that in the first place, and bring about such an incident. Mainly so it doesn't happen again.'

Sarah shook her head in annoyance. 'Well, not everything gets wrapped up in a nice little bow.'

In truth, there was plenty about the whole investigation that bugged Sarah too. Such as why certain information had been freely given over to them by the possessed Father Hus, especially since that information had only served to help them. Sarah had initially put that down to Herman's own arrogance—and that could well have been the case—something about it didn't sit right. Nor did it make sense that Nergal had just stood by while the spirit was exorcised in the crypt.

Maybe I'm just overthinking things.

'What's the situation at the cathedral?' David asked with a strained wheeze.

Father Janosch took a breath. 'It's still closed to the public, but everything has been cleared up. A new altar will need to be built. But the Council is satisfied the Cathedral of Assumption isn't dangerous anymore, so it will be reopened soon... as long as the story about what happened there doesn't grow and hit fever-pitch. And once the pentagram etching in the crypt is concreted over, of course.'

'And what of Sister Maria, Sister Agatha, and Father Hus?'

'Father Hus and Sister Maria are still there,' Father Janosch said with no small amount of disbelief. 'They spent a night away from the cathedral, but from what I understand they were determined to return there and work on setting things right. Sister Maria, especially, was single-minded about it. The fact that she lost so much of her memory has angered her, and she refuses to be scared away.'

In Sarah's opinion, the pair staying at the cathedral so soon after what had happened was a mistake. However, she had to respect Sister Maria's attitude. It had been one Sarah had shared when returning to Perron Manor after the death of her sister.

'What about Sister Agatha?' she asked. The last she'd heard, the old nun was still in hospital.

'She won't be discharged anytime soon,' Father Janosch replied. 'Her condition is no longer life-threatening, though it was touch and go for a while. She'll never be the same person again though. Not just because she's lost her sight—I'm told she doesn't say much now and is in a constant state of fear.'

'I don't blame her,' Sarah said. 'I can't imagine what she's going through. It must be hell.'

'Yeah,' Father Janosch agreed. 'Sister Agatha didn't deserve that. Any of it.'

The discussion then trailed off as each of them reflected on what had happened. Sarah eventually moved things on. 'Anything else of note come out of the debrief?'

Father Janosch looked down. 'Actually... yes. They have something else for us.'

Sarah's head reeled back. 'What, another case so soon?!'

He nodded. 'Afraid so.'

'You're joking. You have to be,' she snapped. 'I'm not even sure I want to keep doing this at all, to be honest, and now those clowns upstairs think they can just send us off again to run their errands and put our lives on the line after what we've been through?'

'There is a situation that needs investigation,' Father Janosch went on. 'I can't force you to go, but I think this is important.'

David held up his hands. 'I'm... not sure,' he croaked out. 'After what happened, I—'

'Actually, David,' Father Janosch cut in, 'there is something else the Council wants you to look into separately. Nothing dangerous, but they feel your expertise could be well suited. Ralph, Ann, and George will be joining you as well, if they're agreeable. Sarah and I will be handling the other assignment on our own.'

Sarah wasn't sure what annoyed her more, the fact that the Council wanted to send them straight back out again, or that they had seen fit to exclude David and cast him aside. She could tell by David's expression that he was caught somewhere between being relieved and insulted.

He eventually shrugged. 'Works for me... for the time being.'

But Sarah wasn't so sure. 'So where the hell are they sending us now?'

Father Janosch raised his eyebrows and waited a moment before answering, 'Ever been to America?'

37

FATHER HUS HEARD a knock on his door, and it pulled him from his sleep. He blinked in confusion and looked around his small room. It was dark and quiet. Father Hus checked the watch he had placed on the nightstand.

It had just turned three in the morning.

The knocking came again, light and slow.

'Hello?' he called out in a groggy voice.

'Father Hus, it's me.'

Sister Maria. He frowned and got out of bed, pulling on a long dressing gown over his nightwear.

'Is everything okay?' he asked.

'May I come in?' was the reply.

After tying the knot in his robe, Father Hus walked to the door and opened it. The nun stood outside in her habit, hands clasped before her waist, with a polite smile on her face.

'What is it?' he asked. He couldn't think of a good reason Sister Maria would be here at this time of the morning. Not unless something was wrong. However, she didn't seem panicked or worried. In fact, she looked calm.

Sister Maria surprised him as she strode past him.

'I just wanted to talk,' she said as she stopped in the centre of the room, then turned to face him. Father Hus closed the door and stepped close to her.

'Talk about what?' he asked.

She took a step closer to him and Father Hus tensed up. There was a look in her eye—one of hunger.

'Us,' she said. A smile danced across her lips. It was almost seductive.

'Us?' Father Hus repeated. *What is she talking about?*

Her hand found his arm and gave it a gentle squeeze.

'Sister Maria,' he said, 'what are you doing?'

She leaned in and whispered in his ear. 'It's not what I'm doing right now,' she said, 'but what I'm *going* to do.'

He pulled away with a frown. 'What's that?' No sooner had the words left his mouth than he drew in a shocked breath. Her eyes burned yellow.

Father Hus didn't have time to react. In an instant, the nun was on top of him, forcing him to the ground with her hands around his throat. He tried to fight back against her, but was overpowered by her unnatural strength. Her fingers, which were now much longer than they should have been, almost claw-like, found his neck and started to squeeze.

Panic flooded through him as he stared open-mouthed at the demonic face above him.

How could this be?

Father Hus tried to shout and scream, but the air was caught in his throat at the immense pressure of her grip. Then, he felt the sharp nails of her thumbs pierce the flesh of his throat and begin to pull it apart.

He began to gargle blood.

~

Nergal grinned down at the dying priest who lay gasping on the ground. The demon still had its hands gripped around his destroyed throat, enjoying the feeling of blood run over the flesh of its host.

The sensation was divine.

After what had happened down in the crypt, the demon had briefly left the body of the nun—so Sarah would no longer sense Nergal's presence. The demon needed Sarah to believe that she and her friends had succeeded.

Nergal squeezed its talons tighter, mushing the flesh out beneath its fingers, pressing hard enough that it eventually found the spinal column of the pathetic man's neck. It twisted and heard a crack. The last of the light left the priest's eyes.

The demon laughed and pulled, riving the human's head clean off as blood spurted free from the stump, coating the floor in crimson liquid.

Nergal hated the soft, weak form of the humans, including the one it now inhabited. Possessing the nun initially had been hard, and had taken time. The ritual that had started all those years ago allowed the demon to reach Sister Maria and chip away at her resolve. But at that time, with the ritual not complete, the link was weak and had to be used carefully.

However, since the events in the crypt, the power in the cathedral was now immense.

Sarah and her friends had failed.

Possession of a human did not taint their blood, as the group had so errantly believed. The person needed to willingly denounce their God of their own volition.

The only other way tainted blood could flow through the veins of someone was if they were born with it.

Like the Daughter of Darkness.

Those blind fools had been led on a merry dance from the moment they arrived, shepherded along as needed: pointing them to the ossuary, making them aware of the skull and the anchor, then making them believe Father Hus' blood was the key.

Herman had then completed the ritual by biting the girl and spilling her blood within the symbol. In order to keep the charade going, he'd forfeited his soul to the exorcism. Nergal, too, had made a show of leaving the nun.

If Sarah realised that they had failed and the doorway had been opened, the priest with her would no doubt have tried to close it again, just as they had done at Perron Manor. He wouldn't have succeeded this time, of course, but Nergal couldn't risk harming or killing Sarah in the fallout.

They needed her.

Things had played out exactly as they had needed to. The arrogant priest believed he had won. But they were blind.

With all Seven Gates open once again, it was now time to call Sarah home.

~

THE END

HAUNTED: MOTHER DEATH

'*THEY STRUGGLE AND PLEAD AND TAKE THEIR LAST BREATH, WITH THAT HORRIBLE OLD LADY: MOTHER DEATH, MOTHER DEATH.*'

Haunted: Mother Death

Book 5 in the Haunted Series.

One of the most famous hauntings in British history took place at a house on South Hill Estate. There, the spirit of Mary Kane was said to have returned from the grave in search of more children.

But that was a long time ago. No further activity has been reported since the 1980s... until now.

David Ritter and his team have been sent to investigate claims that Mary Kane has returned. Is it just a hoax, or does Mother Death once again hunger for the souls of the innocent?

Buy Haunted: Mother Death now.

INSIDE: PERRON MANOR

Sign up to my mailing list to get the FREE prequel...

In 2014 a group of paranormal researchers conducted a weekend-long investigation at the notorious Perron Manor. The events that took place during that weekend were incredible and terrifying in equal measure. This is the full, documented story.

In addition, the author dives into the long and bloody history of the house, starting with its origins as a monastery back in the 1200s, covering its ownership under the Grey and Perron families, and even detailing the horrific events that took place on Halloween in 1982.

No stone is left unturned in what is now the definitive work regarding the most haunted house in Britain.

The novella, as mentioned in Haunted: Perron Manor, can be yours for FREE by joining my mailing list.

Sign up now.

www.leemountford.com

THE DEMONIC

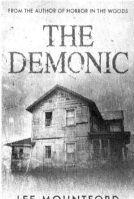

If you liked the Haunted series, you will love The Demonic.

Years ago Danni Morgan ran away from her childhood home and vowed never to go back. It was a place of fear, pain and misery at the hands of an abusive father.

But now Danni's father is dead and she is forced to break her vow and return home—to lay his body to rest and face up to the ghosts of her past.

But Danni is about to realise that some ghosts are more real than others. And something beyond her understanding is waiting for her there, lurking in the shadows. An evil that intends to kill her family and claim her very soul.

Experience supernatural horror in the vein of THE CONJURING, INSIDIOUS and the legendary GHOST-

WATCH. THE DEMONIC will get under your skin, send chills down your spine and have you sleeping with the lights on!

Buy The Demonic now...

OTHER BOOKS BY LEE MOUNTFORD

The Supernatural Horror Collection
The Demonic
The Mark
Forest of the Damned

The Extreme Horror Collection
Horror in the Woods
Tormented
The Netherwell Horror

Haunted Series
Inside Perron Manor (Book 0)
Haunted: Perron Manor (Book 1)
Haunted: Devil's Door (Book 2)
Haunted: Purgatory (Book 3)
Haunted: Mother Death (Book 5)
Haunted: Asylum (Book 6)

ABOUT THE AUTHOR

Lee Mountford is a horror author from the North-East of England. His first book, Horror in the Woods, was published in May 2017 to fantastic reviews, and his follow-up book, The Demonic, achieved Best Seller status in both Occult Horror and British Horror categories on Amazon.

He is a lifelong horror fan, much to the dismay of his amazing wife, Michelle, and his work is available in ebook, print and audiobook formats.

In August 2017 he and his wife welcomed their first daughter, Ella, into the world. In May 2019, their second daughter, Sophie, came along. Michelle is hoping the girls don't inherit their father's love of horror, but Lee has other ideas...

For more information
www.leemountford.com
leemountford01@googlemail.com

ACKNOWLEDGMENTS

Thanks first to my amazing Beta Reader Team, who have greatly helped me polish and hone this book:

James Bacon

Christine Brlevic

John Brooks

Nicole Burns

Carrie-Lynn Cantwell

Karen Day

Doreene Fernandes

Jenn Freitag

Ursula Gillam

Clayton Hall

Tammy Harris

Emily Haynes

Dorie Heriot

Lemmy Howells

Lucy Hughes

Marie K

Dawn Keate

Paul Letendre

Megan McCarty
Valerie Palmer
Leanne Pert
Carley Jessica Pyne
Gale Raab
Justin Read
Nicola Jayne Smith
Sara Walker
Sharon Watret

Also, a huge thanks to these fantastic people:

My editor, Josiah Davis (www.jdbookservices.com) for such an amazing job as always.

Further proof editing was supplied by Diane McCarty. Latin editing provided by Megan McCarty. Their help was invaluable.

The cover was supplied by Debbie at The Cover Collection.

(www.thecovercollection.com).

I cannot recommend their work enough.

And the last thank you, as always, is the most important. To my amazing family: my wife, Michelle, and my daughters, Ella and Sophie—thank you for everything. You three are my world.